HER
PAYBACK

BOOKS BY EMMA TALLON

Her Revenge

Her Rival

Her Betrayal

Runaway Girl

Dangerous Girl

Boss Girl

Fierce Girl

Reckless Girl

Fearless Girl

Ruthless Girl

HER PAYBACK

EMMA TALLON

Bookouture

Published by Bookouture in 2022

An imprint of Storyfire Ltd.
Carmelite House
50 Victoria Embankment
London EC4Y 0DZ

www.bookouture.com

ISBN: 978-1-80314-299-9
eBook ISBN: 978-1-80314-298-2

For my beautiful babies,
Christian & Charlotte

PROLOGUE

They reached the side of the building and jogged stealthily towards the back. There were sounds coming from within. Low voices and something heavy being moved. Rounding the corner first, Lily Drew spotted a door that stood ajar. She pulled her gun from underneath her jacket and pointed it steadily in front of her as she cautiously approached.

She strained her ears to hear the voices as she moved down a dark side corridor that led into the warehouse.

'Seriously, though, what are we going to do with him?' one gruff voice asked.

She held her breath and paused. Were they talking about Cillian?

'Make a fire,' she heard him reply. 'And get rid. The last thing we need is more evidence floating about.'

Lily felt her heart rate shoot up in alarm and she rounded the corner, ignoring Scarlet's desperate call for her to wait, fire blazing in her eyes and gun trained straight towards his head.

'I don't *fucking* think so,' she roared as the others quickly joined her, fanning out to make sure they held everyone in the room at gunpoint.

Straight away, the two other men dropped what they were holding and threw their arms up in alarm.

'Where is he?' Lily yelled as she reached him. 'Where the *fuck* is my son?' She stopped a couple of metres short and cocked her gun, her face contorting in rage.

He pulled back, his eyes locking onto hers. 'What the hell, Lily?' he asked, staring at the gun. 'Put that fucking thing away!'

'Not until you tell me what you've done with my son. Where is he?'

She could feel her panic rising, now that they were here, now that she was faced with the man who had taken him. Cillian needed her – she could feel it. She had to get to him quickly. Where was he? What had they done to him? Were they already too late? All these questions swam around in her mind as she stepped forward again, forcing the gun closer to his head with a growl of frustration.

'I don't know where your son is!' he exclaimed. 'I ain't seen either of them in years!'

'You liar,' Lily spat. 'You've taken him, just like the others. I know you have. I know everything. So save yourself some pain and just *tell* me – or I swear, I will blow your *fucking* brains out!'

She could hear the shake in her voice, knew only too well that for the first time in her life she sounded desperate. But she *was* desperate. That was her son in there. Her firstborn, the one who'd entered this world just minutes ahead of his brother. He was everything to her and she couldn't lose him. Not like this.

Suddenly the world seemed to still, and she zoned in on the man who stood between her and her boy.

'You have thirty seconds to tell me, or I will pull this trigger and be damned with the consequences.'

ONE

TEN DAYS EARLIER

Cillian Drew crossed the road with a jog and headed towards the old orange-and-white brick building that housed Repton Boxing Club. The comforting feeling of being somewhere that was a home away from home washed over him, and a half-smile crept over his face. He'd been coming here for years, since he was barely more than a child. It had been his solace from the outside world back then, a place to let off steam, where he'd learned to practise a bit of discipline. He'd been too busy over the last year or two to come more often than once or twice a month, but Billie, his girlfriend, had urged him to get back into going regularly again. *Self-care* she'd called it. Not that he was sure what punching another bloke around the ring had much to do with self-care. Surely it was the exact opposite? But Billie seemed to know more than him about these things, so he'd just accepted with a nod and redoubled his efforts to make more time for the place.

Slinging his gym bag up over his shoulder, he walked through the front door and breathed in the familiar smell of wood polish and sweat. The punchbags dotted around the sides had seen better days. The green-and-yellow paint on the walls was pockmarked with chips and dents, showing the brickwork beneath, and plastered with old posters, faded and worn with age. Photographed smiles of triumphant boys and men beamed out from all sides, and the ring where they fought whispered tales of blood and sweat, wins and losses, men pushed to their limits and records being beaten.

To an outsider it perhaps looked tired and worn, somewhere that needed an overhaul. But to those who understood the place, it was a palace.

One of the coaches shouted instructions up to the young men sparring in the ring. Others were dotted around on mats or practising with the punchbags. Several of them nodded or lifted a hand in greeting as Cillian headed towards an open door at the far end of the large room. A light was shining, indicating the man he was searching for was in.

Jimmy had been the head coach since Cillian had first set foot in the place as a boy, and although he'd stepped back from a lot of the coaching now, he still ran the club from his small office at the back. He was the one who'd taught Cillian to fight. He'd also taught him when not to fight and how to maintain an edge without losing his cool – some of the most valuable lessons of his life. They'd remained close over the years, and Cillian always popped his head in for a quick chat before training, out of respect.

Now though, as he approached the door he slowed, hearing strained voices from within. He paused a few feet away and leaned against the wall to wait, looking back towards the ring.

'It just ain't like him though, coach,' came a piteous cry. 'He wouldn't go and leave me and Benny like that, he just wouldn't. You know him. You know he wouldn't.' The woman sniffed as though holding back tears.

'I don't know what to tell you, Cass,' Jimmy replied, his tone sympathetic. 'It's news to me too.'

'But that's what I mean – it's news to everyone. It ain't right

– something ain't right.' Her words trailed off into deep racking sobs and Cillian found himself feeling sorry for the woman, despite not actually understanding her troubles.

'Look, Cass, go home. Be with your boy. I'll ask about and see if I can find out where he's gone. Maybe he just needs some time alone – maybe something's going on that he ain't shared with us and he needs to work out by himself,' Jimmy replied.

'There ain't a thing in this world that man wouldn't share with either me or you and you know it,' Cass replied emotionally.

There was a pause and Jimmy sighed heavily, not correcting her. 'I'll call in on you later, Cass. OK? I'll come by tonight and we'll talk some more. Maybe he'll be back by then anyway.'

'I hope so, coach,' Cass replied doubtfully. 'Keep that. Show it around. It might jog some memories.'

There was a noise like a chair being pushed back and a few seconds later a short blonde walked out, wiping the tears from her cheeks as she hurried past Cillian towards the exit. He looked away, not wanting to embarrass her, but she didn't seem to notice him.

He pushed forward off the wall and wandered into the office, knocking on the open door. 'Alright, Jimmy?' he said, noticing how stressed the older man appeared as he frowned at a piece of paper.

'Alright, Cillian,' he replied, glancing up with a smile, the frown not quite disappearing. 'Haven't seen you in here in a few weeks. How's things?'

'Yeah, I've not had the time.' Cillian took a seat opposite the coach.

'If you wanted to, you'd make time.' Jimmy's reply was stern. 'I've told you that before.'

'True,' Cillian conceded. 'I will be doing just that going forward. Gonna start coming in early each day for an hour. Get back on it.'

'Good lad.'

'What's going on?' Cillian asked, gesturing towards the paper that Jimmy's eyes had been drawn back to.

'Oh, it's just Cain,' he said, shaking his head. 'You know Cain?'

Cillian's forehead puckered as he tried to place the name. 'Spars with Danny a lot, tall fella?'

'That's the one. He's gone on the missing list.'

'He's missing?'

'Well, not missing exactly.' Jimmy passed the paper over the table. 'His missus woke up to find this in the kitchen yesterday morning.'

Cillian quickly scanned down the short letter.

Cass,

I'm sorry, but I can't do this anymore. I've taken a job in another part of the country and I'm moving there today. I won't be coming back. Don't look for me – you won't find me. I'm not talking about it as there's no point. My decision's made. I just want to start again, clean slate.

I wish you the best and hope you find your own happiness one day.

Cain

'Bit blunt, ain't it?' Cillian pulled a face. He could understand why the woman had been so upset. 'So he's left her and his kid with nothing?'

'Technically, Benny ain't actually his. He met Cass when Benny was just a baby. But he loved that boy and they always seemed so happy together. Cain was always full of beans, talking about all his plans for them as a family. They were supposed to get married this summer.' Jimmy scratched his head.

'Cold feet maybe?' Cillian asked.

Jimmy shook his head, his frown deepening. 'Nah, not Cain. He acted like he'd won the jackpot with that girl. He couldn't wait to get a ring on her finger. He had so much going for him here too. Good job, some big fights coming up. I just can't believe he'd leave all that. It is certainly an odd one. Very out of character.'

Cillian's mind turned to his mother, wondering how shocked and upset she'd been when their dad, Alfie, had walked out on them all those years ago. He supposed no one ever settled down to be a family with a person they suspected would eventually leave.

'I guess it's always a surprise when it happens,' he said, putting the paper down on the table between them. 'But people change.'

'Yeah, I guess,' Jimmy replied reluctantly. He exhaled, suddenly looking as though he had the weight of the world on his shoulders.

Cillian studied him. 'There something else?'

Jimmy was quiet for a few moments, seemingly debating whether or not to share his burden. 'I've had word from the company that owns this place that they want to sell it to a building developer.'

'*What?*' Cillian was shocked.

'I've looked into the proposed plans. They want to knock it down and build flats.'

'But they can't do that, right?' he asked.

Repton Boxing Club was part of London's history. It had belonged to the local community for decades, a sanctuary for so many people. As sacred as a church, to some. Surely they wouldn't be allowed to just tear it down as if it meant nothing?

'They can,' Jimmy replied unhappily. 'And it looks as

though they will. Not much I can do to stop it. I'll log an appeal to the planning department, get some signatures from all who oppose it, but these people have money and power. Two things I don't. I don't fancy my chances.'

'So the planning hasn't been accepted then?' Cillian asked, his quick brain working over the problem. 'And they haven't actually sold it yet?'

'No. The owner just sent me a notice of intent to sell. I found out about the flats by looking this place up on the government's planning site. The company looking to buy are clearly waiting to see if it passes before they complete the sale.'

'Why do they want to sell anyway?' Cillian asked.

Jimmy gave him a sad smile. 'This place don't make no money. What little we do make goes straight back into the upkeep and to getting the boys what they need. I guess the woman who now owns it – Miranda, her name is – ain't into boxing. The land's worth a small fortune.'

Cillian shook his head. 'She might not be, but all those boys out there are. She don't understand what this place really is, what it means.'

'I know, but I don't think you're gonna find a way to make her understand, mate. She ain't from our world. She's never faced the challenges the people in here have,' Jimmy answered helplessly.

Cillian nodded, his expression dark. 'No. Maybe not. But she's never come up against me either. Give me all the details you've got and let me see what I can do. Because we can't let this place go.' His expression hardened. 'I'll figure this out, Jimmy, don't worry about it. And this Miranda, well, she's about to realise she's got a few changes to make...'

TWO

Scarlet Drew tripped down the long thickly carpeted hallway and stifled a giggle with her hand as she turned back to look at John, her boyfriend. He shook his head with a grin and took her elbow, guiding her more steadily towards their hotel room.

'*I can do more tequila,*' John mocked, mimicking her earlier statement. '*It never affects me.*'

'It's definitely not the tequila,' she argued with a hiccup, pushing her long raven hair back over her shoulder.

'No?' he asked, amused.

'No, I think it's this floor actually,' Scarlet claimed, pointing down at it and wobbling once more. 'It's very uneven.'

John pretended to study it. 'Yes, I think you're right. It must be that.' He looked back at her with a slow smile. 'Definitely not the tequila.'

'No,' she agreed, shaking her head seriously. While John searched his pockets for the key, Scarlet watched him and a warmth flooded through her. They'd been dating – officially at least – for around six months now, and every day had felt like a blessing.

Theirs was an unusual relationship. One that had to be

hidden from everyone except her family and those closest to them within the firm. John was a detective inspector for the Metropolitan Police, and Scarlet, well... She was exactly the kind of person John spent his life trying to put behind bars.

Scarlet was part of the notorious Drew family, a firm that ran various illegal enterprises in the murky underworld of East London. She'd been on the police radar since the day she was born, due to her family name. But John hadn't known this when they'd met, any more than she'd known he was Old Bill. If they had, they'd have steered well clear of each other on a personal level, being natural enemies. But with each of them reluctant to discuss their career with a stranger, they'd avoided talk of work, and a deep bond had formed between them. It had been a shock to them both when they'd later met in a police interview room on opposing sides of the table.

The police had had her in the palm of their hand. Despite how careful she'd been, they had all the evidence needed to send her down for murder. But at the last moment, John had stolen the evidence, leaving them no choice but to let her walk. It had been a huge surprise to everyone, even to John himself, that he'd laid everything he believed in – everything he'd ever worked for – aside, to save her. He'd chosen her above all else. And in that moment their bond had been cemented.

Now they trod a fine line, day to day, protecting themselves from the potential dangers all around, should they be discovered. If the police caught wind of their association, they could put two and two together about the lost evidence. And should any other firms find out, the Drews could be threatened from all sides. The rules of the underworld were unforgiving and very particular when it came to those on the other side of the law. It was one thing having a bent copper on the payroll somewhere at arm's length, but it was quite another having one in your bed.

And so they hid, keeping their relationship behind closed doors, under the cover of darkness. Occasionally they'd sneak out of London for a night, as they had tonight, somewhere that no one would recognise them.

John finally located the key card and swiped it, holding the door open for Scarlet to walk in before him. She kicked off her shoes and sat on the end of the bed, melting backward into the thick duvet. She smiled lazily up at John as he shrugged off his smart jacket and draped it over the back of a chair. He undid the top few buttons of his shirt and smiled back at her.

'What?' he asked. 'What you thinking?'

Scarlet let her gaze roam his taut, athletic body and raised her eyebrow suggestively. 'A few things,' she said. 'And most of them are very rude.'

John laughed, his cheeks dimpling and his bright green eyes crinkling at the side, making him even more attractive to Scarlet.

'Come join me,' she said, holding her arms out to him.

John came down to her level, propping himself up on his elbows and kissing her long and hard on the lips. 'You're irresistible,' he murmured.

'It's my tequila resistance, isn't it?' she joked as he pulled back and stroked a stray strand of hair back from her face.

'It's really not,' he replied with a laugh. He rolled to the side and looked down at her, his smile softening as a more serious expression took over. 'I wish we could do this every night.'

Scarlet turned and propped herself up on her elbow, mirroring his position. 'What, dinner and drinks?'

'Yeah, but not just that. *This*, you know? Coming back home together. Just... being us, whenever and however we want.'

The wistfulness in his tone touched her heart and she shuffled her body closer to his.

'I know,' she said, lightly kissing his shoulder. 'But what we do have is amazing. I wouldn't change it for the world. I wouldn't change *you* for the world.'

'And I wouldn't change you for the world either,' John

conceded, his gaze roaming over her face. 'I just wish...' He trailed off and clamped his jaw shut.

Scarlet knew why he couldn't finish his sentence. He would have to wish for too many things to be different in order for their lives to be publicly compatible.

Her phone beeped in her clutch behind her and she twisted to grab it. It was a text from her aunt Lily.

What time are you back tomorrow? Full house on the tables from seven, need you there.

She pulled a grim expression. She hadn't planned on watching over the poker tables tomorrow, having enough to catch up on from her night away. She quickly typed out a response, shuffling her to-do list in her head.

Around lunchtime and no probs. I'll be there.

The Drews ran a pub in East London, which was frequented not just by the locals who knew and respected them but by others in the underworld. Firms on friendly terms throughout the city went there to enjoy social drinks within the safety of its camera-free walls, to conduct meetings, and often to enjoy themselves in the secret illegal gambling den on the first floor. This floor was invite-only, its existence a closely guarded secret.

The fact that the pub had no cameras put people at ease, but it by no means gave anyone the impression that it was vulnerable. The place was run by Tommy Harding, a formidable man whose rules were hard and finite, and whenever an event was running upstairs, there were several heavies on the premises to ensure order was kept. And on every gambling night there was always at least one Drew on site. Which tomorrow, it seemed, would be her.

Scarlet slipped her phone back into her clutch and focused back on John. Their time together was precious and she didn't want to waste any more of it thinking about work. 'Sorry, just Lil,' she said dismissively. 'Why don't we have a look at that room-service menu, because I'm fairly certain I saw chocolate strawberries on there earlier.'

'That sounds like a good idea to me,' John replied, standing up to go and get it.

As he picked it up, his phone began to ring in his pocket. He pulled it out and cursed when he saw who it was. Putting his finger to his mouth, he answered, trying to hide the annoyance in his tone at the interruption.

'DI Richards,' he said loudly, letting Scarlet know it was a work call. Not that it wasn't already clear. Who else would be calling him at midnight on a Thursday?

'Sorry, guv,' Scarlet heard a female voice say on the other end of the line. 'But it couldn't wait.'

John handed her the menu and crossed to the lounge area of their suite. Scarlet stifled a sigh and sat up, feeling suddenly more sober. No matter where they went, the lives they were hiding from always seemed to follow.

Tuning out John's conversation, his voice hushed and urgent as he gave whoever was on the line some instruction, she looked over the menu. The strawberries didn't seem so inviting now as she eyed the swirling script describing them.

John ended his call, exhaling with a grim lock of the jaw. 'I'm going to have to set off early tomorrow. I need to be back in the office for eight. Everything's kicking off. Sorry.' He sat next to her and shot her an apologetic look.

'Don't worry about it.' Scarlet shrugged. 'That's life.'

'Shall we get those strawberries then?' John asked.

Scarlet crinkled her nose. 'Nah, I don't really fancy them anymore. I'll tell you what I do fancy though,' she added with a half-smile, standing in front of him.

'What?' John wrapped his arms around her waist as she looped hers over his shoulders.

'You.' She winked and pushed him backward, straddling him with a grin.

John flipped her over and leaned down with a mischievous glint in his eye. 'Good,' he said in a husky voice. 'Because I've got plans for you...'

THREE

Isla Carpenter stared at the flimsy lounge door with wide eyes, calculating how much force it would take to break through. Not much, she reckoned. It was nothing but hollowed-out chipboard, the same as every other internal door in these cheap old council flats. At least the front door was slightly thicker, though not by much. She could hear the woman now, punching and kicking and slamming her body against it as she tried to get past *him* and into Isla's tiny one-bedroomed flat. He was pushing her back, standing in her way, but she was putting up a good fight, and Isla wasn't sure exactly who she'd place her bets on. He was a large, formidable man prone to extreme violence, but the woman trying to break down the door was the one person he wouldn't lay hands on.

She was screaming now, cursing and raging like a wild animal, spewing vicious threats. She was going to kill her, she roared. And Isla knew she meant it.

'You hear me, bitch? I will kill you. Get out of my way, you cheating piece of shit, do you hear me? Get out of my fucking way!'

He yelled back at her, their angry voices merging to the point where Isla could no longer make out a word that either of them was saying for a moment.

'Stop protecting her! You let me get to her now or so help me I will make you pay,' she screamed.

A fresh wave of kicks and punches rained down on the door, becoming so loud Isla was sure it would cave in any moment. But still he managed to hold her off.

Another thumping sound was coming from somewhere and she realised that it was the blood rushing through her ears. Her heart beat fast and the panic threatened to overtake her. She locked her jaw and forced herself to stay calm, to stay alert. If she got in here, Isla would have to fight back, but she didn't stand a chance against her opponent. She was bigger, stronger and certainly angrier. And unlike Isla, she had absolutely no limits when it came to inflicting pain on others.

The sound of all the yelling intensified as the front door opened and Isla's jaw dropped in horror. Was she in? Was this it? She braced herself for what was about to come, but when the lounge door slammed back, it wasn't her. It was *him*.

She watched him for a moment, wary as she took in his face. Sweat dripped down his forehead, mixing with the blood from two long parallel cuts above one eyebrow that looked as though they'd been inflicted by sharp nails. He was flustered and angry, glaring down at her, and she fought the urge to flinch, though she reasoned that it couldn't be her he was angry at. Not right now at least.

'My brother's out there but she ain't giving up.' Calvin King glanced back at the door as the furious screeches intensified. 'You need to get out of here for a while.'

'W-What? Where?' Isla stuttered. 'I ain't got nowhere else to go, you know that.'

This tiny depressing flat with its sparse cheap furniture was all she had. He'd made sure of that, she thought resentfully.

Calvin glanced back at the door again, his brow creasing with a frown. 'Here.' He pulled a thick roll of twenty-pound notes out of his pocket.

He started to ease off the rubber band holding them together when the front door flew open with a bang. Isla gasped as the angry, deranged-looking woman surged towards her, Calvin's brother, Jared, barely managing to get in front of her to stop her.

'You fucking bitch, I'll rip your fucking head off!' she screamed.

Out of time, Calvin threw the whole roll of notes towards Isla and ran to help Jared contain her. 'Take it. Just get out of here and find somewhere to stay. Then call me.' He glared back at her. 'You call me straight away, but don't tell no one else. I'll deal with her.'

Isla watched in silence as he left and pulled her front door shut, roaring at the woman in the hallway with a ferocity now that matched hers. Her eyes dropped down to the thick roll of cash and she quickly picked it up, assessing it critically. There must be at least a grand there, she realised. Her heart rate quickened, but this time with hope. This was it. This was her chance.

She rushed into the tiny bedroom, reached under the bed and yanked out an old rucksack. Trying to ignore the row still raging outside, she quickly stuffed a few essentials in and zipped it up, then glanced around, taking in the horrible little flat one last time. She wouldn't miss this place. It had been her prison for far too long. But now she was breaking free. He'd given her an out. A much bigger one than he realised. Because she wasn't sticking around here for him. Oh no. She was getting out of this place altogether. She'd dreamed about it for so long, escaping this run-down estate and her dismal life. And *him*. Now she had some money, it could become a reality. And she had plans – plans that were far away from here.

Opening the bedroom window, Isla swung one leg out and

then the other, lowering herself down onto the rusty fire escape below. Then she carefully pushed the window back shut, pulled her hoodie up over her head and climbed down the ladder, before melting silently into the shadows, the first small ray of hope she'd felt in years spurring her on.

FOUR

Lily zipped her black leather skirt up over her top and twisted in front of the mirror, smoothing her hands down her sides. Satisfied with her classic look, she sat down in the small chair by the window and slipped her feet into her favourite pair of black heels. Work was already at the forefront of her mind, despite the fact she'd been awake only a few minutes. Running an underground empire like theirs meant that she had to be focused at all hours of the day. The family firm was an ever-expanding entity and she thrived on this as she juggled and plotted and reached for the next step in the limitless ladder they climbed.

Ray – her long-term partner, a well-respected face in South London with a firm even bigger than her own – stirred in the king-sized bed under the messy mountain of duvet. Lily looked over to him with a smile as he rubbed his eyes.

'Good morning,' she said, reaching for a pair of small gold earrings.

'It would be better if you were over here,' he replied, his deep voice husky with sleep still. He reached up and crossed his bare muscular arms behind his head, giving her a lazy crooked smile.

Lily's eyes moved down to the soft dark hair on his broad chest and fought the urge to lay her head on it and wrap herself around him as she had been just half an hour before. She looked away with a wry smile. 'You can sit there posing as much as you want, but it's not going to work. We need to get you up and out before Ruby wakes up.'

She glanced at the clock. It was only quarter past seven, but Ruby usually woke around eight and she wasn't in the mood for a frosty daughter today. Ruby and Ray did not see eye to eye these days. They'd never exactly been great friends, but after Ray had taken Ruby off the street the year before and forced her to go cold turkey from the drugs she'd been slowly killing herself with, she'd grown to hate him. He'd done it with good intentions of course, trying to spare Lily the ongoing worry and pain that Ruby's addiction caused. But having suffered a difficult, and at the time unwilling, withdrawal, Ruby couldn't forgive him.

Lily and Ray had been in love for the best part of thirty years and together for a lot of that time. But with two demanding firms to run in different parts of the city, they kept their home lives mostly separate. It had been Lily's choice, firmly declining Ray's pleas over the years to move in with him and even to marry him. It worked, this careful balancing of their relationship and careers. And although she'd never admit it, it also satisfied her inbuilt need for self-preservation.

Their history had not always been rainbows and roses. After her parents had died when she was just fifteen, she'd grown up on the streets, raising her young brother Ronan alone and fighting through every day to survive. She'd been forced to harden her shell and sharpen her wits. When she'd met Ray and fallen in love, she'd let her guard down, and when he'd decided he was too young to be tied down by his first serious girlfriend and her kid brother – telling her he wanted space to play the field – it had crushed her. But she'd survived it, just like everything else, and pushed forward with her life. By the time Ray had realised his mistake, Lily had settled down with someone else. Alfie, a steady stable bet – or so she'd thought. She'd never loved him, not really, but he'd offered her the one thing she craved at that time more than anything. A family.

Her marriage to Alfie hadn't lasted long. After Ruby was born, he'd disappeared into the night, bored of the chaos a tired wife and three kids created, she guessed. And Lily had been left once again holding everything together alone. She'd not just survived this time, she'd thrived, not willing to let the blows of life get the better of her. She'd planted the seeds of the empire they ran today and she'd worked hard, determined to provide her family with everything they'd ever need, with no help from anyone. When Ray took his chance and came back for her, she'd welcomed him with an open heart – but kept him firmly at arm's length. She'd vowed then that no matter how much she loved him or anyone else, she'd never again allow someone close enough to destroy her.

Ray sat up with a regretful sigh and slipped out of her bed, walking over and wrapping his arms around her waist. He buried his face in her neck and kissed it, sniffing appreciatively.

'Mmm. Is that a new perfume?'

'Yeah, it's one Scarlet bought me last Christmas,' she replied.

'I think you should come round tonight wearing that,' Ray suggested. 'That and nothing else,' he added with a mischievous grin at her in the mirror.

Lily laughed and prised herself away. 'I can't tonight, I've got too much on. Come on – get your clothes on. I've got a business to run. And so have you,' she added, shooting him a look.

'True,' he conceded, picking up his shirt and slipping it on. 'I've got a right cock-up to sort out today and all.'

'What's happened?' Lily passed him his shoes.

'One of the lads on my supply chain has gone down with shingles. Which can't be helped, but he was already carrying the load of two and the time it's taken for the message to come up the chain has put us back further. I've got to reroute those deliveries, and clients are getting pissed off at the wait.'

Ray was talking about the cocaine he supplied around South London. Drugs were not something Lily's firm dealt in, a decision she'd made after watching Ruby deteriorate for so many years, but it wasn't something she judged Ray for. Business was business, and drugs made a lot of money in their world.

'You got a fall-back route?' she asked.

'Yeah, but it's top heavy. I don't like to put so much through one person,' Ray answered. 'It's risky.'

Lily glanced out of the window at the sound of a car coming down the street. 'Shit!' she exclaimed.

'What?'

'Cillian's here,' she said, squinting down to make sure she wasn't seeing things.

It was definitely him, but why her son was here so early in the morning was a mystery. She glanced at the clock to check she hadn't misread it before, but it was definitely only twenty past seven. He was never up this early, let alone dressed and at her house. She turned and exchanged a look with Ray, biting her bottom lip. He tried to hide the grin that crept up on his face but didn't quite manage it.

'It's not funny,' she insisted in a loud whisper.

'It is a bit,' he argued. 'How old are we? I feel like a teenager whose girlfriend's parents have come home early.'

'Come on, get dressed. You can sneak out the back while I distract him in the kitchen. Christ, I thought we only had Ruby to hide you from this morning.'

Cillian and Connor, her twin sons, were, of course, fully aware of her relationship with Ray, but they didn't like it. They had naturally assumed it was Ray keeping their mother at arm's length and saw it as a slight. No matter how much she'd tried to explain things to them, they never quite understood. It wasn't that she was ashamed of Ray staying over, or that she *needed* to hide it, but it was just easier to avoid the clash of opinions on her personal life.

She kissed Ray goodbye and went downstairs to find Cillian. *Why on earth was he here so early?* she wondered, a seed of worry planting itself in her stomach. Early mornings in their world rarely meant anything good. She descended the stairs and put on her game face, ready to find out.

FIVE

'Cillian, what's going on? Why are you here so early?' she asked, pushing back her tight blonde curls in an attempt to smooth them.

Cillian was standing by the open fridge, studying its contents. He pulled out a banana and closed the door, leaning back on the side while he peeled it. 'I've started back at the club. Training each morning at six. This was on my way back – thought I'd pop in and grab a coffee with you,' he replied. 'More importantly though, what kind of psycho keeps bananas in the fridge?' He took a bite and looked up at her with a frown.

Her tension evaporated and she felt relief wash over her, thankful that there was no dark, dangerous emergency that required her help just yet. It was far too early for all that. She hadn't even had her coffee yet.

'The kind that like their fruit cold and fresh,' she replied. 'You put a pot on?' She glanced over at the coffee machine and saw that he had, then opened the cupboard and pulled two mugs out.

'Only two?' he asked, eyeing them.

Lily tensed and closed the cupboard door. 'Rubes won't be up for ages.'

Cillian nodded, accepting her answer, and she relaxed. Turning away from him, she briefly eyed the hallway, wondering if Ray was out yet. 'So,' she changed the subject, 'what's motivated you to get back into training?'

Cillian shrugged and pulled a face. 'It don't hurt to be in top condition in our game, does it?'

Lily nodded and assessed him subtly. His handsome, chiselled face was hard, his dark brown eyes filled with the kind of steel that would make men think twice before causing trouble, and his defined muscles showed through his well-cut suit. Both her boys kept themselves strong and in good shape. They had to. Their world was harsh, and respect was often earned through fear and violence. It was just their way. The law of the jungle. The strongest survived and thrived, while the weak fell by the wayside.

'As you're around this morning, can you start the market collections early? We're spread thin tonight, so I could do with freeing one of you up.' Picking up her freshly poured coffee, Lily walked over to the breakfast table and opened the window, pulling a cigarette out of the packet on the sill and lighting it up.

'Sure. I was hoping to talk to you about something first though,' he replied.

'Shoot.' She took a sip of her coffee and waited. She'd known he hadn't just dropped in for a chat.

'Yesterday Jimmy told me he's been given notice that the woman who owns the club is planning to sell it to property developers.'

Lily frowned, shocked by this news, but waited for him to continue before commenting.

'It ain't gone through yet, but I can't sit by and watch that happen, Mum.' He pushed his hand agitatedly through his hair.

'No,' she said. 'You can't.' She took another drag on her

cigarette and then blew out the smoke. She knew as well as Cillian how important the club was to the community.

'What are you thinking?' she asked.

'I did some digging last night. The woman who owns it has a few things on the boil, all quite different. Does a lot of charity work – and gets paid very well for it,' he added with sharp disapproval. 'My guess is she bought this trying to make herself look good, only to realise it don't turn over much. So she's flipping it on the quiet.'

'Who's the developer?' Lily asked.

Cillian grimaced. 'AJ Conway.'

'Oh, you've got to be kidding me,' Lily groaned.

AJ had grown up on the same streets they had, a few years after Lily. He'd been among the next wave of up-and-coming reprobates at a time when she'd already made a name for herself. She'd considered taking him on for a job years before, trialling him out to join the firm, but they'd caught him out on an underhanded scheme that went against their own interests and had moved on, leaving him behind. He'd eventually made his own way in their world, partnering up with different firms job by job until he eventually formed his own – very crooked – building firm. He was the biggest cowboy in the business, but a successful one due to having the gift of the gab and a ruthlessness that knew no boundaries. They weren't exactly enemies, but they weren't really friends either.

'I don't think AJ is going to be open to having his heartstrings pulled,' Lily said.

'If he had any,' Cillian added. 'Jimmy's putting a petition in, but realistically he ain't going to get anywhere. It's a prime piece of land in an area that desperately needs more housing.'

Lily pursed her lips. 'Scarlet and I will go visit him today, see what we can find out. See if there's anything we can negotiate. That's got to be our first port of call. Then we'll have to look into speaking with this woman.'

Cillian nodded. 'Keep me in the loop?'

''Course,' Lily agreed.

Cillian picked up his coffee and drank some of it before putting the mug in the sink. 'I'll go get Connor and do the rounds.'

He began making his way towards the front door. 'Oh, and Mum?' he called back on his way out. 'Next time Ray's over, if you're going to go to the trouble of hiding it and sneaking him out the back, tell him not to park his motor just down the street in full view, yeah?'

And with that he left, shutting the door behind him.

SIX

Lily and Scarlet pulled up outside the builder's yard and stepped out of the car. As they walked through the front gates, Lily noticed that AJ had expanded since the last time she'd seen it, clearly having bought out the commercial plot that used to sit next door. Several brand-new heavy-duty machines were neatly parked to one side, looking as though they hadn't been used yet, not a scratch on their bright yellow paintwork. He'd evidently been doing very well lately.

Several of the men around the yard looked over, suspicion in their eyes. No smiles were forthcoming, but Lily ignored this. She wasn't here to see them.

'Friendly lot, aren't they?' Scarlet muttered sarcastically.

'Indeed. But I'd still take them over AJ,' she added darkly.

'Is he that unfriendly?' Scarlet asked as they approached the largest Portakabin on the site.

Lily pulled a grim expression. 'It's not that he's unfriendly exactly, it's more that—'

'Lily Drew!' A loud voice boomed out at them as the door to the Portakabin was thrown back, and a large ruddy-faced man beamed at them. 'You beautiful thing, you. Finally given old

Ray the boot and come to find a real man?' He winked with a wide grin and pointedly raked her up and down with his eyes.

'Ah. I see,' Scarlet said quietly as they approached.

Lily felt her distaste for the man rise up into her throat, but she swallowed it down, ignoring the comment. This sleazy façade would fade soon enough, once he realised why they were there.

'AJ. It's been a long time.' She stopped just at the bottom of the steps leading up into his office.

He pulled back from the doorway and made a wide sweep with his arm. 'Come in, both of you. I don't think I've had the pleasure of meeting this little vixen.'

Lily saw Scarlet's jaw tighten, her grey-blue eyes cool in her peripheral vision, but the girl kept the response she no doubt wished to deliver to herself for now. She stepped up into the cabin and Scarlet followed. Inside, the place reminded Lily of some sort of budget Hawaiian tiki hut. Posters of bright orange sunsets dotted the walls, a floral garland hung from the whiteboard behind AJ's desk and there was a small circular cocktail station to one side, a glass full of paper umbrellas standing proudly in the centre.

'Fancy one?' AJ asked, noticing that her gaze had rested here.

'No thank you, not for me.'

Scarlet hurriedly shook her head as he glanced in her direction.

'Oh dear. All business and no fun, girls?' He tutted. 'What is the world coming to?'

'Now that's a question I've been asking lately myself,' Lily replied, taking a seat in front of the desk and looking up at him expectantly.

Scarlet took the seat next to her and AJ took his place opposite them. He laced his fingers together on the desk and raised his eyebrows enquiringly.

'So what can I do you for?' he asked.

'You've put in a planning application for a block of flats where Repton Boxing Club currently stands,' Lily said, getting straight to the point. 'Surely you can't be serious?'

AJ looked surprised. 'How'd you know about that? I ain't told no one yet.'

'Planning applications are public, you know that,' she replied. 'When Jimmy got the notice that the owner was planning to sell, he checked the lists.'

AJ pulled a look of resignation. 'Well, there we go. Cat's out of the bag. And yeah, I'm dead serious. That place is a gold mine.'

'That place was where you grew up,' Lily reminded him sharply. 'Where you went when you needed to escape or work out your anger. Jimmy and the others were always there for you.'

'That they were,' he agreed, nonplussed. 'But that was years ago. This is now. Times change and people move on.'

'You might have, but there's a whole new generation of young men, just like you, who go there and get just as much out of it as you did. How could you take that away?' Lily asked. She knew her words were likely falling on deaf ears, but it was worth a try before things got more complicated.

'They'll start it up again somewhere else,' he said dismissively.

'In a place with no history,' she shot back, feeling her anger rise at his flippancy. She took a deep breath and forced herself to calm down.

'Nah, I get it,' Scarlet piped up.

Lily's head shot round in surprise, and her eyes narrowed. Scarlet's expression was fairly unreadable, but the glint in her eyes gave her away.

'At least someone does,' AJ replied.

''Course. It's a prime location and honestly that woman

probably doesn't even know what she's sitting on. But *you* do.'
She shot a dazzling smile in his direction. 'You strike me as a
man who can drive a hard bargain. Go on, what did you get it
for? I bet you charmed your way down to a decent price.'

AJ preened at the flattery and puffed out his chest. Lily had
to hide a grin. So easily manipulated.

'I did, as it happens. A cool three mill. It's easily worth
another three hundred if the planning gets passed,' he said
proudly.

'Impressive,' Scarlet replied, the sarcasm only barely
concealed.

'I like this one, Lil,' he said loudly. 'She's got good business
sense.'

'She does indeed,' Lily replied wryly. 'So what you going to
do if the planning don't get passed?'

'It will,' he replied confidently. 'Ticks all the boxes. And as
soon as it does, I'll be signing the papers.'

Lily nodded. 'But if it doesn't, then the land isn't worth
much at all, is it? And definitely not worth anything to you.'

AJ's blasé demeanour suddenly changed and the mood in
the room shifted. His smile disappeared and he stared at her
icily, holding her gaze.

'So that's the game you're playing,' he said in a low voice.
'There ain't nothing you can do about that planning. I know all
about Jimmy's little petition. The list he's getting them all to
sign to keep the old place running. But the truth is, it's run-
down. It's a fucking health hazard, to be exact.' He looked her
up and down, this time coldly and critically. 'Everything sits in
my favour. I ain't even had to grease any palms on this one, to
get what I want. There ain't nothing that could stop it now,
other than the odd design niggle which I can deal with easily.
So I suggest you back off and get back to your own businesses,
in your own neck of the woods.'

'And if we don't?' Lily challenged, arching one unimpressed eyebrow.

AJ let out a quiet, humourless laugh. 'Don't push me, Lil. I'd hate for us not to be friends anymore.'

There was a loaded silence and then Lily stood up. Scarlet followed suit as she smoothed her knee-length leather skirt and picked a small piece of lint from her black turtleneck top.

'Good to meet you, AJ,' Scarlet said, her tone flat. She walked over to the door and opened it, descending the stairs out into the sunshine beyond.

Lily studied AJ for a few moments. 'Thing is, we're already in our neck of the woods, AJ,' she said, following Scarlet. She paused and looked back. 'And we were never actually friends.'

She shot him a cold smile and then left, leaving the door open behind her, more determined than ever to stop these plans from going any further.

SEVEN

Scarlet cast her gaze across the busy room as she approached her aunt. It was a big night tonight but luckily not a stressful one. On the upper floor of their pub, the Blind Pig, they hosted regular gambling nights for those in the underworld who wanted somewhere to relax and gamble their money without leaving a paper trail or having their movements logged on CCTV. As these evenings were run for business rather than pleasure, the Drews kept the premises neutral, and anyone in the know was welcome so long as they followed the rules. This did mean that on occasion they had to entertain people from firms they didn't personally like, but it was rare. Those firms usually kept their distance.

It was more common that people would accidentally end up in the same room as their rivals and these were the evenings that could prove stressful. The rules were strict. There were to be no upsets of any kind on the premises, and anyone involved in violence or personal arguments would be ejected and banned for life. No one wanted that, so for the most part the rules were respected – but when tempers began to rise at the sight of a foe, it sometimes took some stern reminders and their heavy security presence to keep the peace.

Tonight, though, there was no undercurrent between parties, and the atmosphere was jovial and relaxed. The reason it was a big night was that some of the most notorious heads of the underworld were here. Freddie and Paul Tyler, underworld royalty, were seated at one of the poker tables along with Cos Christou, head of a large Greek firm in the north of the city, drinking whisky, playing cards and holding a casual meeting.

Her Aunt Lily had known the Tyler brothers – and their younger siblings, Michael and Thea, sadly now deceased – since they were small children. She'd apparently lived a few doors down on the estate they'd grown up in, and after their dad had died, had often babysat for their mother Mollie, being a few years older than them. Now, all these years on, her aunt was still close with the family.

Seeing Paul Tyler lift his glass to his mouth and drain it, she quickly changed direction and swung by the bar to pick up the whisky he'd been favouring all evening.

Approaching their table, Scarlet smiled. 'Let me refill that for you.'

'Thanks,' Paul said, his voice deep and craggy as he held out his glass. 'Just leave it here – save you topping us up every five minutes.'

'Sure,' Scarlet replied, placing it between him and Freddie.

'Cos, have you met Scarlet?' Freddie asked, placing his cards down and turning in his chair. The dealer stopped and clasped his hands together, waiting respectfully.

'Not officially,' Cos replied, turning to face her with a warm grin.

'Scarlet Drew. It's great to meet you.' She offered him her hand.

'Cos Christou,' he replied, shaking it. She knew that already of course, but she nodded just the same.

'I like what your aunt's done to the place,' Freddie continued, looking round approvingly.

The room was large and airy, spanning the entire width and length of the pub, apart from the two small offices at the back. The walls were panelled, painted midnight blue with large gold lamps throwing soft light around the room. Tasteful paintings with gilt frames adorned the walls, and comfortable leather chairs were spaced around each of the carefully spaced gambling tables. It was just the right balance of elegant and cosy.

'Thank you,' came a voice from Scarlet's side. She turned to see her aunt had moved to join them. Lily wore a wide smile – a genuine one, Scarlet noted. She was one of the few who could always tell the difference. 'Are you all having a good evening?' Lily asked.

————

Lily cast her gaze around the room, subtly checking that no one on the neighbouring tables was listening in to their conversation. She wanted to casually bring up the situation at the boxing club with Freddie in the hope he may offer some assistance, but she didn't need everyone knowing their business. There were some who might be friendly with AJ and she didn't want to risk this discussion getting back to them.

'We certainly are,' Paul said in reply to her question. 'Though I think your dealer here is cheating, the amount he's had off me tonight.'

Martin, the dealer, stiffened, his eyes widening marginally as they flickered over to his boss.

'I'm joking, mate,' Paul continued with a chuckle. 'Don't get your knickers in a twist.'

'How's tricks?' Freddie asked.

'They're good. Everything's running smoothly.' Lily

nodded. 'Few things going on. I seem to have picked a new fight with AJ Conway today.'

'Oh dear,' Freddie said with a wide grin. 'You're that bored?'

'You know me,' Lily replied with a laugh. 'I don't much like sitting still.'

'Not a fan of smooth waters?' Freddie asked with an amused glint in his eye.

Lily wrinkled her nose. 'Smooth waters never made a skilled sailor, you know that. And I couldn't stand for my skills to be dulled.'

Freddie laughed openly now. 'Dull is not a word anyone would *ever* use to describe you, Lily Drew. Or your skills.'

'True,' she conceded.

'So what's AJ done to rile you up?' The jokey tone was gone and interested concern had taken its place. 'Must be pretty big for you to bother with him.'

Freddie was about as much of a fan of AJ as she was. He and AJ were around the same age and had entered the underworld at the same time, but Freddie had never had much time for the other man. He was too much of a wide boy to have been accepted by someone like Freddie. A chancer who crossed anyone and everyone to get what he wanted. These weren't traits that any of them respected. To get anywhere in the underworld you had to show loyalty and a certain subtlety that AJ had never quite grasped.

Lily pulled a grim expression. 'You ain't gonna like it much either.'

Freddie frowned. 'What do you mean?' he demanded, lowering his voice.

'He's in negotiations to buy Repton Boxing Club,' she replied.

'Right.' Freddie didn't look pleased, but he wasn't furious. Yet.

She delivered the blow. 'He's submitted a planning application to tear it down and built flats there.'

'*What?*' he roared.

The room went quiet, and people turned to see what was happening. Freddie took a deep breath and composed himself, waiting for everyone to return to their own business.

'What?' he asked again, his voice still angry but quiet this time.

'Exactly,' Lily replied. She looked around, checking everyone was OK and not earwigging in their direction. 'We're dealing with it.'

The club was on their turf, so naturally it was up to them to sort out.

'How?' he demanded.

'I'm not entirely sure yet,' she admitted. 'Scarlet got the price out of him – it's too much for us to compete with.'

'You'd buy it?' Freddie asked in surprise.

'I've thought about it.' Lily glanced at Scarlet. She hadn't discussed it with anyone yet, but it had been an option she'd considered. 'But the price is too steep, and to be honest, I think he'd outbid me even if I did counter.'

Freddie tapped his fingers on the table as he thought it over. 'Unless you drove the price down,' he said.

'How?' she asked.

'There are ways. I've got a man in the planning office. I'll have a word and come back to you. There must be a loophole somewhere that would cause AJ so much trouble he can't keep it up.'

'Thanks,' Lily said. 'Any help we can get is appreciated.' She squeezed his shoulder. 'Anyway. Enough business for now, you're here to relax and gamble. Enjoy the tables, and anything you need, let us know – we'll send it over.'

'Thanks, Lil,' Paul said, his deep voice warm as he shot her a smile.

She winked and moved away. Casting her gaze over the room one more time, she caught Andy's eye and signalled for him to keep close watch, then walked through to her office. Scarlet followed her in and closed the door.

Taking a seat, Scarlet pushed her long dark hair back over her shoulder, fanning herself with her hand. 'We really need to get air con in here,' she said.

'I'll see what we can do,' Lily replied, sitting down behind her desk and lighting a cigarette.

'It will be interesting to see what his man comes back with,' Scarlet mused. 'I'm sure AJ was bullshitting us when he said he hadn't had to grease any palms to get this through. Did you see the way his eyes flickered away when he said that?'

Lily nodded. 'I did.'

She took a drag of her cigarette, savouring the warm smoke as she inhaled it into her lungs. They had a battle ahead of them. And this was only one side of it. They still had to deal with this Miranda woman, who wanted to sell the place. But that could wait for now.

'Ruby's birthday's coming up next week,' Lily said, changing the subject abruptly.

'OK.' Scarlet regarded Lily carefully.

'I want to throw her a party.' Lily smiled, grateful that she could even make the suggestion. 'It's her first birthday since she's been back in the fold and I think it would be a nice gesture.'

Scarlet nodded, keeping her expression neutral. 'Sure. Well, anything you need me to organise, the food or—'

'Scarlet, I want you to start giving her a chance,' Lily said, cutting her off.

Scarlet paused, her mouth closing and then reopening to respond, but Lily spoke again. 'Don't tell me you have, because we both know you haven't.'

Scarlet exhaled heavily through her nose, and Lily took

another drag on her cigarette. The issues between Scarlet and Ruby had been brewing for months. Years, really. But this was the first time she'd outright brought it up. Until now, she'd stayed out of it, hoping things would calm down over time. But they hadn't. If anything, they were now more strained than ever and it wasn't good for business.

'Look, Lil, I know that she's family. And believe it or not, for that reason I actually *have* tried.' Scarlet's grey-blue eyes clouded over with a dark, brooding look of concern. 'I've tried to ignore the history and the outbursts, and I've tried to have patience and understanding because of the things she's been through. But I can't ignore it all.' She ran her hands back through her thick dark hair. 'I know you don't like to be reminded, Lil, but this is the same person who lied and stole from us on a regular basis for years.'

Lily pursed her lips but let Scarlet continue.

'And we let her, because she's family. She lied and stole and spent every waking hour doing everything and anything to get her next fix. She treated us like shit and only came around when she needed something. And not just us – she betrayed friend after friend, using them and dropping them like hot shit the second they had nothing more to give. She's used up and dropped absolutely *everyone* she's ever had in her life, like some sort of locust—'

'That's enough.' Lily's tone was sharp, and she flashed Scarlet a look of warning. Lily, more than anyone, knew the history of Ruby's betrayals and lies. But there was a limit to what she would allow others to say about members of her family – even if they were members of that family themselves.

Scarlet exhaled, tired. 'I'm not trying to insult her or upset you. But that's the truth. It's how she was.'

'*Was* being the appropriate word,' Lily stressed. 'She's changed, Scarlet. She's been clean now for a good eight or nine months. Even despite all she went through in that fire.' Lily closed her eyes briefly, the pain and guilt she carried from that time rising up like a wave. She let it pass and then continued. 'If anything was going to set her back, that would have been it. But she's still here. And she's turned up every single day, working hard, learning what she needs to learn. And I'll admit, I was sceptical too at first. But she's proven herself. And it's time for you to recognise that.'

Scarlet looked away, her jaw tightening before she responded. 'I can't promise to become her new best friend, Lil, but I'll try to do better.'

Lily nodded. 'That's all I ask. Now, as for the party, I thought we'd keep it cosy. I'll shut the pub for the night and we'll have just the nearest and dearest as guests. We'll put on food and cocktails, get her some nice presents, let down our hair and make it fun. Something to cheer her up and reward her for all the hard work she's put in so far. Something to show her we're supporting her.' She held Scarlet's gaze until she nodded.

''Course. Let me know if you need me to do anything,' she replied dutifully.

'I will. Why don't you get back out on the floor? I have a few calls to make.'

'Sure.' Scarlet smiled and stood up, walking out of the office and leaving Lily alone with her thoughts.

Lily let out a long heavy sigh and shook her head. Scarlet and Ruby were cousins. They were both part of the firm. They should have been getting on, united in their common goals and their shared blood, the way she and Ronan used to be. Together, two such strong, powerful women would be a force to be reckoned with. Unstoppable. If only they could see that.

Apart, however, they were dangerous. Both so strong-willed and proud and calculating. If they didn't start to ease up on each other soon and find peace in this firm together, she could only see one path ahead of them. And it was filled with destruction.

EIGHT

Cillian slammed his fist with all his strength into the face of the man in front of him. The force sent him flying back onto the floor with a grunt of pain. Bouncing back, Cillian rolled his shoulder and paced from side to side, watching him closely to see if he was going to get up, then lifted his arm, wiping the sweat from his forehead. For a second the other man looked as though he might try to get up and fight back, but then resignation set in and he tapped the floor to indicate that he was done.

'Nice shot, Drew,' the coach training them shouted. 'Barnes, you need to keep your bloody gloves up.'

'Yes, coach,' Barnes mumbled, wiping a small trickle of blood from the corner of his mouth.

Cillian leaned over and offered his arm with a friendly smile. 'Here.'

Barnes gripped it and pulled himself up. 'You're a fast bastard,' he said, grinning back.

'So I'm told, mate,' Cillian replied as they both stepped out of the ring.

'That's what his missus says, eh?' a nearby lad mocked, looking to his group of friends for the obligatory laugh he figured he'd earned with his quick wit. Except none was forthcoming. They'd all fallen silent, looking over to infamous local gangster Cillian Drew to see how the disrespectful comment would be taken. It was clear that they understood who he was – and just as clear that the man who'd spoken didn't.

Cillian turned and walked slowly over to the lad, giving him a hard look. 'What was that?' he asked, his tone dangerously cool.

The lad looked to his group for help, then back to Cillian with a wary grin. 'I'm only messing about.' He tried to laugh it off.

'Oh, you're messing?' Cillian asked, turning to Barnes with a cold mocking smile that didn't reach his eyes. 'He's messing, Barnesy.' Barnes made a sound of disapproval. 'He's messing with *me*.' Cillian shook his head in amazement then turned and looked the man who'd spoken up and down. 'Right. You're, what – light heavyweight?'

'Yeah, that's right,' he answered, his expression nervous.

Cillian nodded slowly. 'Get in the ring,' he ordered.

The man faltered, his smile starting to fade. 'What? With you?'

'Yeah.' Cillian waited, restrapping the glove he'd been about to remove. 'We're gonna do some training.'

He saw the coach step back and lean against the wall to watch, out of the corner of his eye. Not a word was uttered in the silent room. This boxing club was neutral ground, but he was a Drew, and everyone here still naturally showed him the respect that name commanded.

'But you're a heavyweight. I ain't in your league.'

'That's right. You're not,' Cillian replied, his gaze holding the other man's. 'Get in.'

The man looked around, seemingly checking for any other options but, after realising he had none, turned reluctantly and stepped into the ring. 'OK then,' he said, not sounding quite so brave now as Cillian stepped in after him. 'What sort of training are we—'

WHAM.

The hard blow hit fast on the underside of his chin and sent him flying up into the air before he slammed backward onto the floor, crying out in pain. It was a vicious move, one that shouldn't have been allowed. But the coach said nothing, keeping well out of it as Cillian had known he would.

Cillian nodded to him out of respect, to let him know he was done with the man, then calmly unstrapped his gloves and began to unwind the bandages from his wrists. He stared down at the pitiful figure on the ground.

'What sort of training are we doing?' He repeated the man's question. 'That was training on respect. I wouldn't push for a second lesson if I were you.'

Barnes gave the lad a look that told him he'd earned what he'd been given, then turned and walked over to the changing rooms with Cillian. 'He won't do that again in a hurry,' he said.

'Not if he knows what's good for him,' Cillian agreed.

'How's your Billie anyway? She good?' Barnes asked.

Cillian smiled a wide warm smile. 'She's great, mate. Absolutely pukka.'

———

Billie felt Cillian's arms wrap around her waist and his grip tighten as he pulled her body towards his in the bed. She turned into him sleepily and nuzzled into his hard chest. 'What time is it?' she mumbled, still not really ready to get up for the day.

'Half seven. I've just got back from the club,' he replied, kissing her forehead gently.

She looked up with a smile, kissing him back on the lips. 'I probably need to get up then, don't I?' she said resignedly.

'Or...' he said with a glint in his eye, 'you could stay right there all day and not get dressed at all.' She laughed and he pulled her even closer. 'We could turn off our phones, order takeout...'

'And in no time at all your mum would be standing at the foot of this bed demanding to know why you ain't at work, and glaring at me like I've bewitched you and held you captive,' Billie said, cutting him off with a laugh.

'Maybe you did,' Cillian considered. 'Maybe that's why I can't get enough of you.' He kissed her deeply, his hands roaming over her body in the ways he knew she liked.

With difficulty she pulled away and firmly removed his hands. 'Stop it, you naughty bugger.'

She pulled herself up into a seated position and dragged her fingers through her sunshine-blonde shoulder-length hair in an attempt to smooth it down. 'You need to go to work, and I need to get home to change and sort myself out properly before I go to work too.' She sighed, wishing she could give in and spend another hour with him in bed, but she really couldn't.

'Come on.' She slipped out of the bed and shoved one of his T-shirts on. 'Let's have a cup of tea before I go.'

She padded through his flat to the wide open-plan kitchen the other side of the living room and put the kettle on. Cillian followed her, wearing nothing but a pair of jogging bottoms. She gave him a wry smile as he sat at the breakfast bar.

'What?' he asked.

'You know what,' she replied.

He flexed with a slow predatory grin. 'What, this? You like what you see?'

'You know I do,' she replied, turning firmly away from him and pulling two mugs down from the cupboard. 'But I can't be distracted – I have a client at nine thirty and I need to be ready.'

There was a short companiable silence as she made the tea. Handing him a mug, she leaned over the breakfast bar facing him and sipped at her own. He watched her with a thoughtful expression.

'I've been thinking about this whole morning thing, you know,' he said, wrapping his hands around his tea.

'What do you mean?'

Cillian's dark brown eyes moved away from hers for a moment, then settled again with a resolute expression. 'I think you should move in with me.'

'Oh,' she said, surprised by the sudden statement.

'I mean, you're here most nights, and when you're not, I usually end up at yours. And it means you wouldn't have to keep going between places like this in the morning. It makes sense. And, to be honest' – he shrugged and stared at her with a look that completely melted her – 'I just want you here. All the time.'

Billie felt her heart flutter in her chest, and the love she felt for him surged. She bit her bottom lip and grinned. Somewhere in the back of her mind she knew she should probably take some time to consider it properly, but she ignored it. Her heart had already answered and was screaming at her to voice it out loud.

'Yes,' she said with an excited giggle. 'Yes, I'll move in with you.' She put her hands over her mouth, surprised at herself for jumping in so swiftly. She wasn't usually so impulsive when it came to men, but Cillian wasn't just any man. Her heart well and truly belonged to him, and she knew his belonged to her. This was another level entirely, their relationship. It had been from the start, and now she was as ready as he was to take it up a notch.

Moving around the breakfast bar, she wrapped her arms around his neck and kissed him, happier in that moment than she could ever remember feeling before. He returned her kiss with passion before pulling away and looking at her with a smile.

'I'll have the keys cut today and then let's do it,' he said.

'We'll move things around, work out what you want to bring and then I'll arrange a moving van. And then that's it. We live together.' His tone was full of joy, matching his expression.

'Well, that's not quite it,' Billie replied. 'There is one more thing we have to do.'

He frowned. 'What?'

'We have to tell your mum.'

NINE

Lily walked down the side of the Roman Road market watching the shoppers as they hurried from stall to stall in the bright spring sunshine. Sellers were shouting out their wares, from ripe red fruits to plush leather bags, and one or two gave her a respectful nod as she caught their eye. Pushing her hair back to mask the action, Lily glanced over her shoulder, to check that no one was following or watching her. She stopped and leaned back against a wall, lighting a cigarette and staring out at the crowds ahead.

'Young girl, eighteen, maybe twenty. Been sniffing around asking about ya.' The quiet words came from the young man a couple of feet away from her, wearing a dark green tracksuit and a baseball cap pulled low.

Jamie was their watcher. Someone who looked – to anyone not in the know – as though he had no association with them or the market, but who in reality watched over everything like a hawk. He told the sellers when it was safe to peddle hot goods and when to quickly hide them from market inspectors or police. He watched for potential thieves and dealt with them should the need arise. And above all he acted as the eyes and ears for the Drews, with regard to anything they might need to know.

'Who is she?' Lily asked, not looking round. She was sure no one was watching her, but just in case she was wrong, she didn't want to give their relationship away.

'Not sure. She asked around a few of the stalls if they knew you, if this was your market. Said she's after a job, but what kind she wouldn't say. When they asked her name to pass on, she clammed up.'

Lily frowned and took a drag on her cigarette, blowing the smoke out slowly before answering. 'What *do* you know?'

'I watched her yesterday – she was hanging around close to pack-up. Was going to follow her to see where she went.' He shifted, pulling out his own cigarettes and lighting one. 'Turned out there weren't no need. She's staying in the City View.'

Lily didn't need to see the direction he nodded in – her eyes instinctively moved to the tired-looking hotel just down the road. She glanced up at the windows, wondering if the girl was watching the market right now. She couldn't see anyone, but that didn't necessarily mean she wasn't there. Her jaw locked and she pulled a grim expression.

'I don't think she's from here,' Jamie added, puffing on his cigarette.

'Because?' she asked.

'She's got a Northern accent. Plus the hotel,' he added. 'And she don't seem to know the area.'

Lily took another drag on her cigarette, wondering what business the girl had here. 'What does she look like?'

'Short, pale, proper skinny. Dark blondish hair, not short but not long. Scruffy clothes. Jumpy – very jumpy.'

'Thanks.' Lily took one last drag and dropped her cigarette to the floor, grinding it out with her shoe. 'Keep an eye on her comings and goings and let me know when she's next hanging round the market, straight away.'

'Will do.'

Lily walked away, picking up the pace as she made her way back to her car. Passing the hotel, she snuck a glance once more at the windows, but no face stared back at her. Who was this girl who'd turned up out of the blue, seeking her? How did she know who she was? And more importantly, what the hell did she want?

TEN

Ruby went over the production line schedule again and rubbed her head. She'd rejigged it several times but however she played it, at least one of their orders would be overdue, which was not good business. She glanced at the clock and wondered when her mother would arrive. She'd texted, asking if she could come in and work through the problem with her. Lily had replied to say she'd sort something out, but that had been over an hour ago.

She'd rejoined the family business nine months ago. At first, they had all been reluctant to allow her into their precious inner sanctum, giving her the most menial position possible as an unnecessary assistant in their new hairdressing salon. She grudgingly understood why, even if she didn't like it. She'd spent so many years disappearing down the rabbit hole of drugs and using the family coffers to pay for it, that they'd naturally grown wary of her real intentions every time she surfaced.

The salon was mainly a front to launder money, and the job had been created purely to keep her busy somewhere they could keep an eye on her. She'd felt trapped and frustrated there, but eventually, with a couple of nudges from those still quietly rooting for her, she'd seen the opportunity it had presented. She'd thrown herself into the job with as much vigour as she could muster and had proved herself to be hard-working and reliable.

One of the firm's psychotic rivals had tried – and almost succeeded – to burn her alive six months ago, after which her mother's protective instinct had focused almost solely around her recovery. It was then that she'd seized her chance. She'd asked to join the firm properly, to learn the business from all sides. Her mother had agreed, seeing how far she'd come, declaring that she'd earned her rightful place, and the family had celebrated. Or most of them had anyway.

Her cousin, Scarlet, had not been able to mask her feelings. When Lily had agreed, Scarlet's expression had morphed through surprise, to panic, to irritation, before she quickly masked it. It was such a swift contortion that if she'd blinked, she might have missed it. But she'd seen. Scarlet hated the fact that Ruby was now a fully fledged part of the firm. A contender for her place in the hierarchy. She was scared – and she should be.

The door to the office opened and Ruby looked up expectantly. Her mood darkened and her muscles tensed when she saw the object of her dark thoughts walk into the room. Scarlet closed the door behind her and shrugged off her light red jacket, draping it over the back of the chair before sitting down opposite Ruby. Neither smiled at the other. They only kept up the pretence in front of family, and even then it was just the bare minimum.

'Lil asked me to pop down and look at the schedule. What's up?' Scarlet said, cutting straight to the point.

Ruby clenched her jaw and turned round the pages she'd been staring at for the last hour so that Scarlet could see. She felt her cheeks flood red. Why did Lily have to send her cousin to help? Scarlet would be loving this. Yet another chance to gloat over something Ruby had failed at and she had saved.

Scarlet frowned at the papers, her eyes flitting over the pencilled-in columns. 'Why are the lines so packed – did we take on another client?'

'No, same as always, other than that extra run for Toxago. But we've done that before – it shouldn't cause overflow.'

'No, it shouldn't,' Scarlet murmured in agreement. She narrowed her gaze at something and then looked up at Ruby. 'Marlow, when was their last order sent out? Can you bring it up?' She gestured towards the desktop.

Ruby moved the mouse and the screen sprang to life. She clicked through their files until she found what she was looking for, turning the screen slightly so Scarlet could see. She clocked it at the same time Scarlet did and immediately groaned, kicking herself for not seeing it before.

'Their last order was only three weeks ago,' Scarlet said, jumping in before Ruby could say a word. 'They only need a delivery every two months. You've bumped this up a month. Take them out and put it into next month's and all the lines will flow.'

'Yep,' Ruby replied tightly. 'I can see it.'

Scarlet stood up and picked up her jacket, swinging it over her shoulders. 'It's just attention to detail,' she said in an impatient tone as she looked at her watch. 'Try looking properly before you call for help next time.'

Ruby gritted her teeth to halt the response that sat on her tongue and quietly seethed as Scarlet swept back out of the office. It was a simple mistake – anyone could make it. And with anyone else it wouldn't have been a big deal. But she knew Scarlet *would* make it a big deal – would make sure Lily knew that Ruby had fallen short and that she had saved the day. That was just how Scarlet worked.

Ruby and Scarlet had never got on even in childhood; natural enemies right from the start. But that childish feeling of dislike had grown into something far more sinister over the years. Scarlet had learned to play the game quickly when they were younger. If Ruby had drawn her mother a picture, Scarlet had performed a song. If Ruby had done well in a spelling test, Scarlet was top of the class. If Ruby threw a teenage tantrum, Scarlet had angelically cleaned up the mess. And later, whilst Ruby had partied and rebelled her way through early adult life, Scarlet had made strategic moves to nestle into the heart of the family firm, making herself indispensable to Lily. To an outsider, it would look as though Scarlet was everything Ruby wasn't. But Ruby knew better. Scarlet wasn't naturally better – she just had an insatiable urge to win. And Ruby had always been her competition.

But Ruby had grown tired of being the loser in this silent lifelong battle. And she'd now made plans of her own. Plans that would leave Scarlet in the dust, as Ruby took back the position that should always have been hers – that was her birthright. It was a long game, but it would be worth it. And Scarlet would never see it coming.

ELEVEN

Lily left her car on the main road and carefully walked the rest of the way down the steep cobbled loading entrance towards the docks. She felt the warm afternoon breeze on her face and looked out over the wide murky river below and at the skyline beyond. It was a strangely peaceful place, for such an industrious area. She could understand why Freddie favoured this Portakabin office.

A group of men lingering by a stack of crates eyed her as she approached. One slightly older man in a flat cap moved to block her way.

'Alright, Miss?' he asked, his words polite but his tone and expression guarded. 'Can I help you?'

'I'm here to see Freddie,' she replied, coming to a stop.

'Yer name?' he asked.

'Lily Drew,' she answered.

The man nodded and stepped aside. 'He's in there.' He pointed to one of the two Portakabins nearby and she smiled her thanks before heading over to it.

The door opened before she could lift her hand to knock and Paul smiled at her, standing back to allow her entrance.

'Saw you coming from the window,' he explained, before shutting it behind her and half sitting on top of a low set of drawers.

'You always were a good lookout even when you were a kid,' she replied with a smile. 'Especially when you were up to something terrible.'

Freddie laughed from the worn leather office chair he sat in behind the desk. 'It's good to see you again, Lil,' he said warmly.

Lily sat in the chair opposite Freddie, twisting it so that she could see them both. 'How've you all been?' she asked, accepting the offer of a cigarette from Freddie and lighting it up. They hadn't had time to chat properly the previous evening.

'Yeah, all good,' Freddie replied. 'Business is good; everyone is well.' He paused and rubbed his forehead, closing his eyes for a moment.

'You look tired,' Lily commented, knowing she was probably one of the few people left in the world who could make such a personal comment. Freddie was, to all intents and purposes, the king of London's underworld. He'd worked and fought hard for his position, rising up the ladder over the years until he had surpassed them all, and that meant that he was owed an entirely different level of respect. Except, perhaps, from family and old friends.

'It's been a busy time,' Paul said, his deep craggy voice sounding heavier than usual. The brothers exchanged a brief look.

Lily pursed her lips. It wasn't for her to pry into whatever they had going on. 'Well, you should get some more sleep,' she said finally.

Freddie grinned, the creases on his forehead not quite disappearing. 'Sleep is for the weak,' he replied. 'Anyway, you ain't here to scold me for going to bed late. I spoke to my contact at the planning office this morning. He had a look into it and says there's definitely been a palm-off.'

'I knew it,' Lily said resentfully.

'He ain't sure exactly where yet, but it's not as straightforward as it looks,' Freddie continued. 'At first he said to look into spot listing the building, but this could take time and still might not go through.'

'What's spot listing?' Lily frowned, taking another drag on her cigarette.

'Spot listing is where the building is deemed of historical value or great significance to the community. It ain't easy to get it, but if it does...'

'It will stop him building?' she asked, her hope lifting.

'Possibly, but not definitely. It may just add some restrictions,' Freddie replied.

'How can we stop the planning being allowed altogether?' Lily asked. 'It don't have to be above board. Would your guy be open to a payoff to stop it going through?'

'I already asked, but it's gone to a level he can't pull it back from,' Freddie replied regretfully. 'If we'd known as he was submitting, maybe. But not now.'

'Shit,' Lily hissed.

Freddie and Paul exchanged a loaded glance, then Freddie turned to Lily with a slow creeping grin. 'There is another way...'

TWELVE

'Drew?' The name was hollered across the busy gym and Cillian turned to look back over his shoulder. He wiped the sweat from his brow with his forearm and tilted his chin up in question. Jimmy beckoned him over and then disappeared back into his office.

Cillian sniffed and took off his boxing gloves, laying them down near his training bag, then picked up his T-shirt and shrugged it back on before making his way across. He reached the open door and leaned in.

'Come in,' Jimmy said, pacing the small room in agitation.

'What's up?' Cillian asked, glancing back out of the room out of habit, to check that they were alone. A feeling of concern began to creep in. Jimmy was never this flustered.

'You spoken to Barnes recently?' Jimmy asked, watching him closely.

Cillian frowned. 'Not since we sparred yesterday, no. Why?'

'You're mates though, right? Outside of here, I mean.'

'Yeah, we go for a beer now and then. What's going on?'

Jimmy stopped pacing and sat down at his desk. 'He's gone.' He said the words as if the fact they were coming out of his mouth surprised him.

'What do you mean? Gone where?' Cillian asked, totally confused.

Jimmy slid a piece of paper across the table towards him and Cillian picked it up, scanning the neat lines typed upon it.

Mum – I've met someone who's become really special to me. I haven't introduced you as she's a free spirit who prefers not to live by society's rules. We've bought a campervan and plan to live off-grid for a while. Sorry it was so sudden, but when love calls, you have to answer. Not sure when I'll next be on-grid but please don't worry. I'm happier than I've ever been. Love you loads – Jude Xx

Cillian dropped the paper, his frown deepening as he locked eyes with Jimmy. He read it again, to make sure he wasn't misunderstanding the words, then looked back up and shook his head. It didn't make sense on so many levels, but one particular point stood out like a sore thumb, and no matter how hard he tried to wrap his head around it, he just couldn't.

'But he's gay,' he finally managed. 'He's never touched a bird in his life – or not that I know of anyway.'

'Exactly,' Jimmy said gravely. 'That ain't him.'

There was a long silence then Cillian turned and closed the door. He took a seat at the desk and Jimmy did the same, lacing his fingers together and pressing them to his mouth.

'Who brought this in, his mum?' Cillian asked, his eyes searching the note as though it might tell him something more. It didn't. He rubbed his forehead, stressed.

'Yeah, she dropped by his flat before going to work. Apparently, she still does his washing, was dropping it off and found this. She obviously knows it ain't him too.'

'Why did she bring it here?' Cillian asked, confused.

'She's old school, salt of the earth. Doesn't speak to coppers. She don't trust 'em,' Jimmy replied.

Cillian tilted his head in understanding. 'What does she expect you to do?' he asked.

'I don't know exactly. I told her I'd look into it, but here's the thing.' Jimmy shifted in his seat. 'I think there's something bigger going on.'

'What do you mean?' Cillian asked.

'You remember Cain? His letter to his missus?' Jimmy held his gaze, his pale blue eyes full of concern. 'That didn't seem right either. Not what it said and not the fact he'd just left a note and run off. Then there's this. And there was another one too.'

'Another one?'

'A while back. Nice kid but kinda quiet. He didn't really know many people in the area; no family, moved here for a job. He stopped coming in and I went to check on him. He'd been a bit down, you know? So I just wanted to make sure he was OK. But the flat was empty. Caught the neighbour who said he'd just gone one night and left the landlord a note to say he wasn't coming back. I didn't think much of it at the time, and maybe I'm reading too much into it now – I don't know.' He pushed his hair back and shook his head. 'But all these people disappearing and leaving notes. It seems kinda sus. Something's going on.'

Cillian thought it all over. It did seem a bit sus – Jimmy was right. Especially knowing, as they did, that whoever wrote Jude Barnes's note was definitely not him. He studied the words again.

'Whoever wrote this knew he was close to his mum, but didn't know Barnesy personally,' he said. ''Cos he don't hide who he is – he never has. Assuming he was straight was a real rookie error. But how did they know his mum would be the one to leave the note for, if they weren't close enough to know that?'

'Beats me,' Jimmy answered. He eyed Cillian. 'I know you already have your hands full with saving this place, but I need your help figuring this one out too, if you can spare the time.'

Cillian nodded without hesitation. 'Of course.' Jimmy had done so much for him over the years. If he needed help, Cillian would always be glad to give it. He looked down once more at the note. 'What do you think has happened? Any ideas at all?'

'None.' Jimmy looked as flummoxed as he felt.

What had Barnes got himself into? Who would want him to disappear? Cillian felt at a loss. They'd been friends since they were young, but despite this they never really discussed personal stuff. He knew Barnes was close with his mum because he was always praising her cooking and making jokes that she'd forever be the only girl in his heart. He knew as well that Barnes sometimes played football at the weekend. But other than that, they mainly chatted about boxing and laughed at the stupid videos Barnes shared. Barnes knew who he was but never made a big deal of it or asked questions, and it was nice having a friendship where things were kept simple. Barnes was the one person he could go for drinks with and just relax. But right now he wished he'd delved deeper into his personal life. Perhaps he might have had some idea where to start looking.

'Did he ever tell you where he worked?' Cillian asked.

'Nah, but I got the impression it was pretty fluid. He was in here at all times of the day. Sometimes would rush off to see to something, but often he had time to kill.' Jimmy shrugged. 'He never talked about work to me.'

Cillian bit the inside of his cheek. 'You got his address?' he asked.

'That I do have,' Jimmy said, standing up and walking over to a tall filing cupboard. He rifled through the drawers until he found the file he was looking for, pulled it out, thumbed through to the contacts page, then handed it to Cillian. 'Here.'

Cillian looked at the address and narrowed his gaze with a grim expression.

'What's up?' Jimmy asked, glancing at the file and back at his face.

Cillian exhaled through his nose. Barnes's flat was in an area just outside of their turf. It was a bit of a grey area, not really within anyone's jurisdiction. Not that anyone was particularly interested in those few streets. It was all residential and held no special appeal. But that meant no rules applied there. Which could work in his favour, but could also become a problem, depending on who or what they were dealing with.

'Nothing.' He pushed his reservations aside. 'I'll start asking around and looking into things today, then if I'm still no closer, I'll check his place out tomorrow night, see if I can find anything there.'

Taking one last look at the address, Cillian handed back the file and stood up. Jimmy stood up too and returned the file to the drawer.

'These three with the notes, did they know each other?' Cillian asked.

'Cain and Barnes would often spar together and they got on, but I don't think they were close. Gary, the third one, didn't know either of them. At least not to my knowledge. Kept himself to himself.'

Cillian nodded. 'OK. I'll let you know if I find anything.'

He turned to walk out but paused as Jimmy spoke. 'He'll be alright though?' The question sounded as though he was trying to seem confident, but the uncertainty underneath shone through.

Cillian chose not to answer, instead nodding his goodbye and leaving the office to go back to the bag. He felt ten times heavier than he had when he'd entered the club that morning. He needed to figure out what had happened to his friend before it was too late. But the question was: how deep did this situation go? And if the three men really were all tied up in the same mess – who was next?

THIRTEEN

Scarlet opened the front door to John with a wide grin and ushered him quickly inside, double-checking behind him as had become habit. He had a hoodie pulled up over his head underneath his jacket and he shrugged both off as she closed the door.

'Bit warm for that, ain't it?' she asked, taking them from him.

John shrugged. 'Doesn't matter how warm it is, so long as it keeps my face from being seen on the way over.' He put his hand to her cheek and pulled her in for a kiss.

'Come on – I'll get you a drink,' Scarlet said, drawing him into the kitchen by the hand.

Up until a few months ago, the sacred Sunday family lunch had been strictly for Drews only. No one, no matter how close, had ever been allowed to join them. Not even Ray, though he and Lily had been together for decades. But then one day Cillian had broken that rule and had brought Billie along. Lily had practically exploded and the rest of the family had stayed well out of it. But Cillian had stubbornly held his ground and she'd had no choice but to open up invitations for significant partners going forward.

Now the table was more full than ever, with the additions of

Billie, Ray and John. And if Ray was annoyed that it had taken Billie five minutes to undo that family rule after he'd been excluded for so many years, he didn't show it. Not that he attended every week – his firm, south of the river, needed him there, so he only came now and then when he could slip away. Today he hadn't come, much to Scarlet's disappointment. He always brought some extra entertainment to the table, and his presence always riled Ruby, who would then slink off as early as she could, which Scarlet secretly rejoiced about.

Lily had music playing in the background as she and her sister-in-law Cath put the finishing touches to the roast dinner that filled the air with mouth-watering aromas. Scarlet felt her empty stomach respond to the sight of the juices running out of the lamb joint as Lily placed it on the platter, and the crispy-edged potatoes her mother was tossing into a large bowl. Ruby took the plates out to the dining table, looking John up and down rudely as she passed.

'Can I help?' Scarlet offered, looking to her mother and aunt.

'No, we're good, love,' Cath replied cheerily. 'Alright, John?'

'Hi, Cath, Lily,' he responded politely.

Scarlet opened the fridge and pulled him out a beer, knowing that this was what he'd ask for. A warm relaxed smile rested on her face. She'd come to know so many of his little habits over the course of their relationship. Some days it felt as though their time together had passed in a flash, but at other times it felt as though they'd never been apart.

This – bringing him to Sunday lunch, where for a few hours every week they just enjoyed each other's company and ate good food – felt like perfection. It felt like they were *normal*. As though they were just a normal, average, happy couple. For a few hours she could pretend that their only problems were ordinary things like diary clashes or disagreements over holiday destinations, rather than whether they'd coordinated their lies well enough or if their next trip would be to a high-security prison.

Scarlet handed John his beer and picked up her wine from the kitchen island, then led him across the hallway to the lounge where Connor and Cillian sat talking quietly. They stopped as she approached and shared a look which she knew meant, *We'll finish this later.*

'Alright?' she asked, sitting down on one of the sofas and gesturing for John to take the seat next to her.

'Mm,' Connor murmured, his expression distracted as his gaze still rested on his brother. Whatever they'd interrupted was still on his mind.

Cillian's expression was equally as thoughtful, but his gaze was trained on John. Scarlet frowned, wondering why. It was rarely a good thing when Cillian paid attention to John in any way. She tensed, ready to combat whatever quip was about to come out of his mouth, but his next words surprised her.

'Actually, John, you might be able to help with this,' he said, no trace of the sarcasm she'd been expecting.

Immediately she felt John tense beside her, but he showed no sign of it as he replied. 'With what?'

'Jude Barnes, a friend of ours, has gone on the missing list. There was a note left basically saying he'd met a girl and was going off-grid, riding into the sunset and all that, sorry, Mum, bye,' Cillian explained. 'Except it ain't him. He couldn't have written it. For starters this imaginary girl ain't his type. Missing a rather important body part, if you know what I mean.'

'You know,' Connor added, looking at them both earnestly. ''Cos he likes men. So she'd be missing a—'

'Yes, thanks, Connor,' Scarlet said, cutting him off. 'We did actually all get that.'

'We did,' John confirmed.

'So it ain't him,' Cillian continued. 'And he wouldn't have just gone off like that anyway. Also it might not *just* be him.'

'What do you mean?' John asked with a frown.

'There have been a couple of others disappear too – both left similar notes. They were all members at the boxing club.'

'How do you know all this? Have their families gone to the police?'

Cillian shook his head. 'People like them don't trust the filth.'

John's jaw clenched slightly, she noticed, but he didn't comment.

'They're old school. Barnes's mum and Cain's bird came to Jimmy. He runs the place. Coached for years. It's who everyone goes to when they have a problem. Except he don't have a clue what's going on.'

John rubbed his forehead and then looked out of the window for a few moments with a thoughtful expression. 'If someone else has written this note and Barnes is in some sort of situation he doesn't want to be in, this girlfriend thing might have been his way of trying to send out a signal. He may have purposely fed some wrong information. It's a possibility.'

'Yeah, I thought that,' Cillian replied. They eyed each other, obviously not impressed that they actually agreed on something for once.

'So if you don't want to go to the police, what is it you want from me?' John asked.

'I need to look into this – Jimmy's asked for my help. You can help me. Off record.'

John blew out his breath through his cheeks and raised his eyebrows. 'I don't know, I mean—'

'That's what you signed up for, ain't it?' Cillian said, interrupting before he could say no. 'To help people? Well, Barnes needs help.'

John closed his mouth and leaned back into the sofa.

'I'm not asking you to do it all, I just need someone who knows what they're doing to help us figure this out.'

John nodded. 'OK. The first thing you need to do is look into anything they could have had in common other than the club. Hobbies, people, geographical locations, anything that might link them. And the club is a big link, so you need to start looking into the people there.'

It was Cillian's turn to bristle. 'It ain't anyone there. We're like family.'

'It's usually someone they know,' John replied frankly. 'You can take my advice or not, but that's where I'd start.'

For a few moments they eyed each other challengingly, and then Cath walked in, breaking the tension.

'Alright, you lot, dinner's ready. Come on,' she said.

'Perfect,' Scarlet replied brightly.

Everyone got up and headed to the dinner table, their conversation parked for now. John slipped his arm over Scarlet's shoulder as they fell in behind the twins. In turn, she wrapped her arm around his middle, marvelling once more at just how much she felt for him.

———

Ruby watched the pair as they pulled apart from each other to take their places at the dinner table. Scarlet's smile sent a stab of burning-hot hatred through the pit of her stomach. Scarlet Drew, the golden child. Scarlet Drew, who could do no wrong. Scarlet Drew, who'd had everything handed to her on a plate. The classic good looks, the respected position, the handsome boyfriend – it all came so easily to her.

She tore her gaze away and clasped her hands together respectfully as her mother said grace. It wasn't that she was jealous. She didn't want to *be* Scarlet. She didn't envy her looks or her relationship. She just hated that no one else saw her the way she really was. Calculating. Spiteful. And it *was* spite, the way she had trampled all over everything Ruby had held dear since an early age. It was spite, forcing the attention back on herself every time Ruby tentatively tried to step onto the stage. It was spite the way Scarlet looked down her nose at her as though Ruby was nothing but an annoyance, when really she had more right to be here than her cousin did. At this table, in the firm, by her mother's side, all of it.

'Ruby?' She looked up into the inquisitive eyes of her aunt. 'I said, would you mind passing the carrots?'

Grace was over – she hadn't even noticed, too caught up in the thoughts that plagued her day and night. Quickly unclasping her hands, she grabbed the carrots and passed them over to Cath.

A general chatter filled the room as everyone asked about each other's lives. Ruby quietly listened as she plated her food and poured the rich gravy over her vegetables. She began to eat as the stories that were exchanged went on and on. Connor's hot water wasn't working and he needed to call a plumber. Cath had a funny feeling that Roxy was going to leave the salon. She definitely wasn't, but Ruby wasn't interested enough to add that to the conversation. Billie had a client in a nursing home with dementia who, every now and then, would turn over on the bed and ask if she offered extra services. Ruby had to grin at that one as everyone laughed around her.

Just then, John's phone pinged. Ruby watched him look down and then roll his eyes at Scarlet.

'Is that her again?' Scarlet mumbled behind her hand through a mouthful of food. She followed his nod with a laugh.

'Who?' Cath asked. 'Come on – share the joke.'

Scarlet swallowed and took a sip of her wine. 'It's just this woman he works with. Ascough. In fact, you might remember her – she came to the house once, with Jennings.'

'The one with the short red hair?' Cath asked, squinting as she tried to recall the memory.

'That's the one,' Scarlet replied. 'She's got a bit of a thing for

John. Keep's trying to ask him out.'

'Check Dickie out, all popular with the ladies,' Connor remarked with a smirk.

'And this one's in your own world,' Cillian added, a subtle barb behind his words.

Ruby watched with interest as Scarlet shot him a sharp look.

'Well, you're a handsome lad, John,' Cath said. 'You can't blame her.'

'She's harmless,' John said dismissively. He rested his arm along the back of Scarlet's chair and touched her shoulder in a reassuring gesture. 'She knows I'm not from round here and thinks I don't know anyone and that I'm single, so she keeps sending me invites to go out for drinks or join her and her friends.' He shrugged. 'Not much I can do except keep dodging it.'

'Oh come on, it's more than that,' Scarlet scoffed. 'She follows him home!'

'What?' Lily asked, confused.

'No.' John rolled his eyes at Scarlet. 'She doesn't *follow me home*. She knows I live in Tooting and she does too. We went the same way home a couple of times, so now when we finish shift at the same time, she waits and walks with me. Which is fine, except when I'm actually supposed to meet Scarlet, which obviously I can't tell her, so I end up having to go *all the way* back to Tooting only to wait until she's gone and come *all the way* back this way.'

There was a wave of laughter as he made an expression of mock weariness and soon the conversation moved on. But Ruby turned the information John had just imparted over in her mind. She took a sip of her wine and studied John across the table as he joined in with the family fun.

Don't get too comfortable, she thought darkly. *Because you're not going to be around for very much longer at all.*

FOURTEEN

Lily matched the pace of the girl striding through the market a few metres ahead of her. Unobserved, she assessed what little she could see from this distance and angle. The girl was slight, a slip of a thing really, all sharp angles and awkward movements. Her outfit was casual, clearly chosen for comfort. A hoodie with skinny jeans and a pair of trainers. Her blonde hair was pulled up off her face into a neat ponytail and, from what Lily could see, she wore no make-up. She was the kind of girl that wouldn't stand out in a crowd. Nothing about her really stood out to Lily at all, in fact. Other than the fact she'd been hanging around the market asking for her by name.

The girl stopped and looked up and down the market once more with a big sigh. Her shoulders drooped a little and then she wandered off to the side, out of the main strip. Lily watched her walk into one of the little cafés on the side of the road. What was she doing here, this girl? How did she know Lily's name and association with the market?

She waited a couple of minutes and then followed her in, ordering a cup of tea and taking a seat at the table behind her. The girl opened up a purse, hiding it from view as much as she could with one hand and searching through the change section with the other. She counted out enough for whatever she'd ordered and placed it neatly on the table, then bit her lip as she peered inside and looked at what was left. Pressing her lips together grimly, she zipped it up and pushed it back into the front pocket of her hoodie. She leaned her elbows on the table and rested her face on her folded hands, staring out the window with a worried look.

The woman behind the counter bustled over with Lily's tea. ''Ere you go, Miss Drew,' she said respectfully, as Lily had known she would.

'Thank you,' she replied, taking it with a smile of gratitude.

At the sound of the name Drew, the girl's head shot round. Lily pretended not to notice. Out of the corner of her eye, she saw her quickly smooth her hair, tucking away the strands that had fallen forward, and then stand up. She approached with caution, moving to get into Lily's line of sight.

'Hi, sorry, I couldn't help but overhear the lady,' she said in a broad Mancunian accent. 'Your name's Drew?'

'It is,' Lily replied levelly.

'Are you Lily Drew?' she asked, watching her intently.

Lily took a sip of her tea and studied her over the rim of the mug before answering. 'That depends who's asking.'

'Oh, yeah.' The girl shook her head and closed her eyes for a moment as if reprimanding herself. 'I'm Isla. Isla Carpenter.'

'Is that name supposed to mean something to me?' Lily asked.

Now she was closer, Lily could see the girl's blonde hair was bleached, her roots showing her to be naturally more of a mousy brown. She'd been right about the make-up – Isla wore none and Lily could see that this was because she didn't really need it. Her young skin looked fresh and taut, dappled with pale freckles that were only visible up close. Her big brown eyes were fringed with long lashes and they watched her now, tense and hopeful.

'No, you don't know me,' Isla said. 'But—'

'So how do you know me, Isla Carpenter?' Lily interrupted, raising one eyebrow in challenge.

'I don't,' Isla replied. 'Not yet anyway. I only know *of* you.'

Lily narrowed her gaze for a few moments, then gestured to the empty seat opposite her.

'Thank you,' Isla said gratefully, sitting down with a breath of relief that she hadn't been dismissed. 'I know that must sound weird coming from a stranger. And a Northerner at that,' she added with a crooked smile. 'But you're known outside of London too.'

'How?' Lily asked.

Isla licked her lips and cleared her throat. 'I worked for a firm up in Manchester. They make knock-off handbags and that. I was listening in one day when the bosses were arguing. One of them wanted to look at expanding down this way, but the other warned him off, pointing out that territories are already drawn here. First one weren't having none of it, so the other went away and came back with details of the bigger London firms and showed him on a map.'

Lily's eyebrow rose again, but this time in disbelief. 'And you just happened to remember my name and exactly where to find me from a chance comment in a meeting you overheard?'

'Well... Yeah,' Isla replied simply. 'I couldn't recall everyone, but I remembered you and one or two others. I was trying to memorise as much as I could. Just in case...' She trailed off.

'Just in case of what?' Lily asked, suspicious now of this girl and her far-fetched story.

Isla's cheeks warmed. 'In case I could find a way out.' She jutted out her chin, trying to replace her embarrassment with forced confidence. 'I knew if I left, I'd have to find somewhere me skills would see me right.'

Lily sat back in her chair, unsure what to make of it all. 'You want a job?' she asked.

'Yeah. If you've got one. I mean, I'll do anything. Run errands, help out on the markets. I'll clean toilets if you need me to – long as it's somewhere I can climb the ladder once I've proved meself,' she said earnestly.

Lily didn't answer for a few moments. The whole situation reeked of an undercover police operation. 'So how long *have* you been on the force then?'

Isla's expression turned to one of surprise and then swift revulsion. 'I'm no pig!' she declared.

Lily lifted an eyebrow, her intense gaze unwavering.

'I'm *not*,' Isla reiterated, bringing her tone down to a calmer level. 'I hate them as much as you do. Look, I know I'm a stranger to you. But I'm willing to prove myself in any way you want. All I'm asking for is a chance.'

Lily exhaled, unsure what to do with the strange young woman in front of her. 'Even if I could trust you, we ain't exactly hiring right now.'

'You must need something,' Isla pushed, her eyes pleading.

'You say you worked making knock-off goods for a firm up North?'

'Handbags, trainers, coats, belts – you name it, I made them,' Isla replied with a spark of hope.

'What firm?' Lily asked.

Isla hesitated and her eyes flickered downwards.

'Right,' Lily replied grimly. 'If you can't even tell me who you supposedly worked for, then I can't check that out. Which means this conversation is over.' She made to move but paused when Isla spoke.

'No, wait, please.' She held her hands out to stop Lily from leaving, desperation written all over her face. 'I'll tell you, but I need you not to tell them I'm here. See, I was sort of... tied up with one of the bosses. And I didn't exactly tell him I was leaving. And, well, he isn't the type that would take that very well.' Her cheeks burned and her gaze dropped to the table. 'I just really don't want him to know where I am,' she admitted.

Lily saw it then. The hollow fear in her eyes. The driving force behind this attempt to start over somewhere new. 'If you're just looking for a fresh start, why not go straight?' she asked. 'There are plenty of jobs going for someone young and smart and able.'

Isla shook her head. 'It just ain't me. I was brought up on this side of the law. I don't know no different and don't particularly want to.'

Lily nodded. She could understand that. *If* the girl was telling the truth. For all she knew, she could still be an undercover trying to worm her way in. And Lily wasn't taking any chances. She looked down to her tea and drummed her fingers on the table next to it as she thought things over.

'Where's your family?' she asked, picking up the mug and taking a deep sip.

'Dead,' Isla replied, holding her head a little higher. 'Me mam died when I was young, and me dad went missing nearly three years ago. Technically a mystery, but...' She trailed off as her voice wobbled and turned her gaze towards the window for a moment. 'But, um, I'm pretty sure it was a rival firm. Me and Dad both worked for them, you see. He was one of their closest men for years.' She looked down and pursed her mouth, clearly not wanting to discuss the subject further.

'And who are they, this firm? I'm going to need names. You have my word that we won't tell them you're here.' Lily waited.

Isla bit her bottom lip. 'OK,' she said. 'Calvin and Jared King, they're the brothers who run the operation. Calvin was the one that...' She pulled a face. 'We were a thing.'

'And you're not now?' Lily probed.

'No. It's why I had to get out.' Isla looked away again, a shadow falling over her expression.

Lily studied her for a few moments and then abruptly stood up. 'I'll need to think on things and look into your story. I suggest if anything you've told me is untrue that you take this time to pack up and leave. Otherwise, I'll be in touch in a few days.'

Isla stood up too, startled by the sudden turn in the conversation. 'It's all true,' she said hurriedly, stepping out of the way as Lily swept past her. 'How will I—'

'I'll contact you,' Lily said, cutting her off.

'OK, well, I'm in the—'

'City View, I know.'

She looked back at Isla and saw the look of surprise on her face that her movements were already known to Lily before she'd approached her today.

'This is my city, Isla Carpenter. I make it my business to know everything I need to.'

With one last look at the girl, Lily turned and departed the small café, calling over her shoulder as she went, 'Time will tell what there is to learn about you. And you'd better hope I like what I hear.'

FIFTEEN

Cillian sat on one of the hard wooden benches at the edge of the club and looked around. A couple of younger lads sparred in the ring while one of the coaches barked out orders to correct their moves. Nearly all the bags dotted around were in use, each man pummelling away, training as hard as they could, fighting whatever demons plagued them on the inside. A group of friends stood in one corner, talking and laughing amongst themselves. One of them looked Cillian's way and nodded respectfully as he caught his eye.

John had said to start here, to look into anyone who might have beef with Barnes. But no one did as far as he could tell. Cillian exhaled heavily, frustrated, and leaned forward on his knees, running his hands back through his hair. There had to be *something*, some clue that would point him in the right direction. But he and Jimmy had gone through all the files, talked to everyone who knew him in the gym, and there had been nothing suspect at all. Now time was ticking and every second that he just sat here without a clue was one second more that Barnes was stuck in whatever predicament he'd got himself into.

He'd go to Barnes's flat tonight, have a look around. Though he wasn't sure what he expected to find. If Barnes was involved in something dodgy then it wasn't likely he'd have evidence lying around at home. But maybe he'd find some clue as to where he worked at least. That would give him something to try next.

Standing up, Cillian wiped a hand down his face and walked towards the vending machines. He needed a drink and to clear his head.

As he passed the ring, the two boys who'd been sparring jumped down and the two men waiting by the side took their place.

The drinks machine was being restocked, so Cillian leaned against the wall beside the open door and waited, watching the new pair begin to spar. He recognised their faces. They were training for some of the upcoming matches. They weren't ready – he could tell by watching them, but he knew with Barnes and Cain gone, the club was running out of options in their weight range.

'What you after?' came a voice from behind the door of the drinks machine.

Cillian turned to see a pale, angular face surrounded by a mess of ginger hair peeping around the side, looking up at him inquisitively. 'Oh, um, just a Red Bull.'

'Hang on, let me check what I've got. I'm sure there's some at the bottom.' The man began to rummage through his cart, pulling out boxes of cans and piling them up beside him.

'Come on, Carl, put your hands up. Hands *up*, I said!' the coach bellowed from beside the ring. Cillian turned back to watch while the drinks-machine guy searched for the Red Bull. 'Christ, a five-year-old could have blocked that.'

'It's in here somewhere – I definitely had it in the van,' the drinks guy continued. 'Ah! Here it is.'

'Come on, gloves up, get on with it!' the coach barked. He shook his head and Cillian knew he must be internally cursing the fact he was training two lost causes for a competition they would definitely lose.

In his peripheral vision, he noticed two people entering the building. It wouldn't have been notable in the slightest if the flash of neon yellow hadn't caught his eye. His head swivelled and his frown deepened as he watched DC Jennings, along with a uniformed police officer, enter their sacred building. What the hell was *he* doing here?

'Here.' The drinks-machine guy held out a can towards Cillian, but Cillian shook his head, backing away.

'Nah, forget it – I gotta go.' He began walk away.

'But you said...'

'I said I've gotta go,' Cillian snapped.

He sidled to the other side of the busy gym in the policemen's direction, careful to stay out of sight. They were headed for Jimmy's office. Was this about Barnes? He hung back as Jennings knocked on the door. Jimmy answered and welcomed them in, surprise written all over his face.

As Jimmy made to shut the door behind them, he caught Cillian's eye and at the last moment left it ajar so that he could listen in. Cillian shoved his hands into the pockets of his gym hoodie and casually leaned on the wall just outside the door. Several of the others in the room were looking over warily, some giving a nod to indicate they'd come to him later to find out what was going on.

'We need to speak to you about a Mr Gareth Oldham,' he heard Jennings say as he leaned a little closer.

'Who?' Jimmy asked.

'I believe you knew him as Gary,' the female officer said.

There was a short silence and then Jimmy spoke up. 'Gingery lad?' he asked. 'Quite tall and—'

'We wouldn't be able to tell you much about his height, Mr Smith, but we were told he used to box here and that after he disappeared, you went round his neighbours asking after him,' Jennings said, his tone hard and almost accusatory.

Cillian frowned. He already hated DC Jennings and for good reason, but this rudeness towards Jimmy was endearing the man to him even less.

'Well, yeah, 'course I did. He disappeared without a word and I knew the lad had been a bit down. I wanted to make sure he was OK. Why are you asking me about him?' Jimmy's tone grew worried. 'What's happened? Has he done something wrong? Has he asked for me?'

'No, he hasn't done anything, Mr Smith,' the female officer said gently.

'Jimmy,' he corrected.

'Jimmy, I'm afraid Gary's body has been found. Or parts of it anyway,' she said.

'*What?*' Jimmy exclaimed.

Cillian's breath caught in his throat and he felt a heavy veil of foreboding settle over him. Gary had been the first one to disappear, according to Jimmy. The first one with a note left behind.

'A dog walker found a bag on the shore of the river a few miles away. Heavy-duty, wrapped up. Looked like it had been weighted down but had come loose and been dragged up by the tide,' Jennings continued in an unemotional tone. 'The dogs were a bit too interested so she opened it and... Well. Here we are.'

'And you're saying...' Jimmy faltered. '*Parts* of Gary were in there?'

'Yes,' the female officer answered. 'We're still searching for the rest of his body, but for now we're making enquiries into how he got there. Were you on good terms with Gary?'

'Yeah, he was a nice lad. He hadn't lived here long, didn't know many people. He'd got a building job locally and was saving money up for a nicer place. I can't believe this has happened.'

Cillian heard the squeak of Jimmy's chair as he sat down heavily.

'I know this must be hard to take in, Jimmy,' the officer said. 'But if there's anything you know that might help us work out what's happened—'

'I don't,' he said, cutting her off. 'I really don't. He kept himself to himself. Hadn't really made friends with anyone. I mean he sparred and passed the odd comment with people here, but he was shy. It's why I kept an eye on him.'

'Do you know of any girlfriend he might have argued with or any neighbour he may have riled up the wrong way?' Jennings asked.

'No, I only spoke to the woman next door and she seemed to like him well enough. I'll ask around in case any of the lads know something I don't,' he replied, sounding deflated.

Cillian pulled a sympathetic grimace. This news would have hit Jimmy harder than the plods knew. To Jimmy, each and every man he trained in here was family. The man lived and breathed this place, and he cared for his boys almost as deeply as their own parents did. Sometimes more.

Distracted by this thought, he realised that Jennings and the other officer were leaving the room just a moment too late. He turned to walk away but Jennings clocked him just as he pushed off the wall. The light of recognition flashed in his cold dark eyes, followed swiftly by disdain.

'Well, if it ain't one of the Drew twins,' he said, looking him up and down. 'It's funny, whenever I find a body these days, one of you always seems to be nearby. Now why is that, do you reckon?'

Cillian restrained himself from answering quite as strongly as he'd have liked to. 'No idea,' he said, forcing a cold, fake smile. 'I'm just waiting here to see me coach.'

'Is that right?' he asked with a menacing look.

Cillian held his gaze, letting his own cool and harden as the tension between them increased.

Jennings stepped back and smirked. 'We'll see. Why don't you come down to the station tomorrow morning? Have a chat about our mutual friend Gary.'

'I don't know any Gary and I ain't got time to join a pissing contest down the station either,' Cillian remarked.

Jennings walked away, the other officer in tow. 'You'll be there tomorrow, or I'll get a warrant,' he warned. 'And I can detain you a lot longer with that.'

Cillian's lip curled and his hand made a fist as he stared after Jennings with a mixture of hatred and frustration. He bit his lip to stop himself telling the DI where he could stick it and instead watched in stony silence as they left the building. All eyes were on him after the public exchange. He glared around at them all, then felt Jimmy tugging on his arm.

'Come on. Come in here,' he said. 'Let's talk.'

SIXTEEN

'Seriously though, that was the funniest thing I've heard all week,' John said with a laugh. '*Your chicken pie is toast, mate.*' John repeated the words he'd heard her say earlier to a man arrested for attempted murder and laughed loudly once more.

'I honestly can't believe all he cared about was getting his bloody pie out of the oven!' Ascough exclaimed, joining in with a chuckle and shaking her head in disbelief. 'I mean, I'd have been more worried about losing my freedom, personally.'

'You and me both,' John said, his laughter slowing as the seriousness of the risks he took on a daily basis crept back into his mind.

These days he thought about his freedom a lot. It was some-thing he'd always taken for granted. He'd slept easy, knowing he lived on the right side of the law. But then he'd met Scarlet and everything he'd ever believed in, everything he'd thought he'd known about the world, had gone out the window. His entire focus had shifted. Now, he lived for her. For the moments they shared together. And every day when he came into work and sat behind his desk, he felt as though he was on borrowed time. His freedom was no longer a genuine right, it was an overlooked error. His freedom no longer belonged to him. Not really. And at any point someone in law enforcement could realise that and take it away.

John looked up to the bright blue sky, criss-crossed by wisps of cloud, and took in the sounds around him. He prayed he would be walking freely down streets like this for many years to come, but although he'd done his best to ensure this, he could never be certain. He would always need to keep looking over his shoulder.

'You OK, guv?' Ascough asked, looking up at him with a small frown.

'Yeah, sorry.' John quickly plastered on a smile. 'Just thinking about another case.'

'All work and no play, you are,' Ascough teased. 'That was fun the other night though.'

'Yeah, it was a laugh,' John agreed. They'd been out as a team for drinks after work and it had turned into an amusingly eventful evening. 'We should do it more often. Once a month or something.'

'Good idea. Though don't think Ronnie's wife will be too pleased,' she replied, pulling a face.

John didn't reply but couldn't help the grin that escaped. He tried not to talk ill of anyone's people, but Ronnie's wife was a particularly horrible person. The poor bloke was miserable every day of his life and John could understand why. His wife gave him the hardest time of anyone he'd ever known, constantly berating him in person and down the phone without a care who heard, spending every penny he had, flirting with his co-workers and kicking off any time he did anything for himself. She'd screamed at him down the phone when he'd told her he was going out for drinks, not letting him get a word in edgeways. In the end, he'd snapped and turned off the phone. The other night had been the first time he'd seen the man actually relax and have some fun – though he guessed he'd probably paid for it dearly the next morning.

'Maybe next time we could go for some food as well,' Ascough suggested.

'It's a nice idea but I don't think the others would be up for it,' John replied. They were a hard-working bunch and on team nights like this, they just wanted to let their hair down. They didn't want to sit and talk over food.

'Well, then maybe we could grab something on our way home after, if you're up for it,' she said, her tone hopeful. 'Save us both a night of microwave meals for one at least, huh?'

John stifled a sigh and gave her a tight smile. It was getting harder and harder to put her off. As far as Ascough was concerned, he was just a single guy going it alone in his little bachelor pad, which – rather inconveniently for him – happened to be only a few streets away from her flat. Now they travelled home together, chatting amiably until he split off towards his flat and spending time together as friends. And John really did value Ascough as a friend. She was funny and good company and they liked a lot of the same things. But that was all it ever would be for him. Friendship.

Ascough had been making her feelings subtly clear for a while now. She wanted to go out just the two of them, suggesting cosy late-night bars and nice little restaurants whenever she got the slightest inkling that John might be alone. She wanted to push their friendship towards something more. If he'd been single, he might have considered it. They got on so well and she was attractive. But he only had eyes for one woman. A woman whose existence he had to hide completely. And because of that, he could never quite explain to Ascough why he couldn't take her up on all these offers.

'Sure,' he said eventually. 'I've actually just started this new diet where you fast in the evening,' he added, hoping it didn't sound as fake as it really was. 'So I'm kind of hibernating while I do that. But yeah, maybe afterwards sometime.'

Ascough's face dropped but then she smiled and nodded, the way he'd known she would. He felt like an arse. He wasn't the kind of bloke to not be straight with a woman usually. He didn't believe in leading people on or dangling their hopes on a piece of string the way he seemed to have ended up doing here, but what else could he do?

They reached the Tube and John hesitated, trying to figure out a valid excuse to not follow her onto their usual line. She stopped and looked back at him.

'You coming?' she asked.

In his head he flicked through all the excuses he'd used lately and decided against it. ''Course,' he said resignedly, following her down the steps. He'd just have to go home and double back to get to Scarlet again tonight. Another long night. But it was worth it. What they had was something else. What they had was worth all the hassle and the risk in the world.

SEVENTEEN

Cillian played with the toothpick, turning it round and round between his teeth with his tongue. He felt tense, being so far out of Drew territory right now. He paced beside his car, parked at the dark end of the run-down car park. There were a few other cars around, but no people. Which wasn't exactly surprising, considering that it was nearly midnight.

His run-in with Jennings earlier and the discovery of Gary's body had increased the urgency of this situation tenfold. The police had no idea about Barnes's disappearance or the link between him and Gary, but it was likely only a matter of time before they did and then he wouldn't be able to do anything to help his friend. He needed to find answers *now*. Before it was too late. If it wasn't already.

He checked his phone again hoping he might see a missed call from Connor, but there was nothing. They had planned to come together. Usually, Cillian wouldn't do something like this alone, but Connor had ended up being called away by Lily to deal with other things. They hadn't told her about this little escapade to Barnes's flat yet.

Glancing back towards the empty road once more, Cillian

flicked the toothpick away and clamped his jaw grimly. It was time to get on.

As he walked across the car park towards the tall block of flats, he decided he was probably better going in alone anyway. It would be a quick in-and-out job, and should anyone happen to see him, a man alone was a lot less interesting and recognisable than twins. He reached into his pocket and pulled out a pair of leather gloves.

The front door of the building had no passcode, so Cillian walked straight into the tired-looking ground-floor hallway. A light came on and he tensed. Two bikes leaned against a wall, and a pair of muddy boots stood outside one of the front doors, but no one appeared. He realised he must have triggered a motion sensor. His tension evaporated and he pushed on, wanting to be done with this place as quickly as possible.

As he climbed the stairs, the light on the first floor came on and he stopped there, counting the door numbers until he found the one he was looking for.

'Six, seven... There you are,' he said under his breath.

He paused and eyed the door with interest. These flats were old and not all the doors were the same, having been replaced over the years, but the one thing that the rest had in common was that they looked cheap and basic. Barnes's front door, on the other hand, was completely out of place, a sleek contemporary metal affair that would be a lot harder to break into than Cillian had anticipated. The crowbar he had under his jacket had been rendered useless. He exhaled slowly and glanced back over his shoulder before pulling a small box out of his pocket.

'You can avoid it being smashed in, mate, but you can't escape my skills,' he said to himself quietly. He opened the lid, pulled out his lock-picking pins and pondered the odd choice of door.

Why *did* Barnes have such a heavy-duty door? It was the sort of thing he'd seen many times before, on residences belonging to those who lurked in the underworld. Doors to keep them safe, doors to keep enemies out. But who would Barnes be trying to keep out? He rolled the pins between his fingers for a few moments, thinking it over. The light in the hallway switched off, flooding the place in darkness once more, and he swore a little louder than he'd meant to, taken by surprise. He waited a few moments to check no one had heard, then paced back down the hall until he triggered the sensor again.

The door had now added to his growing list of questions about Barnes, but he could think about that later. He needed to get on, get into the flat and look for something that could point them in the right direction. He bent down and pushed the pins through the lock, carefully manoeuvring them until everything clicked into place. Moving slowly so as not to lose the tension, he turned the lock and pushed the door open.

Cillian stepped into the hallway, pushing the door closed behind him. Inside, the flat was in darkness. He felt along the wall for a switch and flicked it down, finding, as the place was illuminated, that he was standing in a long, thin hallway with closed doors off to each side. A couple of jackets hung on pegs, and several pictures – of Barnes with his mum and some other people Cillian didn't recognise – hung neatly in a line. A table stood at the end of the hall, a lone piece of furniture in the otherwise empty space. Was this where Barnes's mum had found the note? It seemed probable.

Cillian walked over and checked the contents of the large wooden bowl on top. There was nothing of interest. Just a padlock, some change and a small screwdriver.

Discarding these, he opened one of the doors and peered in. It was the bathroom. He was about to turn to leave but then paused and entered, switching on the light. His eyes flickered between a couple of places he knew people commonly hid things they didn't want to be found, the odd choice of front door making him curious. As far as he was aware, Barnes wasn't into anything dodgy, but how much detail did he really know about his personal life? On a hunch, he lifted the top off the toilet and peered into the cistern, and as he found what he'd partially been expecting, his mouth formed a grim line. There, hanging down in the water, was a plastic bag on a string.

Setting the lid down, he pulled the bag out and opened it up. Whatever Barnes had been hiding was no longer there. It was empty. Cillian frowned. What would he have here that would need to be hidden this way? What was he tied up in?

He dropped the bag back in the water and secured the top, deciding to check the bedroom next.

He turned and nearly jumped out of his skin as he saw he was no longer alone. Two large, serious-looking men stood watching him from the hallway, one of whom had a baseball bat in his hand. As they made to move towards him, Cillian instinctively slammed the bathroom door shut, throwing his weight behind it as they tried to shove it back open. He held fast, digging his heels into the floor and pushing back against their attempts, cursing loudly as he realised it was only a matter of time before they forced their way through.

Who the hell are they? And what are they doing here? he wondered.

He looked around, searching for options but there was no way out, no window to climb through, even if he was able to move away from the door. He gritted his teeth and pulled the crowbar out from inside his jacket, thankful that he at least had this. There might be no escape, but he wasn't going out without a fight.

Next to his head, the flimsy wood of the door splintered as the bat smashed through.

'Jesus *fucking* Christ,' he roared.

Taking a couple of deep breaths, he pulled away from the door and let them break through, lifting the crowbar and ploughing back towards the pair as they fell into the room.

They pulled back quickly though, and Cillian missed hitting one of them by just inches.

Fuelled by adrenaline, he lifted the crowbar again and charged after them into the hallway, not noticing until it was too late that one had slipped to the side and stuck his leg out across the bottom of the door. He tripped with a curse and fell head-long across the hall, the crowbar flying out of his hand and landing with a clatter a few feet away. Not pausing for breath, he pushed himself along the floor towards it, but he was too late.

'I don't think so,' said one of the men in a hard voice as he kicked it out the way. 'Someone wants to talk to you.'

Cillian opened his mouth to reply, but before he could utter a word, he felt a hard blow to the head and heard the sickening crack of wood upon bone before he passed out into a void of complete blackness.

EIGHTEEN

Connor took another deep drag on his cigarette and paced restlessly outside the front of the family pub, mobile held to his ear. It rang off and went to voicemail.

'Hey, it's me. I've only just finished with the Hussains. Some racist cunts tried to smash up the front. We smashed them up in return. They won't be trying that again any time soon. Honestly, I really don't know what's wrong with some people. We've patched up the window, but we'll have to sort out something proper in the morning. They don't pay protection for nothing.' He took another drag and glanced down the road at a passing car. 'Anyway, it's late so you'll have been in and out of Barnes's ages ago. Probably tucked up in bed with your bird by now. Lucky git. I've still got to give Mum the rundown before I can clock off. I've just got to the pub now. Hit me up in the morning.'

He ended the voicemail and shoved his phone down in his pocket before walking into the closed pub. It was gone one in the morning, but that wouldn't matter to Lily. She was a creature of the underworld, and night was her day. They were all used to late nights and long hours. In their line of work, it was often much easier to get things done throughout the hours that people on the other side of the law spent sleeping.

Inside, the place was empty, other than Lily and two men sitting at a table at the far end of the bar. The lights were low and the curtains pulled across the windows. A bottle of whisky sat between the three on the table and all had a drink in hand. As the door closed behind Connor, they turned their heads towards him, and one of the men stood up and walked behind the bar.

'You're late. Was there trouble?' Lily asked, her cool voice carrying through the empty pub.

'Yeah.' Connor pulled up a chair and sat down at the round wooden table. The man who'd stood up came back with a glass and handed it to him. 'Thanks, Tommy.'

Tommy nodded. 'I'll be off then. You're OK to lock up the front?' he asked, looking to Lily.

Lily nodded. 'Catch you tomorrow.'

Connor poured himself a measure of whisky and swirled it round in the glass. Lily had pulled out the good stuff tonight, he noted, though this wasn't a surprise considering who else was at the table. You didn't pull out the cheap stuff for Bill Hanlon.

'Alright, Bill,' he said respectfully.

'Alright, Connor,' came the deep gravelly reply.

Bill Hanlon – or Billy the Banker as he'd been known for years before he stopped pulling bank jobs and moved towards illegal technology and information instead – worked as a free-lancer throughout the underworld. Or at least, throughout the network of firms who were on friendly terms with the Tylers, with whom his loyalties lay. He was well respected, quiet and powerful. A good ally to have. He'd worked with the Drews many times over the years, though Connor wasn't yet sure what he was doing here tonight.

'So what went down with the Hussains?' Lily asked as the front door shut behind Tommy.

'Couple of thugs messed up the front of the shop. Racist little shits trying to terrorise them. We sent them off with broken ribs and a warning not to show their faces again,' Connor replied.

'Will they become a bigger problem, do you think?' Lily asked, reaching into a packet of cigarettes that sat on the table and lighting one up.

'Nah.' Connor shook his head. 'They were just bully boys. Could dish it out but couldn't take it back. They're done. The shop, on the other hand, was a right mess. We patched up the windows, but we'll need to get someone in to fix the front properly in the morning.'

Lily nodded. 'Leave it with me – I'll call the glazier. Where's your brother?'

'That's a longer story,' he said, taking a sip of his whisky.

'What do you mean?' Lily asked sharply.

Connor glanced at Bill. He wasn't part of their firm but he was someone they could trust. 'This is just between all of us for now,' he said carefully. Bill conceded with a nod, and, satisfied with this, Connor looked back to his mother. 'Jude Barnes has gone missing. Long story but someone left a note claiming to be him, saying he'd run off with some girl to go travel the world and not to worry about him.'

Lily frowned. 'Some *girl*?' she queried.

'Yeah, exactly. It ain't him. Thing is, according to Jimmy, this is the third person from the club to go missing and have a random note left behind. He asked Cillian to look into it, then today out of the blue, Jennings turns up at the club—'

'*Jennings*?' Lily exclaimed, cutting him off with a horrified look. 'What the fuck is he doing there?'

'That's what I'm trying to tell ya,' Connor replied. 'Jennings turned up to tell Jimmy that the first bloke that went on the missing list has turned up.'

'Where?'

'In a bag in the river,' he replied grimly. 'In pieces. Not even all the pieces.' Connor reached for his mother's cigarettes and pulled one out, lighting it and taking a deep drag.

'So where's Cillian?' Lily asked, confused.

'Home by now,' Connor replied, blowing his smoke out across the table. 'But earlier he went to Barnes's to see whether he could find any clues in his flat. We're drawing a blank. The only thing they all had in common was the club, but they weren't even friends.' He rubbed his forehead. It didn't make any sense to either him or Cillian, so far.

'This boy whose body's turned up, was he local?' Lily asked.

'Nah. From what I gather, he moved to the area because there was work going. Didn't know anyone,' Connor replied.

'What kind of work?' Lily asked.

'Building work. He was a contractor, a bricky.'

There was silence for a moment and Connor watched Lily's thoughtful expression, until suddenly something seemed to click. Her frown deepened.

'Building work,' she said. 'Who do we know who's expanded lately and would be taking on more contractors? Someone who has a very warped interest in that club and its goings-on?'

It was Connor's turn to frown. 'You don't think that AJ would have done this, surely?'

Lily thought about it, taking another long, slow drag on her cigarette. 'I think AJ is the kind of man who'll stop at nothing to get what he wants,' she said. 'Maybe if people are going missing – if the place looks like a hub of criminal activity – it would work in his favour. A safeguard against the place ever being spot listed.'

'Spot listed?'

'Listed as a place of community importance. It can't be noted as a place that's important to a community if the people in that community are disappearing and getting murdered.' She held Connor's gaze seriously.

He nodded. 'I guess that makes sense. In a really fucked-up way.'

Bill cleared his throat. 'It would be worth checking to see if the others have a connection to AJ,' he suggested. 'I didn't have him down as the murdering type, but...' He considered it and shrugged. 'The man will go pretty low for the things he wants.'

'Yeah, we'll get onto it,' Connor replied.

Lily nodded. 'Do.' She turned back to Bill and picked up the whisky, topping up his tumbler. 'Just circling back to what we were talking about earlier, Bill...' she prompted.

'Yeah. I checked out what you asked me to.' Bill picked up the drink and took a sip. 'I've been keeping tabs on the Manchester scene anyway, since Freddie had a run-in with them several years back. All that business with Thea, you remember.'

'Yeah, of course. Such a waste,' Lily replied, shaking her head.

Connor took a couple of seconds to recall the name, then suddenly realised the significance of Bill's comment. The Tylers' sister Thea had been caught in the crossfire between them and a rival gang from Manchester. He couldn't remember the details, just that she'd died and that it had shocked the underworld because she hadn't actually been part of the firm. She was, to all intents and purposes, a civilian. And civilians were off the table for any kind of retribution. It just wasn't done. Though apparently that didn't matter much to AJ either, considering the issues they were currently dealing with.

'It wasn't too hard to dig the information up,' Bill continued. 'Isla's family is connected to a firm run by two brothers, the Kings. Or rather, they were. From what I gather, the parents are now dead and she's done a runner. The Kings deal in drugs and black-market merch. They're a vicious lot when crossed, a lot of hot tempers within the family from what I can gather. But they're efficient. Their businesses are thriving. They've got people looking for her – seem quite put out by her disappearance.'

Lily pulled a grim expression. 'That adds up to what she told me. Did you find out why they're so intent on finding her?'

Bill shook his head. 'That much I could get, but when I tried to probe further, they clammed up.' He shrugged. 'Why is anyone's guess. But the main thing is, she's kosher.'

'OK. Thanks for looking into it, Bill,' Lily replied.

Connor wondered who they were talking about but kept quiet. He'd no doubt find out soon enough.

'What you gonna do with her?' Bill asked.

'I'm not sure yet,' Lily said, looking across the table at him thoughtfully.

Bill nodded and downed the last of the whisky in his glass, then stood up. 'I've got to shoot. Amy will be wondering where I am.'

'Sure,' Lily replied with a warm smile. 'Send her my regards, won't you?'

''Course. See ya later.'

With a nod to them both, Bill walked out of the pub, and the door swung slowly closed behind him.

'What was all that about then?' Connor asked.

Lily stood, gathering the glasses and placing them on the bar along with the bottle. 'This girl turned up at the market asking for me. Knew the market was ours, but she ain't from the area. Said she was after a job. Seemed a bit sus.'

'Smells of bacon to me,' Connor replied with a frown.

'It did to me too,' Lily agreed. 'But she was persistent, seemed pretty determined. So I got Bill to check out her story.'

Connor bit his lip, still concerned. 'And you're sure that's enough? What if Bill is wrong?'

'Christ, I should wash your mouth out with soap, boy,' Lily

replied with a grin to show she was joking. 'You should know by now that when it comes to information like this, Bill Hanlon is never wrong. He was pulling jobs and staking people out before you were even born. He's better than any PI in the country.'

Connor held his hands up in surrender. It had been a stupid comment, but it was late and he was tired, and his brain no longer wanted to function.

'I need to go to bed,' he said, stifling a yawn.

'Go on then,' Lily replied. She grabbed her jacket and followed him out the door, checking the time on her watch. 'It is late.' She leaned over and gave him a quick one-armed hug as they reached the car park. 'Go and get some sleep. And don't rush in the morning. I don't really need either of you till lunchtime.'

'OK, see you then.' Connor stepped into his car and waited until his mum had driven off before starting the engine. A lie-in was exactly what he needed, and Cillian would be pleased too. He'd text him to tell him not to bother rushing in the morning. For once he could just enjoy a nice morning in bed with Billie, with no one bothering him at all.

NINETEEN

Scarlet woke to the sound of her mother opening her bedroom door and turned over with a start, pulling the covers up over her naked body.

'Mum!' she cried, her voice still hoarse from sleep, as Cath entered with a cup of tea.

'Oh Christ, sorry!' Cath exclaimed as she saw Scarlet wasn't alone. 'I'd have brought two up, if I'd realised.'

'Not my point!' Scarlet replied, shaking her head and looking to the heavens. 'Can we not just have a bit of privacy? Jesus!'

John propped himself up on one elbow and ran his hand back through his messy brown hair with a laugh. 'Morning, Cath,' he said, shooting her a winning smile.

'Morning, love,' Cath replied. 'Fancy a tea?'

'Mum!' Scarlet exclaimed again.

'Would love one, thanks,' John replied.

'I'll bring it right up. Two sugars, isn't it?' she asked, ignoring Scarlet's indignant glare.

'Yeah, lovely,' John answered.

'OK then. Be back up in two ticks.'

Cath put Scarlet's tea down on the bedside table and disappeared as Scarlet pulled the covers up over her face with a sound of frustration. John laughed and pulled them back down again.

'Don't be mad at her,' he said, nuzzling into her neck. 'She's just being nice.'

'She's a pain in the arse,' Scarlet shot back, her tone melting slightly as she arched into his kisses and pulled him close.

'She just loves you. Don't take it for granted.' He pulled back and kissed her lightly on the end of her nose, his piercing green eyes meeting hers. 'I'd do anything to have my mum bring me a cup of tea in bed again.'

Scarlet looked down, suitably chastened. John's mother had died three years earlier and he missed her greatly. It was one of the things they'd bonded over, when they'd first begun to date, the fact they'd both lost parents that meant the world to them.

'I know,' she said, kissing him deeply on the lips. She pulled his warm body closer to hers and snuggled back down under the covers. 'Still, another hour in bed would have been nice,' she added with a wry smile.

'True,' he agreed. He pulled her in close and rested his chin on her head as she lay on his chest. 'What's your day like?'

'Not too bad. Got some stuff to catch up on at the factory, then we've got a poker night tonight. Few bits in between.' She didn't elaborate. She was visiting some dangerous places today to meet with dangerous people. Places and people John would find dangerous, that was. To her they were familiar haunts and good business associates.

'I thought Ruby was handling most of the factory stuff now,' John commented.

'In theory,' Scarlet replied, the disapproval in her expression sneaking into her voice.

'But?' John prompted.

'She's just not very good.' Scarlet shifted slightly to look up at him. 'She's sloppy, gets things wrong all the time. I end up having to unpick all her mistakes and redo things correctly. It would just be quicker and easier for me to do it from the off. But, of course, Lil won't see it that way. Says we have to be patient, that she's still learning.' She pulled a face to show him what she thought of that.

'Is she really still that bad?' he asked.

'Yes,' she answered resolutely.

She felt the usual resentment and irritation rise up at the thought of her cousin.

'It's been nearly a year now that she's been back in the fold,' John reminded her. 'You said so yourself. And she's shown no signs of being back on the gear.'

'True, but...' Scarlet pulled a grim expression. 'I don't know. There's just something that still makes me feel like she's going to suddenly tip the tables. And when she does, it will be a big problem.'

Everyone in their family, their firm, had to be fully committed at all times. It was a dangerous game they played and one wrong move, one second with their eye off the ball, or one loose cannon in the ranks could end it all for good. The police lurked in the shadows, waiting for their chance to put one of them away – she'd barely escaped a life sentence for murder only six months earlier. And rivals hovered constantly on the sidelines, searching for any sign of weakness that could be manipulated and turned against them. They had to be vigilant. And they had to be a team, have each other's backs at all costs. But Ruby didn't have their backs. The only back she wasn't ready to stab at a moment's notice was her own.

'Knock, knock,' Cath called gaily from the hallway, just a second before entering. 'Here's your tea, love.' She handed a steaming mug across the bed to John.

'Thanks,' he said, taking a sip.

Scarlet looked at her mother with a wry smile.

'What?' Cath asked, holding her arms out in question. 'I did say *knock, knock* this time. Gawd, there's no pleasing you this morning, is there?' She rolled her eyes with a tut and walked away.

'Mum?' Scarlet called.

Cath paused and popped her head back into the room. 'Mm?'

They'd been through a lot together, her and Cath. More than most mothers and daughters. They'd weathered the worst things in life standing solidly at each other's side, and the bond they shared was deep. She shouldn't get annoyed by the little things, Scarlet knew. As John had reminded her in his earlier words, life was too short.

She smiled at Cath gratefully. 'Thanks. I love you.'

'Translation – I now realise I also want some toast.' Cath winked and disappeared, calling back over her shoulder. 'I love you too, Little Doll.'

TWENTY

The first thing Cillian noticed as he started to come back round was the pounding ache in his head. It was almost unbearable, resounding through his skull as though every single atom was vibrating. How long he'd been out he had no idea. All he could remember was being in Barnes's flat, trying to fight two guys and then the feel of the bat on his head. At least, he assumed it was the bat. There had been a bat, but he hadn't actually seen it swing at him. They'd hit him from behind like total cowards.

'Cunts.' The word escaped his mouth in a mumble as he drifted in and out, his eyes still closed.

'Eh,' a voice said near him. 'He's waking up. Get the boss.'

The words roused him properly and he immediately regretted his unguarded comment. He should have stayed silent, tried to get his bearings. But it was too late now. A scrape of a chair moving across a hard floor sounded and then the footsteps of someone hurrying away. His senses snapped to full alert, but still he kept his eyes closed. He needed to try and work out what was going on before he opened them and allowed whoever had taken him to think he was ready for another round of whatever the fuck they'd started last night.

Who *were* the man who'd taken him? Were they something to do with Barnes's disappearance? They had to be, surely. The empty bag hidden in the cistern and the expensive heavy-duty front door came back into his mind. So much didn't make sense.

He moved his head slightly and realised he was lying down on what felt like a bed. He carefully rolled his wrists and ankles, just enough to test the area around them. No binds as far as he could tell. He could be wrong, but hopefully he wasn't. They were cocky then, whoever they were, laying him down without restricting him. Unless there was something between them like a gate. He risked opening one eye and immediately regretted it as the pain intensified in his head. He squeezed it shut again. It felt like the worst hangover he'd ever had. He hoped he got to repay the bastard who'd caused it.

The sound of footsteps returning came through, this time clearly those of more than one person. The two – or three, he wasn't quite certain – people who came back into the room stopped not far from him.

'Cillian? Eh, can you hear me?' came a deep craggy voice.

Cillian forced himself to open both eyes this time, ignoring the searing pain that shot behind them into his brain. He pushed himself up awkwardly, holding one hand to his head as he steadied himself, and as his blurred vision finally cleared, he frowned.

'You have *got* to be fucking kidding me,' he spat.

Ray was sitting on a chair a couple of metres from the bed Cillian was now perched on, leaning forward on his knees, an awkward cringe on his face. 'I'd love to tell you I was,' he said. 'There's been a bit of a cock-up.'

'Damn right there fucking has!' Cillian exclaimed heatedly, his anger rising swiftly. 'Why the *hell* did your goons attack me and drag me back here? To what I assume is your gaff,' he added, looking around. 'What? You got some sort of fucking fetish for kidnapping me mum's kids or something now? Connor next, is he? Three for three?'

'Watch your mouth,' snarled one of the other men in the room. 'Don't you know who you're talking to?'

Cillian glared at him with pure fury, bristling. 'You obviously don't know who *you're* talking to,' he replied, a dangerous undertone to his words. It was one of the men who'd taken him. The other stood silently behind Ray.

'Alright, that's enough dick measuring,' Ray said, holding his hand up to silence them both. 'Look, they didn't know who you were last night. My men were waiting there in case whoever messed with Jude Barnes came back – and then you broke in in the middle of the night, sniffing around the place. They figured you must have been who they were waiting for and didn't take a proper look at ya before they knocked you out.'

'*What?*' Cillian asked, completely confused. 'I don't understand – how do you even know Barnes in the first place?'

'He's one of my runners. One of my best actually,' Ray replied. 'Been working for me for a couple of years now. But then suddenly he disappeared, along with a bag full of gear.'

Cillian blinked, taken aback. Barnes worked for Ray? How could his friend have started working for Ray and not told him? But even as the question entered his head, he knew the answer. He and Barnes had kept just the right balance of familiarity and distance over the years. Barnes knew exactly who he was, but they never talked shop. And he wouldn't want to start by telling Cillian he'd started working for another firm.

'He hasn't run off with your gear,' Cillian stated, following what he thought must be Ray's natural train of thought. 'He wouldn't do that – he's a good bloke.'

'I didn't say he had,' Ray replied. 'He's always been solid, Jude has. Plus it weren't even a particularly big bag. If he was gonna try and do me over, I doubt he'd have wasted the attempt for that amount. Why were *you* at his gaff anyway?' he asked, looking at him with a sharp gaze. 'What have you got to do with it all?'

'Nothing!' Cillian exclaimed, irritated. 'I was there as a friend.'

'Breaking into someone's home don't seem very friendly,' Ray replied.

Cillian made a grunt of frustration. 'He's gone missing – I ain't just gonna ring the doorbell, am I? I'm trying to find out what happened. Someone's taken him.'

'What do you mean?' Ray asked with a frown. 'What makes you say that?'

'There was a note. His mum found it. Someone was trying to make it look like he'd written it, but it was clearly not from him. Said he'd met a girl, fallen in love and had decided to go off-grid.'

Ray's frown deepened. 'Well, that definitely ain't him.'

'Exactly.'

Cillian eyed Ray, wondering whether or not to tell him the rest. Despite his personal feelings towards the man, he couldn't deny that Ray was an absolute powerhouse. He had eyes and ears in more places than the Drews and had a much longer reach. Much as he disliked the idea, he could probably use his help.

'It isn't just Barnes,' he said grudgingly. 'There are two others from the boxing club. Both disappeared with weird notes left behind. Then one turned up in the river. Or parts of him did anyway.'

Ray's eyebrows shot up in surprise before he righted his expression. 'Repton?'

'Yeah. Guy called Cain, and the one whose body they found was Gary. Were they working for you too?' Cillian asked. Perhaps this was all to do with Ray, a rival firm picking off his men.

'Nah.' Ray shook his head. 'No one else is missing, and I

don't know anyone by the name of Cain.' He scratched his chin as he thought it over. 'So they're all from Repton Boxing Club. Did they know each other?'

'Barnes knew Cain but they weren't close. The only link between the three that I can find is that they were all in the same weight range,' Cillian replied.

'Now, that is interesting,' Ray mused. 'What weight is it? Heavyweight? Barnes looks like a heavyweight.'

'Yeah.' Cillian rubbed his head, the throbbing still going strong. 'You got any painkillers? Tweedle Dum or Tweedle Dee here did a right job on my bonce. Which one of you was it anyway?'

They both shot him dirty looks, but one then glanced towards the other, giving him away. Cillian turned to him with a raised eyebrow.

'Yeah, it was me,' he replied cockily. 'No point crying over it now though, mate. What's done is done – put your big-boy pants on and get over it.'

'Come through to the kitchen – I've got some in there,' Ray said, ignoring the exchange. 'I'll get you a coffee too. You've been out cold all night.'

Cillian stood up and rubbed the back of his neck, rolling it to crack the tension. As he passed the man who'd knocked him out, he pulled his arm back and smashed his fist hard into his face, sending him sprawling onto the floor. As he made to try and get up, Cillian leaned over him and pointed a finger in his face with a menacing expression.

'You deserved that. And I ain't your *mate*.'

'What the hell!' the man on the floor exclaimed, holding his jaw with a groan of self-pity. 'Ray?' But Ray had disappeared, seemingly bored of their issues with each other.

'Eh – put your big-boy pants on, yeah?' Cillian mocked, turning his earlier words against him. 'Get over it.' Then, with a smirk, he walked out of the room to follow Ray.

Inside the kitchen, Ray was popping some paracetamol out of a packet. He handed them to Cillian with a glass of water. Cillian took them and sat down at the table.

'It's interesting that they're all in the same weight range,' Ray said, turning on the coffee machine on the counter. 'Think it might have anything to do with the competitions?'

'Maybe.' It was something Cillian had been mulling over after he'd left the club the day before.

There was a long silence as they waited for the coffee to brew.

'If it is, then I have an idea as to how we could find out for sure,' Ray said thoughtfully.

'How?' Cillian asked.

'We lure out whoever's doing this with bait. We put another heavyweight contender back in the running and wait for them to start making moves. They won't know we're expecting them, so they'd likely show their hand without realising. Get to the bottom of it that way,' Ray said, pulling two mugs out of the cupboard.

'Who you thinking of putting in?' Cillian asked.

Ray turned and looked him in the eye with a challenging expression. 'You.'

TWENTY-ONE

'Connor, what you doing here again?' Sandra asked with a fixed smile. 'Can't seem to get rid of you these days. You just keep turning up like a bad penny.' She laughed to soften the joke.

'Well, the way I see it there ain't no such thing as a bad penny, Sandra,' he responded cheerily, walking over to the reception desk where Scarlet was looking through some paperwork. 'Any penny can be spent on something that makes ya happy, can't it? So how can there be such a thing as a bad one?'

Sandra contemplated this for a moment, pushing her shiny blonde hair back out of her face with a tilt of the head. 'I guess that's a reasonable point,' she conceded.

'Exactly. Think of me more as a bright shiny new penny, ready for you to grab and use however you wish.' He winked at her with a cheeky smile, and she rolled her eyes before walking away to the backwash.

Connor chuckled and leaned over the high barrier of the reception desk. Scarlet narrowed her eyes and looked up at him.

'You know she's got a boyfriend now,' she warned.

'I do,' Connor replied, his grin dropping ruefully. He'd been in love with Sandra for a while, though she'd made her disinterest in him painfully clear.

'What you doing here anyway?' she asked. 'There's no drop-off today.'

'Nah, I know. Just had some time to kill before Mum needed me – thought I'd pop in and say hi.'

Just then the door swung open behind him and he looked around to see Cillian march in. 'Alright, bruv?' he greeted him merrily. 'How you doing? Good lie-in?'

Cillian stopped beside him, his eyes shooting daggers and the small muscles in his cheeks contorting angrily. He stared at Connor for a moment, then whacked him around the back of the head with the palm of his hand.

'Oi! What was that for?' Connor complained loudly, putting his hand up to his head.

'I've been looking for you all morning. I've called you about ten times,' he snapped, looking fit to burst.

'What?' Connor pulled out his phone. 'Oh yeah.' He tutted as he realised what had happened. 'It must have turned on silent in me pocket. Oh well, you're here now. And—'

'Yeah, I am luckily,' Cillian shot through gritted teeth, cutting him off. 'But you know what?' He glanced at Scarlet. 'Just get in the fucking car,' he managed.

'What on earth has got—'

'*Get* – in the *fucking* – car,' he bellowed, cutting him off.

'Alright, Jesus!' Connor shouted back, putting his hands up in surrender.

He exchanged a wide-eyed frown with Scarlet, who seemed equally as confused. He straightened up and rolled his eyes, annoyed now by his brother's bad mood.

'You know there's no need to get your knickers in a twist,' he said, walking out of the salon. 'Billie dumped you or something?'

For a moment Cillian looked as though he might actually

burst, but instead he stormed off towards the car. Connor shook his head.

'He's definitely been dumped,' he muttered confidently to himself.

———

'How was I supposed to know you'd been knocked out and kidnapped?' Connor asked helplessly, looking sideways towards his brother.

Cillian stared back at him from the driver's seat of the car and shook his head. 'You didn't even check to see everything went OK! I went *off – fucking – territory* on a break-in that only *you* knew about, and you didn't even think to check it was all OK when you were done for the night? I mean *Jesus*, Connor!' he cried. 'I'd been knocked out cold by fucking strangers—'

'Well, Ray,' Connor argued.

'Yeah, *luckily*!' Cillian shot back. He ran his hands through his hair, wincing as his fingers touched the lump where the bat had hit. 'That was bad enough, but what if it hadn't been Ray, eh? What if it had been the fucker who took Barnes? What if the next thing you knew, there was a note from me on the kitchen bloody table?' His voice had risen an octave and he stopped, realising this, turning to stare out the window, his jaw clamped.

There was a short silence, and Cillian could feel Connor's stare as he kept his own gaze fixed pointedly away. He knew he was being irrational, but the last twelve hours had shaken him up more than he cared to admit. It had proven just how fragile their own safety was.

'Look, we ain't gonna find you gone with some note left, alright? I'm sorry, I shouldn't have assumed things had gone to plan,' Connor said, his tone more subdued and apologetic now.

'And you're right, I should have kept trying to get hold of you and raised an alarm when I couldn't.'

'Well, it's probably good you didn't on this particular occasion,' Cillian admitted grudgingly.

'Mum don't know?' Connor asked, surprised.

'That Ray took me? No. Much as I'd love to tell her and drop that bastard in her line of fire, I could actually do with his help,' Cillian admitted. 'We may hate him, but he's got more weight in this city than we do.'

Connor pulled a face and stared off out the window. 'OK.'

'And you may very well find me gone with a note on the table soon,' Cillian added.

'What?' Connor asked with a frown.

Cillian sighed. 'Ray had an idea. Not a very fucking good one, in my opinion,' he added resentfully. 'But I agreed to give it a go.'

'What's the idea?' Connor asked.

'Whoever's doing this is picking off the strong contenders in the heavyweight category at the gym. Or at least it looks that way. I'm going to start competing, which means if we're right about that, they should very soon go after me.' Cillian watched Connor's expression turn to one of horror.

'You're right, that's a fucking terrible idea,' he said.

Cillian's face registered his agreement, then he took something out of his pocket. 'This is a tracking chip Ray gave me. Apparently, it's the best – he got some off Bill for a job he pulled a while back. I can link it to your phone and you'll be able to track me.' He turned the tiny chip over in his hand. 'I'm going to conceal it in my waistband every day, and from now on, we'll start checking in every couple of hours. If I go off-radar suddenly, you go to Ray and you can track me down with this.'

'But what if you go off-radar and it don't work? Or it gets taken off you somehow?' Connor asked, unconvinced.

'It will work,' Cillian said confidently. 'It's straight from Bill.

And I'll make sure it's secure. There's no chance someone would figure out that I've got that attached to the waistband of my underwear. It's tiny.'

Connor's expression remained unconvinced, but he nodded and took the chip from Cillian, turning it over in his hand. 'If you're sure you wanna do that, then OK. But I still don't like it.'

'Me neither, but I do think it's our best shot at finding Barnes,' Cillian insisted. 'Time's ticking and with Gary turning up in pieces...' He stared out the window with a grim expression. 'Look, I'm hoping he's still alive, but I'm beginning to doubt our chances.'

'Don't think like that,' Connor said, shaking his head with a frown. 'He ain't dead. Not Barnes. He's a fighter. Whatever situation he's in, he'll be fighting to get out of it. He just needs our help. So we're going to get to him and bring him home safe. Because we look after our own. Even if they are working for Ray bloody Renshaw,' he added.

Cillian took the chip from his brother and slipped it back into his pocket. 'We'll set this up tonight and then tomorrow morning I'll announce I'm going to compete.' He turned on the engine and pulled out into the road. 'Now we'd better get moving. There's one last thing I need to do before we can get on with work, and I ain't looking forward to it.'

'What?' Connor asked.

Cillian exhaled heavily. 'I've gotta tell Mum.'

TWENTY-TWO

'I don't bloody well think so!' Lily said strongly, placing her hands on her hips and staring at her son as if he'd gone mad. 'You ain't putting yourself in danger like that.'

'I am actually,' Cillian replied, his stubbornness meeting her own.

They stared at each other across the factory office while Connor sat down in a corner armchair, sighing wearily.

Lily sifted through various arguments in her head as she considered her more stubborn son, unaware that their expressions were matched to a T, and tried to decide on her strongest angle. She knew Barnes meant a lot to him – they'd been friends since they were kids – and she supported his need to find him. But putting himself in a direct line of danger like this was foolish.

'Whose idea was it?' she asked. 'Which one of you thought *this* was the way to go?' She raised an eyebrow.

Connor opened his mouth to reply, but Cillian quickly jumped in. 'I did.' They exchanged a glance, and she just shook her head.

'I know you think you're doing the right thing, but this ain't the way to go about it,' she said, sitting back down behind her desk. 'If they really are targeting that weight range, then you're just lining up to be next. If they didn't know what was coming, neither will you.'

'Nah, see, that's where you're wrong. Think about it,' Cillian replied, sitting down opposite her. 'To get that close, they'd have to have been tailing them or have invited them somewhere. They wouldn't have known to watch out for a tail or be wary of an unusual invite. But I do.'

Lily pursed her lips. 'That's a fair point, but still, I think you're wasting your time anyway. I don't think they're targeting a weight range – I think that's coincidence.'

'Why do you say that?' he asked.

'Gary was a building contractor. From what I understand from Connor, he came here because of work. Well, there are lots of building companies around, granted. But how many would be expanding to the extent they search further than the local pool for more brickies?' She raised an eyebrow.

'I don't follow,' Cillian replied.

'When Scarlet and I went to Conway's yard, I noticed he'd taken the next plot along. He's doubled the size of his company since I saw it last. New men, new JCBs, the lot. If Gary had come here to work for him, well, that would be more than just coincidence, wouldn't it?'

'That's still a big if,' Cillian said. 'And why would he kill off one of his own?'

'Because he would be an easy-access starting point. Conway is a bloke who will do absolutely anything to get what he wants, and he's never let the laws of the underground get in his way. It's why no one likes him. He's ruthless but in a way that can't be respected.' She reached for her cigarettes and tapped one out onto her desk. 'What if he wanted this land that badly and knew that sooner or later Jimmy would find out and start petitioning – the way he is now – to get the place spot listed as an important building to the community—'

'And wanted to make sure it looked so shady that it wouldn't be,' Cillian finished, cottoning on.

'Exactly.' She lit her cigarette and took a drag. 'If there are men going missing, bodies turning up, police investigations, fingers being pointed and all the rest, no one's going to want to preserve that. They'll be glad to see it gone.'

Cillian pulled a toothpick out of his pocket and placed it between his teeth, rolling it with his tongue as he thought it over. 'I don't think he meant for the body to be found,' he said. 'But the rest could be plausible.'

'It's more than plausible,' Lily replied.

He nodded and glanced at Connor, looking for his opinion.

Connor shrugged. 'I think right now we're shooting in the dark,' he said. 'It could be Conway. It could be someone in the league, from another club, who's taking things way too far. It could even be something else entirely. But we ain't gonna find out unless we start properly digging.'

'Which is why I'm signing up to compete. I'm heavyweight. If it's that, we'll know soon enough,' Cillian said firmly.

'I'm not OK with you doing that,' Lily replied, her tone just as firm.

'I'm doing it whether you like it or not,' Cillian snapped, his eyes flashing hotly as his temper flared. 'Mum, there are men disappearing and turning up in fucking pieces. People from *our* turf, the area *we're* supposed to protect. These are people we grew up with. Maybe not this Gary, but the others are.' He held her gaze, and she felt his resolution strengthen. 'We can't let this carry on – we have to figure it out. Fast. Before it happens again – before, hopefully, Barnes also ends up in a bag in bits,' he spat. 'Because if we can't do that, if we can't even protect our own, then who the fuck are we?'

The tension between them hung in the air like a weight but

finally Lily relented with a long slow breath. He was right – she knew he was. But he was her son, one of the people she needed to protect above all others. Allowing him to put himself in what was potentially harm's way didn't sit easy with her. Then again, it didn't seem to be her decision at all anymore. Cillian had obviously made up his mind, no matter what she had to say about it.

She lowered her gaze with a nod. 'Just stay vigilant. No fucking around. You stay on the ball. No drinking, no forgetting to check over your shoulder. And you' – she pointed at Connor – 'you stay right behind him, all the time, to catch anything he misses. You got that?' She stared at him sternly.

'Got it,' Connor replied.

'I'll start poking around Conway. And on that matter, there's something else we need to do.' She stubbed out her cigarette and laced her fingers together on the desk. 'We're gonna be taking a little trip out to Oxfordshire tonight, the three of us. I need you in full heist get-up.'

'We're pulling a job?' Connor asked. He and Cillian exchanged frowns of surprise. 'We didn't know about that.'

'Not exactly. But what we're doing is still illegal and apparently taken quite seriously. So no chances. Now...' She couldn't help the grin of amusement that crept out. 'Either of you got a trowel?'

TWENTY-THREE

'I did not sign up for this,' Connor complained moodily. 'I made certain life choices and I made them for a reason. One of them being to live in a flat. You know why? I fucking hate flowers. They make me sneeze. And now here we are, gallivanting around the countryside, picking fucking flowers.'

'Oh do put a sock in it, Connor,' Lily said half-heartedly. 'I'll buy you some antihistamines on the way home. And we ain't picking flowers – we're uprooting some plants. Very carefully actually, because they can't look damaged.'

Connor sniffed, crossing his arms and staring out the window. 'Well, it better be Beconase. None of that shop-brand crap.'

Beside her in the passenger seat, she saw Cillian turn away to hide his grin from his brother.

'You really think this is gonna work?' he asked, changing the subject.

'I hope so. Freddie said, according to his contact, if we can find some of this creeping marshwort and do a good enough job of relocating it, he has someone who will sign it off as kosher.

But it has to look proper.' She pushed her curls back and slowed to turn down the road they needed according to the satnav.

'And that will mean they can't tear down the building?' Cillian asked, sounding doubtful.

'Apparently, yes,' Lily answered. 'It's one of the most endangered plants in the UK. It only grows here and one other place.'

'And we're going to steal it,' Connor said miserably from the back.

'Only a bit. We need to get it back and planted in that little bit of mud out by the back wall of the boxing club by morning,' Lily confirmed. 'Then we can get the ball rolling and hopefully scupper Conway's plans before the planning goes any further.'

They travelled in relative silence for the next ten minutes until Lily slowed down and pulled to a stop on the side of a road.

'This is it,' she said quietly. 'Hats on, let's be quick.'

They all jumped out, and she led the way down a dirt path that took them to a borderline of trees. Beyond was a wide stretch of grass that went as far as they could see, only a few pale lights twinkling in the distance.

'Where are we?' Cillian asked. 'I thought we'd be pilfering from some old lady's garden.'

'No, it's a wild plant. Grows on the ground, spread out near the river,' she replied.

'Right.' He pulled a face but said no more.

They walked down the path and then onto the uneven terrain of the large meadow. The night was dark and eerily silent, only the occasional sound of a car or motorbike engine carrying through the air from the nearby sleepy town.

'How far do we have to go?' Connor asked quietly.

'We should be getting close, from what I was told,' Lily answered, pulling her phone out of her pocket.

She switched on the torch and shone it on the ground. Grass tufts cast their shadows in dancing shapes across the mud as she scanned back and forth, slowing her pace to make sure she didn't miss anything. The sound of moving water became louder, indicating that they were nearly at the river. They should have reached it, if Freddie's instructions were correct.

Suddenly, her light fell across a cluster of small white flowers nestled in a tangle of dark green leaves and she silently rejoiced. She'd found it.

'Here,' she said urgently. 'This is it.'

She moved her torch and could see the creeping marshwort had spread across a wide area.

'You're sure?' Cillian asked.

'As sure as I can be from the pictures,' she replied. 'Connor, get the bag out. Cillian, give me the scissors and one of the trowels.'

Moving quickly, she nipped the tendrils neatly and efficiently with the scissors, careful only to do so where she had to. Then she grabbed the trowel and pushed it down hard into the earth. They had to get the roots up in the hope that they would soon take in the mud by the boxing club. The ground was stiff and she had to push hard to get low enough.

There was suddenly a low whistle from somewhere much closer than the road and all three of them froze.

'What was that?' Connor whispered.

Lily's heart began to beat a little faster. This was one of the rarest plants in the country. Was there security in the area? Were these fields monitored? She pushed down harder, willing the soil to break quicker. They needed to get out of here before whoever it was spotted them. This was highly illegal. It was funny really – or would be, if they weren't in such a precarious position – of all the things they'd done, all the ways they flouted the law, surely this wouldn't be what tripped them up?

'Come on, boy,' came a voice through the darkness.

'It's a dog walker,' Connor said quietly, sounding relieved.

'Not necessarily,' Lily replied tensely. 'That could still be security of some sort. Let's just get this done and get out of here.'

She sped up in her digging, all the while aware that whoever was out there was drawing closer.

'Come on, Mum,' Cillian whispered, and she could hear the same tension in his voice that she felt inside.

Eventually, after what seemed like an eternity, she got all the way round the section of plant she was trying to uproot. Reaching down into the earth, she yanked and pulled, the remaining roots she hadn't yet severed from the masses still stubbornly holding on.

'Jesus, this just doesn't want to give up,' she said, pulling harder.

Cillian picked up the trowel and started hacking at the ones still clinging on and she felt it slowly give way.

'Hey, this way.'

The man's voice was a lot closer now and Lily felt a prickle of fear run up her neck. Soon he would be close enough to see them even through the darkness. They needed to get out of here fast.

'That's it,' Lily said as Cillian broke the last of the roots.

Connor held out the big black bag, and Lily quickly but carefully moved the plant into it as Cillian picked up the tools she'd left on the ground.

'What the—? Hey!' came a shout.

They could see him now, walking towards them, squinting at them in the moonlight.

'What are you doing? You can't take that!'

'Quick!' Lily yelled, shoving the plant the rest of the way down the bag without ceremony. 'Run!'

The three of them bolted, circling around the man towards the path as fast as they could.

'Oi!' he called after them. 'Bloody—'

They didn't hear the rest of whatever he'd muttered, and

when Lily turned to glance back at him, she saw that he hadn't followed them. He must have just been a local, after all, out with his dog.

They broke out of the field in seconds, reaching the car together, and she fell against the passenger door, stopping to try to catch her breath.

'Oh God,' she said, between big gulps of air. As she looked back towards the dark opening that led through the trees and thought about the man with the dog, she suddenly let out a loud laugh. 'I feel like a teenager running away from a prank.' She pulled out the car keys, not quite able to stop laughing as she did, and squeezed both her sons' arms. 'Come on.'

She slipped into the car and her smile faded as her thoughts returned to the boxing club. If only stopping the planning from going ahead was the single challenge that lay ahead of them. If only the threat of being knocked down was the one dark cloud hanging over the place that had once been a haven to so many young men.

With men disappearing, body parts turning up in bags, and no definitive explanation as to why, it would seem that there were darker days and dangerous roads ahead of them yet.

TWENTY-FOUR

The girl awoke and stared at the tired magnolia wall for a few moments before turning onto her back and stretching her arms up above her head. She yawned, a slow lazy yawn of someone who'd woken up with no particular plans for the day. But the yawn soon turned to a startled yelp as she saw that she wasn't alone in her small, sparse hotel room.

'Jesus Christ, you scared the life out of me,' she said, pulling herself up into a sitting position and pushing her straggly morning hair back in an attempt to smooth it.

'Lily will do,' Lily responded, with a touch of humour, from the chair in the corner.

She looked the girl up and down. She was wearing a faded oversized Guns 'N' Roses T-shirt that Lily was more than certain she hadn't bought at a concert – she was far too young to have attended one herself. She wondered idly whether perhaps it had been her father's.

'Your story checks out,' she continued. 'Which leaves me with the question of what I'm to do with you.'

Isla's expression lifted in hope. 'I can do anything you need. I've got all kinds of skills that could make me an asset. Like—'

'Theft?' Lily asked, cutting her off. She lifted the brown leather wallet from her lap and held it in the air with one raised eyebrow. She'd found it on the desk beside the window when she'd arrived, Isla still fast asleep. It contained a family picture of a couple with a little girl, a few receipts and a library card. The girl had clearly already taken the cash and cards.

Isla coloured, a wariness reappearing. 'I needed money,' she admitted. 'I was as careful as I could be, but I ran out. I had to do something. I'm sorry.'

Lily shrugged. 'Save your apologies – it wasn't me you robbed.' She chucked the wallet back onto the desk and folded her hands in her lap. 'So you can pickpocket, that much I know. And you mentioned before that you used to make counterfeit goods. Tell me more about that.'

'Oh, um...' Isla slid her legs over the side of the bed and quickly pulled on some leggings as she spoke. 'Well, it was quite a big operation, and over the last few years, I learned pretty much all of it.' She pulled the duvet up and sat back down on it, crossing her legs and facing Lily.

'How old are you?' Lily interjected, curious. Isla didn't seem old enough to have worked anywhere for a few years.

'Twenty-one. I don't look it, I know.' She grinned. 'A blessing and a curse. I worked the production line to begin with. Learned all the tricks, how to work leather and cloth and all the machines. Weren't no different from a normal factory set-up really, only that it weren't legal.'

Lily's interest was piqued. They weren't exactly skills she needed, but the girl must have been used to working in their world and could keep her mouth shut. That was worth something.

'After a while I moved up the ranks. Worked with the suppliers and made sure the floor ran smoothly. Some said it was due to Calvin. *Favouritism*,' she said bitterly. 'But it weren't. It were because I was good.'

'Calvin – he was the one you were seeing, right?' Lily asked.

'Yeah.' Isla lowered her gaze for a moment, her expression clouding.

Lily's eyes narrowed as she wondered what had gone on between the two of them. 'Why did you leave?'

Isla's gaze shot up to meet hers. 'I had to,' she replied, her voice heavy.

'Because?' Lily prompted, not satisfied with the vague answer.

Isla moved her gaze away once more, looking towards the window. She swallowed and Lily saw a look of shame pass across her face.

'When my dad was killed... I mean, officially he's still missing, but he isn't. When he was killed, I was left on my own. I still lived at home, I'd only just turned eighteen, but someone tipped off the council and after a while they wanted his flat back. It was in his name, you see. They rehoused me in a one-bed flat. Horrible place. I felt so lost and alone. And Calvin came by and started acting like he cared. Said he'd look after me, that everyone in the firm was family. Paid for a get-together in the local pub to celebrate my dad, sorted out all the moving arrangements. I knew it was a bad idea to let him in, but I was scared and it felt nice to have someone take care of things when I was still in shock about it all.' Isla shifted on the bed and pushed a stray strand of hair behind her ear. ''Course, soon after I was moved in, he wanted payment for all his supposed kindness,' she said resentfully.

'What kind of payment?' Lily asked.

'Me.' Isla smiled sadly. 'He came over one night, after him and the rest had been out for drinks. He was steaming. Said he needed me, needed some comfort back the way he'd comforted me. I said I'd make him a hot drink to sober him up and that he could stay over on the sofa, but he wasn't having none of it. He laughed and grabbed me. I did try saying no.' She looked at Lily, unhappiness shining out of her big brown eyes. 'But he got angry and asked why I'd led him on. Asked why I'd accepted all I had from him, if I was going to go cold. Told me I couldn't do that, that we were beyond all that now. And then he, um...' She gazed off into the distance with a detached expression, exhaling tiredly. 'Then he took what he was owed.'

'He raped you,' Lily said, feeling deep pity for the girl.

'I didn't fight it, so no, it wasn't rape. When he pushed me down, I gave in to what he said and I didn't stop him. Even though I wanted to. Even though it was my first time.' She looked down again.

'Isla, that *is* rape,' Lily corrected her firmly. 'You said no. He did it anyway. It doesn't matter that you felt you couldn't fight it physically.' She felt anger rising up in her at the way the young girl had been manipulated and used. Men like Calvin, who preyed on the weak, were the worst kind of scum.

'Well, it don't matter now,' Isla said resolutely, looking back up at her. 'I didn't stop it. And then it became a regular thing between us. I even liked it at times. And I became his side thing. Another person he owned.'

'Side thing?' Lily queried.

'He's married. His wife is crazier than a box of frogs. She's the only person he's actually afraid of. And she was the only person who didn't know. It was the worst-kept secret in the firm. Part of me wanted her to find out, because I knew she'd put an end to it. But she'd have also put an end to me, and to my job in the firm.' She pulled a face. 'I couldn't afford that. My pay barely covered my bills and food. He said it was because anything I needed, he paid for already. But really it was because he knew if I ever had enough to save up to get out then I'd be gone. He kept me poor so I had no choice but to stay with him. I tried to argue it now and then but usually got a black eye and an earful for my troubles.'

'He sounds like a right charmer,' Lily remarked.

'Yeah, well, they all are until they're not,' Isla replied.

They were words that were bitterly wise for her tender years and they reminded Lily all too sharply of her own early ascension to adulthood. She hadn't gone through the same hardships as Isla, but she recognised the journey all too well. She too had lost her parents young and had been left to struggle on alone. She too had had to deal with things that no one of her age should have had to deal with. That was the harsh reality of the world. Life wasn't always fair and the stories were rarely fairy tales.

'How did you get out?' Lily asked.

'Someone eventually told her. I'm amazed she didn't find out sooner, to be honest. It'd been going on for nearly three years,' she said bleakly. 'She stormed over to mine spitting feathers. Somehow, she got hold of my number and called me first, telling me she knew and was going to kill me. That saved my life really. She would have done it. I managed to get hold of Calvin though, and him and his brother Jared got there just in time. But she fought them like a wildcat, ripped all down Calvin's face with her nails.' She smiled briefly at the memory. 'He came in while his brother held her off and threw a roll of cash at me. Told me to go somewhere and lie low, then contact him. I saw how much was there and knew it was going to be my only chance to get away. So I grabbed what I could carry, climbed down the fire escape and came here.' She held her arms out to the side for a moment, then let them drop.

Lily nodded, twisting her lips to one side as Isla's story sank in. The girl had been through a lot. And that wasn't Lily's problem. She could walk out of here now and tell the girl to find her way somewhere else. But she couldn't help but remember the days when she had struggled with no one to help.

Lily sat forward, lacing her fingers together on her crossed knee. 'I'm going to give you a chance,' she said. She saw relief flash across the girl's face, followed by a smile.

'It's just a chance,' Lily warned, staring her down with a serious look. 'You cross any lines, steal, lie or cheat us in any way, and I'll not only hunt you down, I'll hand you back to your old firm wrapped up in a bright red bow.'

Isla blinked at the cold, hard promise Lily delivered. 'I won't do anything like that,' she insisted. 'Why would I? I'm just pleased to be here.'

Lily let the tension hang in the air for a few seconds, then continued. 'I'm not giving you a solid position yet. You'll do some running around, errands, information gathering, filling in at the factory, whatever I need. And there ain't no set hours. I might need you in the day, I might need you at 2 a.m. You'll be on call as and when I need you.'

'Of course,' Isla replied, nodding. 'Whatever you need.'

Lily looked her up and down. 'We'll see how you do and then assess whether there's a position for you going forward. I'll be in touch over the next few days.' She stood up and brushed down her skirt.

Isla stood up too, clasping her hands together anxiously. 'OK, how do I contact you? Should I wait here? Or...?' She closed her mouth, unsure what else to suggest.

Lily opened her bag and brought out a phone and a thick envelope, dropping them both onto the desk. 'This has my number in it. It's a burner; do not use it for anything else other than to contact me. And that's your first pay packet. You're on my payroll now. You understand what that means?'

Isla nodded, the relief obvious on her face. 'My loyalty, time and skills are all yours,' she answered.

'Good. And no more of *that*.' Lily pointed to the stolen wallet. 'I don't need you bringing unnecessary attention to yourself.'

Isla nodded her agreement. 'No more, I promise.'

'I'll be in touch.'

With that, Lily left the room and made her way out of the hotel.

Back on the busy market street, she questioned once more whether she had done the right thing. They didn't exactly need anyone right now, but then a gem like Isla, someone already used to the underworld with a willingness to hand over her allegiance and loyalty, wasn't something one came across often. And when opportunity knocks, only a fool would ignore it.

She just hoped that she was right about this being an opportunity, and that she wouldn't find herself regretting this move entirely.

TWENTY-FIVE

The car slowed to a stop outside Conway's building yard and Scarlet looked over at it with a grim expression. 'What's your take on him?' she asked George in the driver's seat beside her.

George pulled a face. 'Bit of a twat. Someone who wants it all, but who never quite grasped the subtleties of the underworld. He's always been too eager, rushing in and trampling everything in his way to get to the prize. That's what people don't like about him.'

'Yeah, so I keep hearing,' Scarlet replied.

They got out and walked through the yard, heading towards the Portakabin Scarlet had been in days before. This time the door was open, letting in some of the mild afternoon breeze, and she could see AJ on the phone at his desk. She paused at the bottom of the steps and turned to George, who was looking stonily at the men shooting interested glances their way.

'Wait here, would you?' she asked. 'Keep this meeting private?'

He nodded.

Satisfied that George had her back, she climbed the steps into the Portakabin and took a seat in the chair opposite AJ, waiting with a pleasant smile as he finished up his conversation. He eventually put down the phone and looked across at her with a curious expression.

'Two visits in a week – I do feel special,' he said in his loud, brash voice. 'So what's the ploy then, eh? Why send you?' He leaned back in his chair and looked her up and down with a greasy smile. 'Let me guess, you're going to offer me some very friendly gratitude, if I drop the build? Get a bit of skin out, service my desires?'

'Why would you think that?' Scarlet asked in a matter-of-fact tone. 'Is that what you offer people when you want something? Your sexual services?' She blinked innocently and tilted her head enquiringly.

'I...' His jaw slackened as she threw his attempt to put down her worth back in his face.

Scarlet shrugged. 'Hey, each to their own, I don't judge.' She crossed one slender leg over the other and relaxed back in the chair as if she were completely at ease. 'No, I actually don't disagree with you about the boxing club. I think it's an eyesore.' She softened her expression to look as though she was being genuinely friendly.

AJ pulled back and frowned, then dropped his hands down to the desk and searched her face. 'You do?' he asked suspiciously.

'Well, between us anyway,' she replied, wondering if he was really buying this lie. He'd be much easier to trick into showing his hand if he thought she was sympathetic to his cause. 'Obviously I have to support my aunt and her feelings on the matter officially. But yes, between us, I don't get the big deal. It's just a gym – they could rebuild it anywhere. The land though – it's a prime location for a build like this.'

'Huh. At last, a Drew with actual business sense,' AJ cried with a grin.

Scarlet forced a smile in return, all the while throwing

mental daggers right at his heart. The fact he couldn't understand what lay at the heart of that place was the reason he'd
never succeeded in integrating himself fully into their world.
He thought himself a gangster, one of their own, but in reality
he was just a dodgy builder playing by himself on the sidelines.

'So let's get down to why you're actually here then, Scarlet,'
AJ continued, eyeing her with curiosity once more. 'What do
you want?'

Scarlet studied him for a moment. He had a face that gave
away so much more than he realised when he spoke. And his
pudgy cheeks and easy grin made him appear quite friendly, if
you ignored the rudeness and blatant sexism. But this was an
illusion. He wasn't friendly; he was a ruthless snake, and one
that was potentially incredibly dangerous – if he *was* the one
who'd killed Gary and kidnapped the others.

'The gym should be gone, and I really do wish you the best
in getting that planning through, even if that does have to stay
between us.' She smiled, watching his gaze as it slipped to her
mouth. 'And I'm sure it will. I mean, you've got it sewn up as far
as we can see.'

'I certainly do,' he bragged, puffing his chest out.

'So why did you do what you did to Gary Oldham?' she
asked.

The question came out of the blue and AJ's expression was
unguarded. The reaction was instant: recognition when she
uttered the name followed swiftly by fear before a hard wall
was quickly pulled up, barring her from any further insight.

'Who?' he asked, folding his arms across his middle. 'I've
never heard of a Gary Oldham.'

'Really? You seemed to recognise his name just then.' She
studied him, wondering if he'd crack further, but his guard was
well and truly up.

'Not at all. Never met *any* Garys, as it happens, so whatever
you're on about, you're barking up the wrong tree, love.' He

pointedly glanced at his watch. 'Anyway, this was fun, but I've got to get on.'

Scarlet smiled, the action not reaching her eyes. 'Of course.' She stood up and walked over to the door, pausing to look back at him. 'I'm actually really glad you didn't know Gary.'

'Yeah? Why's that?' AJ asked, his gaze flickering in a nervous action that gave him away.

'Because I believe in karma,' she replied, her voice low and her expression cold. 'It always comes around, whether you want it to or not.'

With one last look at him, she turned and left, having seen all she needed.

TWENTY-SIX

Cillian held his breath as he watched a tall, slim man crouch on his haunches by the back wall of the gym. The man was scruffy in an oddly elegant way, his shirt rumpled but tucked neatly into beige chinos and his boots expensive but scuffed and worn down. He pushed back his messy mop of hair and straightened his thick round glasses as he peered at the creeping marshwort now sitting proudly in the patch of mud against the wall.

He looked up at Cillian with a flat, unimpressed expression and Cillian gave him a nod of encouragement. This was one of Freddie Tyler's contacts, a plant specialist and green activist he paid a lot of money to in return for the odd favour. This was one of the favours. The deal was that he would officially recognise this as a site upon which a rare, endangered plant grew. This would mean all plans to tear down the building that the plant grew around would be thrown out immediately. Whilst the plant remained, no one would be able to build here and potentially put such an organism at risk. The only caveat had been that the Drews had to make it look realistic – at least to some degree. The man knew that this was a set-up of course, but he would have to take photos to document the proof. And this was clearly what he was considering now. Had they made it look good enough for him to pass?

He stood and stared down at it for a few long moments, then sighed, placing his hands on his hips before turning to face Cillian. He raised an eyebrow.

'It's certainly a very unusual place to find such a plant,' he said in a flat tone. 'Even if finding them at all wasn't extremely rare, these plants like very wet and green environments, hence why you'd usually find them on a flood plain, not in a muddy part of a concrete car park in the middle of London.' He let his comment and heavy glare linger for a moment.

'Did I mention how much I like you, Harry?' Cillian said with a winning grin. 'I think us working to help each other will really benefit you more than you realise.'

'Yes, yes...' The other man waved the comment away dismissively. 'I work for Freddie Tyler, Mr Drew, I know exactly the sort of reward that will come my way from *helping you out*. And it's *Henry*.' He glared at Cillian and pushed his thick glasses back up his nose with a sniff.

Cillian grimaced. 'OK, well, what's the score here, Henry?'

'It's incredibly unbelievable,' he said frankly, 'that this would be here, that it would thrive here...' He pulled a face and shook his head, and Cillian felt his heart sink. It had all been for nothing.

'That being said, whoever planted it has done a good job. It doesn't look like it's been moved.' He pointed to where a few other weeds were nestled up against it, and Cillian had to admit that Lily had done well on the finer details. 'I'll write it up and get this passed through against the building plans. But you're going to have to think about what to do long term,' he warned.

'What do you mean?' Cillian asked.

'This plant won't survive here,' Henry said as though the fact should be obvious. Cillian supposed it probably was. 'The reason it's so rare is because out of its optimum environment, it wastes away quickly. So I'll take photos and you should keep it alive for as long as possible – keep it wet – but eventually it will go. And if the place is revalued, the restriction will be lifted.'

Cillian nodded. He hadn't thought that far ahead, but hopefully his mother would have. 'Got it,' he replied.

'I'll send the details over to Ms Drew this afternoon as soon as it's all logged,' Henry said, walking away. 'Goodbye, Mr Drew.'

Cillian waved him off then walked around the building and in through the front door. Jimmy was hovering just inside, waiting for him.

'So? All OK?' he asked anxiously.

'Yeah, should be, for now,' Cillian answered.

Jimmy breathed out a sigh of relief. 'Thank God,' he said with feeling. 'I knew I could trust you to see this place right.' He looked around the well-worn venue with a look of pure love in his eyes. 'I couldn't imagine it being gone.'

'Not many of us could,' Cillian replied.

'Right, come on then,' Jimmy said, his tone snapping back to business. 'Let's get you started on your training.'

They exchanged a look and Cillian nodded, heading over towards the far ring. This was it, his first day training to officially compete. Competing had never been his bag, but now he was sure it was the only way to root out the culprit behind the disappearances and Gary's murder. He knew his mother had her bets on Conway, but he didn't buy it. The man was many things, but a killer wasn't one of them. He didn't have the balls. It *had* to be something to do with the league. He was sure of it.

Cillian slowed as he reached the ring, jumping up and slipping through the ropes.

'I'm going to have to ask you to move to the bags. I've got a training session starting here,' the coach said gruffly.

'That's OK, I'm in your session,' Cillian replied, eying him. He'd never warmed to this coach much. He always seemed in a bad mood and didn't seem to like people in general.

'What?' the coach asked, his bushy greying brows rising in surprise. 'But you don't compete. I'm training competitors for the next season.'

Jimmy crossed the busy gym floor towards them. 'He's just signed up, Dave,' he said, joining the conversation. 'And just in time, in my opinion. We were in desperate need of a decent fighter in his weight range.'

It was true. The young men that were being trained up for next season were amateurs at best, nowhere near ready to enter the league. They would be taken out in the first round and the club would drop out of the league entirely. It would be a first; their club usually produced most of the league winners – men who went on to be some of the best in the world. But perhaps that was exactly what someone was hoping to do – topple their crown by picking off their strongest contenders.

'Right. OK then,' David replied, evidently unhappy with the new arrangement. 'Wait to the side anyway. I'll let you know when you're up. These two are first.'

Cillian jumped out of the ring and sat down on one of the benches lining the wall nearby, watching the coach – David Higgs, if he remembered rightly – with interest. It was odd that he wasn't more excited to have a prize fighter like himself join their ranks. And he wasn't blowing his own trumpet – he was one of the best in the club. Jimmy had been trying to recruit him for years. So why was David Higgs so annoyed? It didn't make much sense.

'Sidelined before you've even begun, eh?' came a voice from beside him.

Cillian turned to see the drinks guy offloading a cart of crates next to the drinks machine nearby. 'It seems so,' he replied.

He pulled a face and gave Cillian a quick, uneven grin. 'You always come in this early?' he asked, opening the door to the machine. 'Seen you here a few times at the crack of dawn now.'

'Yeah, clears the head before the day begins,' Cillian replied, glancing over towards David thoughtfully. 'You're an early riser too then?' He'd also noticed the guy tended to visit to restock at this kind of time in the morning a few times a week.

He shrugged. 'Roads ain't so bad – can get more drops in.' He looked up at the ring and Cillian noticed a slightly wistful look cross his features.

'You box?' he asked, already guessing the answer must be a no. The other man was thin and gangly, not an ounce of muscle to be seen, and his posture was too off-centre for him to be a boxer.

As suspected, he shook his head. 'I used to want to give it a go, but...' He pulled a face and shrugged, turning back to the drinks. 'Anyway, I'm Joe.'

'Cillian.'

'Nice to put a name to the face. I've been thinking of you as Red Bull Guy.' He grinned again. 'Want one?' he asked, as he started to unload.

'Yeah, go on then,' Cillian replied, taking the offered drink. 'Cheers. I'll grab some cash for you.' He made to stand up but paused as Joe protested.

'Nah, don't bother. It ain't like the company are gonna miss one can. I nick 'em all the time.' He looked quite pleased with himself at this shocking confession and pulled a smug smile.

'Proper rebel, you are,' Cillian teased.

'Right, Mulsoe, out of the ring,' barked the coach. His eye swept over the few men who'd turned up for the training session and lingered for a moment on Cillian before he called up one of the others.

'Did you piss on his cornflakes or something?' Joe asked.

'What?' Cillian looked back towards him with a frown.

'Him. He don't seem to like you.'

'No, it seems he doesn't,' Cillian replied.

'Oh well,' Joe replied lightly, closing the door to the now fully stocked drinks machine. 'You can't please everyone. You ain't chocolate cake.'

Cillian grinned at this. 'My aunt Cath likes that saying.'

Joe piled the empty crates back onto his cart and started to wheel it back towards the front door. 'Sounds like a smart woman. Anyway, I've gotta shoot. I'll catch you later.'

'Have a good one,' Cillian called.

'Head down, hands up,' Higgs yelled at one of the men in the ring. 'For God's sake, how many times do I have to tell you?'

'Alright, Dad, I can hear ya,' the boy replied irritably.

'Oi,' Higgs shot. 'It's "coach" in here.' He glanced around and lowered his voice before finishing his sentence, but it was too late. Cillian had caught it.

The boy in the ring was Higgs's son. A cold chill crept over him. With all the usual contenders in the picture, this boy would never have stood a chance of getting into the league. Surely Higgs wouldn't have gone so far as to kidnap and kill off all the men who stood in the way of his son reaching the league fights, would he? That would be absurd.

But as Higgs's cold, wary gaze flickered round to meet his and then dropped away, Cillian had to force himself to consider that this might be exactly what had happened – and if this was the case, then he had just put himself directly in the man's line of fire.

TWENTY-SEVEN

Scarlet and Cillian stood side by side in front of Lily's desk in the factory arguing their cases while she sat in silence, listening. Both seemed equally sure that they had figured out the situation, but their stories didn't match. They didn't even come close. Lily laced her fingers together and put them to her mouth as she took all the information in and turned it over in her mind.

'It's definitely him,' Scarlet pressed. 'You should have seen him, Cillian. The moment I mentioned Gary's name he froze. He looked downright guilty. Then he couldn't get me out fast enough. It's *him*.'

'We don't even have a proper link between them though, Scar,' Cillian argued.

'We know Gary moved here because there was a load of new opportunities for those in the building trade and we know AJ expanded. And we know he definitely knows him, because—'

'Because you saw a look on his face?' Cillian grimaced in a way that showed just how little he thought of that.

Scarlet's expression turned hard, and annoyance flashed across her features. 'I *know* what I saw, Cillian. I watched his face – there is no other reason a man would look that scared at a name.'

'And I know what I saw this morning,' Cillian countered. 'The son slipped up. Higgs got pissed when he called him Dad, looking all round super cagey, checking no one heard.'

'So he wants to hide their connection in the gym,' Scarlet said with a shrug. 'He probably just don't want people thinking he's getting preferential treatment through training.'

'But that's just it, Scar,' Cillian exclaimed. 'He never had a shot of being in training, not before everyone who *should* have been there just disappeared off the face of the Earth. I know it sounds crazy, but I know it's him, Mum.' He turned to Lily, his eyes beseeching her to agree with him. 'He's got everyone who was in his son's way *out* of the way. They were all set to compete, and now they're gone, *his* boy is being pulled forward.'

Lily pursed her lips and looked up at them both. 'I see what you mean, Cillian; it *is* suspect, considering the circumstances. But at the same time, it could just be coincidence that they happen to be in the same weight range, if Conway *is* targeting people from the gym. He could even be targeting the competing boxers because he knows it will draw more attention and can't as easily be swept under the carpet. Remember, he has a much higher stake here, a much stronger motive than just a dad trying to bump his kid up the competition.'

Cillian still looked sceptical. 'Maybe. But I just don't think Conway has it in him. He's hot air and lies, sleight of hand and daylight robbery, not kidnap and murder. He's just a bully boy through and through.'

Lily shook her head. 'Don't underestimate AJ Conway. I've seen him pull some dark and dirty things over the years to get what he wants. I think with the prospect of a job this size, he'd do anything.' She weighted her glance between them both. 'Keep watch on both sides for now. Let's just see where it takes us. I'll have someone follow AJ, and Cillian, get Higgs's home address from Jimmy.'

There was a sudden frantic knocking on the door and it opened almost immediately. Don, one of their workers, fell into the room, looking flustered.

Lily frowned. 'What's wrong?'

'Old Bill's just arrived. That moody bastard that kept turning up with questions over the Snow boy last year,' he said breathlessly. 'They just got out the car, thought I'd best warn you quick.'

'Jennings?' she said in disbelief. She and Scarlet locked gazes, and Scarlet paled.

'Fuck's sake,' her niece hissed.

'He ain't here for you,' Cillian said with resignation.

'What?' Lily asked, her frown deepening. 'Who's he here for then?'

'Me,' he said with a heavy sigh. 'Fucking bastard. He saw me in the gym when they came to tell Jimmy about Gary. Told me to go into the station the next day but...' He trailed off for a moment, a dark look flashing across his eyes. 'I got waylaid and then totally forgot.'

'Oh, Cillian!' Lily tutted, realising that chastising him wasn't going to help the matter now.

'Scar, you stay here out of sight,' Cillian said, rubbing the bridge of his nose. 'No point adding fuel to the fire. I'll go deal with this. I'll likely be arrested so send Robert, will ya?' he asked his mother.

'Yeah, fair point,' Scarlet replied. 'Don't give him anything.'

'There ain't nothing to give,' he replied, turning to walk out.

Lily quickly stood and marched around the desk. 'I'll do more than call Robert,' she said, annoyed. 'I'll tell Jennings where he can go!'

Cillian grinned. 'Well, don't get yourself arrested too – that won't help us much.'

They walked towards the front of the factory where they could see Jennings and a younger officer walking towards them. Lily sped up until she was just a step in front of her son and pulled herself up to full height, shooting daggers at the man who'd hassled their family so much over the last year.

'Can I help you?' she demanded.

'As a matter of fact, you can,' Jennings replied cheerily. 'This happens to be just the man I'm looking for.'

'What do you want with him?' she demanded, placing her hands on her hips.

Cillian stayed silent and pushed his hands down into his trouser pockets, looking resigned to the fact she'd taken over.

'He needs to come with us to the station, where we'll discuss that with *him*,' Jennings replied.

'Not without a fucking warrant, you ain't,' she replied.

'Christ, who are you, his lawyer?' the other officer asked with a small laugh.

Lily stalked towards him and his grin faltered at the look on her face. 'Nah, I'm his mother, sunshine. Someone you should fear much more than his lawyer.' She saw the penny drop and the officer stepped back, casting his gaze to the side.

'What's the matter, Cillian?' Jennings taunted, turning his attention back to him. 'Cat got your tongue? Need your mummy to do the talking for ya?'

'Not at all. But I do enjoy watching her work,' he said with a smirk, nodding towards the now silent and red-faced officer next to him.

Jennings pulled a piece of paper out of his pocket and showed it to Lily. 'There's my warrant,' he said, the joviality gone from his tone. 'Didn't take too long after you evaded questioning, given your name.' Walking past Lily, he pulled out the cuffs and slapped them on Cillian's wrists.

Lily looked on in horror as her son was arrested right in front of her eyes. Cillian's glare bored into Jennings as he reeled off his rights, but he didn't fight it. They all knew that would be a stupid move. She felt her heart beat harder as her anger and hatred rose, but she couldn't lose it. It wouldn't help.

'I'll send Robert. He'll have you out in minutes,' she insisted as they led her son away. 'And then we'll get back to life, while these fucking idiots find some other mug's time to waste,' she added loudly as they reached the front door.

As it slammed behind them, she felt her stomach flip uneasily and a deep worry settled over her like a thick cloying fog. Cillian had no reason to be in there – or at least not the reason they were trying him for. But they knew how desperately Jennings wanted to put away one of the Drews. Which begged the question, how far would he go to make that happen? Was Cillian truly safe, or was he walking into a trap?

TWENTY-EIGHT

'I've lost count of the times I've had your little cousin sat in that chair,' Jennings said. 'Had her bang to rights at one point. And yet she still managed to slip away like an oily snake.'

They were sitting in the interview room, a sparse white box with three blue plastic chairs around a table and an irritatingly bright electric light that buzzed constantly on the ceiling. Cillian reached for the thin plastic cup that held the last of his water, put it to his mouth and drained it.

'Probably says more about you than it does her,' he replied, staring at Jennings levelly across the table.

He saw the muscle in his cheek spasm in response as the dig hit home, and he smiled.

'I'm going to ask you again, and this time I want a real answer. How well did you know Gary Oldham?' Jennings snapped.

'And I'm gonna tell you again, in as simple terms as I can – seeing as you ain't grasping the concept – I never met Gary Oldham. Ever. In any capacity. We weren't even training at the club at the same time. I don't know who he is, what he looks like, where he lives, nothing. The first I heard of him was when I overheard you telling Jimmy you'd fished him out of the river.'

This wasn't strictly true. Jimmy had mentioned him as being the first of the men to go missing from the club, but that was a situation the police weren't yet unaware of – and Cillian wasn't going to be the one to enlighten them.

'And you really expect me to believe that?' Jennings asked. 'A body turns up, with ties to the boxing club that one of the infamous Drews hangs around, and you had nothing to do with it?'

'I was in church the day the last Pope died, d'ya reckon that was me too?' Cillian asked, raising his eyebrows in question.

Jennings narrowed his gaze contemptuously. 'Very funny,' he replied.

'Thanks.' Cillian gave him a cold smile.

There was a knock at the door and Jennings barked at whoever it was to come in. The door opened and a young officer appeared, offering an apologetic smile.

'Sorry, guv, a Mr Cheyney for Cillian Drew.' She stepped aside and Robert strode in, briefcase first, brandishing it in front of him like some sort of shield.

'My knight in shining armour,' Cillian said with an amused grin.

Robert sat next to him with a face like thunder as he glared at Jennings, and Jennings's face fell with a frustrated sigh when he saw who it was. Cillian knew they'd met before when he'd interrogated Scarlet.

'Why have you detained my client?' Robert demanded, jumping straight in.

'Your client is here for questioning, regarding a murder investigation, Mr Cheyney,' Jennings replied.

'And why is that?' he continued, not relenting in his glare. 'Was he the one who found Mr Oldham?'

Clearly, Lily had given him all the information he needed, Cillian noted.

'No...'

'Has he been traced as being in the area of the murder around the time it was committed, making him a suspect?' Robert asked, cutting him off.

'No, but—'

'Does my client have a personal connection of any kind to the victim?' he demanded, a glint of triumph beginning to gleam in his eye.

Jennings looked as though he might explode. Cillian watched transfixed.

'No,' Cillian answered before Jennings could.

Jennings pulled himself to full height. 'Mr Drew is a member of—'

'The same boxing club that Mr Oldham once went to a long time ago,' Robert finished. 'Are you going to question *all* the members of that boxing club? It's a long list – I expect that will take you some time.'

'Mr Drew was brought in due to his known connections—' Jennings started to argue.

'Oh, so you're profiling him based on hearsay and other people's so-called reputations,' Robert declaimed. 'Because as far as Mr Drew's actual record goes, other than a couple of small misdemeanours in his youth, his slate is clean. Yet again we find ourselves at this juncture where I have no choice but to consider putting in yet *another* complaint of harassment for a member of the same family as last time.'

'Mr Cheyney,' Jennings shot back through gritted teeth, 'we are perfectly within our rights to pursue all avenues of questioning relating to this murder. We have not yet accused your client of anything – we are merely trying to establish whether he knew the victim or whether he may know anything that might assist us in our investigations.'

'Well, like I told ya,' Cillian piped up, 'I didn't and I don't. Can I go now?' He raised one eyebrow to Jennings and then turned to Robert. 'They arrested me, you know?'

'You evaded questioning,' Jennings replied. 'Which made you look like you had something to hide. I had no choice but to bring you in.' He reached for the recording device. 'Interview ended at sixteen twenty-two.' He pressed the stop button and sighed heavily.

'I didn't know it was mandatory. There was me thinking it was just an offer of a friendly chat,' Cillian said, holding his gaze with a slight smirk. 'I had no idea I was being targeted.'

'You little shit...' Jennings muttered, unable to stop himself.

'I think that's quite enough of the insults, DC Jennings,' Robert replied. 'There's more than enough already for my report. My client and I will be leaving now, as there are no grounds whatsoever for you to keep him here. Come on, Cillian.'

Robert stood up and Cillian followed suit, flashing Jennings a wide grin.

'I wouldn't look so pleased with yourself, Drew,' Jennings said, a flare of irritation crossing his face. 'You might not have anything to do with this, but if you do, I'll find it. And if you don't, that's fine. You get as comfortable as you like. Because one of these days you're going to slip up,' he said menacingly, 'all of you are. And when you do, I'll be there waiting. And I'll make sure you pay for every single one of your fucking sins.'

Cillian kept the smile on his face as though Jennings's words meant nothing, but as they stepped out of the little room and moved down the hall, it dropped to an expression of sombre foreboding. Jennings was a problem. He always had been, since the first time he'd set his sights on Scarlet. But now it seemed his obsession wasn't just with her, it was with the whole family. And by the look in the other man's eyes, he wasn't going to stop until he got exactly what he wanted.

TWENTY-NINE

After a long and trying day, Cillian pulled up with a screech of brakes into the small car park outside the Spoiled Pig and rubbed his eyes tiredly. Connor was standing down the side, almost hidden from view, pacing up and down and puffing on a cigarette. He threw this away as soon as he saw his brother arrive and marched over.

'There you are!' he exclaimed accusingly as Cillian got out of the car. 'You're late.'

'Alright, keep your hair on. I had shit to do. And I *was* actually on time before I realised I'd forgotten Rubes' present, so I had to go back and then got caught in the Friday night traffic,' Cillian replied, pulling out a small powder-blue bag neatly tied with a white satin bow.

Connor's mouth dropped slack for a moment. 'We were supposed to bring presents?'

Cillian stared at him. 'It's our sister's birthday, Connor. Of course we're supposed to bring presents.'

He pushed his hands back through his hair, messing it up. 'How was I supposed to know that?'

Cillian just blinked and shook his head. Sometimes he was

unsure how the two of them were even related, let alone twins. 'You're literally here to celebrate her birthday at a party in her honour. A situation otherwise known as a *birthday party*. What birthday party have you ever been to where there ain't fucking presents?'

Connor floundered. 'Yeah, but I mean, it's Ruby. I didn't get her nothing last year, so I didn't think we were doing that, like, you know, in general.'

'She weren't around last year, but now she is,' Cillian replied. 'What is wrong with you?' Cillian's voice grew more irate by the syllable.

'Alright, you've made your point,' Connor snapped. He glanced back at the pub with a regretful sigh and a worried look. 'What *you* got her?' He stepped closer and tried to peer in the bag.

'I got her a bracelet from Tiffany's. It's got a ruby in it. You know, a ruby for Ruby,' Cillian replied.

He'd thought long and hard about what to get his sister before deciding on this. He'd wanted to get something special this year to quietly show her how glad he was that she was back home with them all again. Something that showed her how much her big brother loved her whenever she looked at it. But also something understated and subtle, as Ruby had never been one for showy jewellery. This had been the perfect gift to encompass all of that.

'Ahh, that's lovely, that is,' Connor replied, nodding sincerely. He caught his brother's eye. 'Put my name on it, will ya?'

'What?'

'Go on, quick, before we go on. I've got a pen in my pocket. Where's the card?' Connor fumbled in his inner jacket pocket and produced his pen, looking at his brother expectantly.

'No!' Cillian protested, pulling his gift away with a frown. 'This is from me – get your own gift.'

'But I didn't, did I? Come on – don't be an arse. Put my name on it. You always used to.'

'Yeah, when we were kids and it was a box of bloody chocolates.' Cillian scowled and gave in, handing the card over resignedly. 'Fine. But you owe me big time.'

'You're a legend,' Connor said, scribbling his name next to his brother's, then shoving the card back into the envelope. 'Right, come on then.'

Connor marched off full of confidence and excitement towards the door of the pub and Cillian followed, shaking his head. He loved his brother dearly, but he was pretty sure Connor wouldn't last a week without him by his side.

———

Ruby reached the pub car park and paused. She wasn't sure why exactly; she just wasn't ready to go in yet. She had no idea what to expect, and it unnerved her slightly. It had been years since she'd had a birthday in which the family was involved.

The door opened and a pretty blonde woman stepped out, peering over towards her through the darkness. 'I thought that was you,' came the cheerful voice. 'What you waiting for? Come on – everyone is here.'

Ruby smiled, her anxiety fading as Sandra held the door open for her. Until recently she'd never really had any real friends. But now, for the first time in her life, she did. And it felt good to have people who genuinely cared around.

She crossed the car park and entered the pub, feeling a warmth run through her as Sandra gave her a quick one-armed squeeze on the way in.

'Here she is,' Lily said, popping the cork on a bottle of champagne with a flourish.

Ruby looked around as everyone cheered her arrival. There were gold and black balloons pinned up over the bar and a large matching banner that read *Happy Birthday, Ruby*. One of the tables had been dragged over to the side of the bar, laden with trays of party food. Ruby recognised her aunt's signature rosemary sausage rolls in the middle. It was all a bit much, really, for something as unimportant as her birthday.

As well as her mother and Sandra, her aunt and brothers were there, along with Billie, George, Andy, Scarlet and John. Her gaze lingered on John for a few moments, the usual resentment she felt at the sight of him turning suddenly into something else. Into resolve. Into anticipation. She had plans for John that had swum around in her mind until she could think of little else. They were bold, but seeing him here tonight had cemented her resolution to carry them out. He wasn't part of her family. He shouldn't even be part of their world. And as no one else seemed to be thinking clearly, it was down to her to ensure he wasn't.

Upbeat music began to play from the sound system George turned on, and Ruby accepted the glass of champagne that was handed to her. 'Thanks,' she said, taking a sip.

Lily handed one out to everybody, with the help of Cath, and then raised hers high in the air. 'To Ruby,' she said. 'It's so wonderful to be able to celebrate with you this year. Here's to being twenty-five, fighting fit and fucking fabulous, my angel.'

Ruby felt something catch in the back of her throat as her mother used the nickname she hadn't heard since she was a child. She swallowed it down as everyone else wished her a happy birthday and took another sip of her drink.

'Ahh, happy birthday, love,' Cath gushed, coming over and rubbing her arm in a warm gesture. 'I've put your pressie over there with the rest. Want to open one?'

She looked so eager, Ruby couldn't say no. 'Sure, OK then,' she said, a little reluctantly. She wasn't used to being the centre of attention.

Cath led her over to another table stacked with presents.

Her hand moved over them and paused on a small, rough wooden carving of a girl on a boat. She picked it up and admired it, noticing the likeness to herself. As she looked up, she saw George shrug.

'I couldn't think what to get ya, but I remember you used to like those as a kid,' he said.

'I loved them. Still do,' Ruby replied. 'Thanks.' She gave him a smile, and he winked back at her before returning to his pint.

'This one's from me and Scarlet,' Cath said, passing her a posh-looking paper bag.

She looked over at Scarlet automatically and saw her cousin's unreadable eyes staring back at her. Eyes that would soon be filled with pain and devastation. Smiling coldly, she looked away, moving her gaze back to Cath. This wasn't from Scarlet. It was from her aunt. Ruby pulled out a cream-and-beige Louis Vuitton scarf and her eyebrows rose in surprise. She'd never owned any designer gear before.

'It goes with the present from your mum,' Cath carried on, pointing to a box to the side. Ruby opened the box and pulled out a Louis Vuitton handbag of the same colours and looked over at her mother.

'It's beautiful,' she said. 'They both are. Thanks – that's really nice of you both.'

'Well, you're part of the firm now,' Lily said. 'Helping to run the businesses and joining us at events. It's only right you look the part too.'

'Thanks,' she repeated, unsure how to take that comment. Everyone was still watching her expectantly and she felt the urgent need to get out from under their scrutiny. 'Can I do the rest a bit later?' she asked.

''Course, love,' Cath said. 'Come, enjoy yourself.'

As everyone fell back into their conversations and returned

to their drinks, Sandra slipped her arm through Ruby's and led her off to talk to Billie.

'It's a lot, ain't it?' she said quietly. 'I know.'

And Ruby knew that she *did* know. Sandra always seemed to have a way of just understanding these things. Understanding how after years of living the way she had, things like birthday parties – just simple, everyday things for others – didn't come as naturally or as comfortably to Ruby.

Soon, with Sandra's help, Ruby relaxed into having a good night. Jokes were made and stories were shared. Drinks were poured and food was eaten. Ruby couldn't remember the last time she'd had such fun, but even despite that, there was one niggling thorn that wouldn't quite be banished from her side. Scarlet.

To her credit, Scarlet had steered clear of her all night. But still, it was there, this thick, dark tension between them. It was never not. No matter how much others may wish they could get along, there was a lifetime of hatred and dark competition at an ugly, unhealthy level that couldn't just be pushed aside. Now, her mere existence, the way she walked and talked with an air of confident superiority and smug contentment needled Ruby constantly. Along with the way she paraded around with her law-loving copper boyfriend as if the union was natural and something to somehow be proud of. She sat there now, holding his hand and giggling with him, as if his very presence here didn't put their entire firm at risk.

But it *did* put them at risk, not so much from the law he served – only Scarlet was at risk on that front – but the entire firm was at risk of comeback from their own kind. If any of the other firms found out about Scarlet and John, the Drews would no longer be trusted or respected. The underworld would close ranks and they would slowly fall from grace until eventually everything they'd worked for would be lost. As independent as they were, they still counted on the security that being part of the underworld network provided.

Cillian sidled over towards the end of the evening, whilst she sat quietly to the side watching the groups of people chat among themselves throughout the room.

'You alright?' he asked.

'Yeah, 'course,' she replied. 'Why wouldn't I be?'

'Well, you ain't started a fight with anyone or stormed off yet, so I figured something must be wrong,' he joked.

'Ha-ha,' she replied sarcastically.

He grinned and took a sip of his pint, then handed her a small bag and card. 'Here. I wanted to check you like it.'

She put her drink down and took the bag, opening the card first. She read it and put it aside, reaching into the bag and pulling out a small box. She opened this and let out a small gasp as she saw what was inside.

'Cillian, that's beautiful,' she breathed. 'Too good for me,' she continued uncertainly.

'Don't be stupid. It's just right. A ruby for our Ruby,' he replied.

The gold Tiffany bracelet was delicate and stunning with one shining red ruby set right in the middle. It must have cost him a small fortune. Suddenly, out of nowhere, Ruby felt her eyes well up with tears. The gesture was so thoughtful, she didn't know what to say.

'Christ, I didn't mean to make you cry,' Cillian said with a surprised laugh. 'I'll take it back if you hate it that much.'

'It's perfect,' Ruby said emotionally, swiftly turning towards him and grabbing him into a hug. She buried her face into the shoulder of his suit jacket and squeezed him tightly. She knew she shouldn't have a favourite brother, but she'd always been closer to him than Connor, and this bracelet – that he'd obviously chosen with such care – meant more to her than words could say.

She got her emotions back under control, took a deep breath and pulled away, immediately aware of the spectacle she was making of herself.

'Help me put it on?' she asked.

'Sure.' Cillian took it from her and placed it on her pale, slim wrist. 'Glad you like it, Rubes. Just something to make you think of me and Connor when you look at it.'

'I know it's really from you,' she said.

Cillian's dark brown eyes flickered up to meet hers, then moved back to the clasp. 'What makes you say that?'

'You wrote the card in blue ink,' she said.

'And?' he questioned.

'He added his name in black.'

She grinned and Cillian did too.

A peal of laughter pulled Ruby's attention back across the room towards Scarlet and John, and her hackles were instantly raised. Cillian sat back with her and followed her line of sight with a look of irritation.

'It's a fucking piss-take, ain't it?' she said quietly.

'It is,' he agreed, equally as quietly.

Ruby noted this with interest. He never usually spoke out against the John situation. Their mother had been quite clear that they had to accept it and keep their opinions to themselves on the matter. But then again, their mother couldn't hear them right now.

'Someone needs to do something about it, before it ends up destroying this firm,' she said carefully.

There was a long silence before Cillian finally replied. 'I can't see how anything could be done without causing some very big problems.'

He hadn't disagreed with her. In fact, it rather sounded as

though he'd given it some thought himself too. Ruby's hopes lifted.

'But if there was a way, with minimum impact on the firm...' She let the idea linger in the air between them.

Cillian ran his hand down the lower half of his face. 'Then it would be in everybody's best interests,' he replied. 'But like I said, I can't see an option that works. And we need to be careful right now, with Jennings on the war path.'

Ruby nodded, and her gaze rested on John, the cuckoo in the nest. Cillian didn't need to see a way out of this situation that kept the firm safe. She already had. And now that she knew she wasn't alone in wanting John gone, it just bolstered her resolve to see it through and rid them of this dangerous stranger in their midst for good. Ruby would be a hero, and Scarlet would be broken into little pieces – and this act of dating their enemy, when it was over, would finally place her in total disgrace with the rest of the family, the way it should have in the first place.

THIRTY

The dull thuds of glove on skin came one after the other as Cillian pressed forward on his opponent. The man pulled back the way he always did. It was so predictable it barely felt like a fair fight, yet they were in the same weight category. He jabbed slightly to the side to make the man move half a step, then slammed his other fist right into his diaphragm.

A sound of acute pain escaped his lips and he doubled over, falling to one knee. On his way down, Cillian shot a sharp uppercut into his face, then smirked and stepped back with a sniff.

'Alright, time for a break,' David snapped, barely able to conceal the look of irritation that crossed his face. He stepped into the ring and tilted the kneeling man's head upwards, then made a sound of annoyance as he saw the blood that was flowing freely from his nose. 'OK, come on. Let's get you cleaned up.'

Cillian leaned back against the ropes and draped his arms over them as he watched the two men leave the ring. The smirk on his face swiftly faded as they disappeared. Usually, Barnes would be here now. He'd roll over to him with a deep, slow laugh and a quip about his last move. They'd laugh over it and maybe grab a drink. But right now, not even God seemed to know where he was. And the only person who Cillian was sure *did* know was currently cleaning up his son's bloody nose.

It had taken so much inner strength to get this far. To pretend like he didn't suspect. To come in and train under David while waiting for him to make some sort of move or let something slip, so that he could find out where the hell Barnes and the other man was. But time was running out. He didn't know *how* he knew that, but he sensed it. Barnes was a strong man, but it had been a week since he'd disappeared and they had no idea what condition they would find him in.

Jumping down from the ring, he walked over to the drinks machine. Joe greeted him with a grin as he closed the door, having just stocked up. 'Nice moves,' he said. 'He needed his face rearranging anyway, that one. He's a bit of a dick, like his dad.'

'You don't like him?' Cillian asked.

'Nah. Had a falling-out over a parking space a while back. Pathetic, really, but he's given me dirty looks ever since, whenever I come in,' he replied.

'A lot then,' Cillian said.

'Yeah. Here,' Joe handed him a drink. 'Swiped it for ya before I came in. Figured you'd want one.'

'Cheers, mate,' Cillian said with a warm grin.

It had already become a bit of a ritual between them, Joe stealing him a drink and making a play for friendship. Evidently, the man was quite lonely, and Cillian could tell how much he wanted to box by the wistful looks he always shot at those in the ring. He pulled the tab and drank deeply from the can, savouring the sharp sweetness.

'You said before you'd wanted to box in the past but didn't anymore,' he said, watching Joe's face. 'What changed your mind?'

Immediately Joe's features flushed pink and he looked down. 'Ah, I don't know. I'm not really the boxing type.'

'No one is till they train,' Cillian replied.

'I tried once – to join a class. But it was more like a heavy-lifter-type place and – well, they laughed me out.' He pulled a face and laughed himself, but it was clearly forced. 'That's what you get for being the skinny ginger kid,' he finished with a shrug.

Cillian frowned. '*Anyone* who laughs at someone who's had the guts to show up and who wants to learn and improve them-selves is a cunt,' he said frankly. 'Fact.' He took a deep breath and exhaled, shaking his head.

'Well, it don't matter now – it was a long time ago,' Joe replied, brushing it off.

'It *does* matter,' Cillian argued. 'Whatever the situation, you can never let people like that get the better of you in this life.' He looked Joe up and down critically. 'I'll train ya,' he offered.

'What?' Joe's eyebrows rose in surprise.

'I'll train you. If you can work out your drops to spare, say, twenty, thirty minutes a day around this time after I'm done here' – he gestured towards the ring – 'then I'll work with you. Teach you what you need to know. It don't matter what your starting point is, it's all down to training. It's up to you if you want to or not, but the offer's there.'

Joe blinked and shifted his weight from one foot to the other, taking it all in and thinking it over. 'Yeah, alright then,' he said eventually. 'Thanks.'

'No problem.' Cillian tipped the can of Red Bull back and drained what was left. Looking at the clock on the wall, he said, 'I need to grab my bag and shoot. I'll see you here tomorrow?'

'OK, see you then,' Joe replied.

Cillian picked up his towel from the bench and wiped his face, then wrapped it round his shoulders. He dropped the empty drink can in the bin outside the locker room and walked inside, heading to the locker he'd left his bag in.

Someone cursed on the other side of the row of lockers just out of sight. 'Alright, watch it, yeah?' he heard them say. It was Carl, Higgs's son.

Having made a silent entry, Cillian slowed his movements to keep his presence undetected. Luckily he hadn't bothered to lock the locker door – he'd just slipped his bag inside and left it partially open. He reached into his bag and pulled out his phone. There was a text from Connor checking in. He began to text back, listening carefully in case anything of interest was said between Carl and his dad.

'He's a right vicious bastard, that Drew,' Carl complained.

'Keep your voice down,' David hissed.

There was a short silence and on instinct Cillian quickly began to record.

'He is though,' Carl muttered.

'Well, don't worry about it. He'll be gone soon, and then we can resume some proper training. Get you ready for the big fights,' David replied.

'I don't know.' Carl sounded reluctant.

'Hey,' David barked. 'Don't you back out on me now, boy. The plan's already underway. We've got this.'

Cillian felt a tingle go down his spine as David finally said the words.

He'll be gone soon. He was right.

Looking down at his screen, he stopped the recording and pressed send. He pulled his bag out of the locker, careful not to make a sound, then turned and walked back out into the main gym. Glancing behind him, he lifted his phone to his mouth and sent Connor a voice note.

'That recording I just sent you,' he said in a quiet, urgent tone, 'it's Higgs talking to his son. They're gonna make a move on me soon.'

As he said the words, a feeling of dread washed over him. He shook it off, annoyed at himself. They had the upper hand. They knew Higgs was coming. Whatever the man had in store, they were ready to turn this advantage against him. He just needed Higgs to make his play first.

'I don't know how soon,' he continued. 'But he said his plan's underway, so I guess we can expect it pretty sharpish.'

He looked over his shoulder again and saw David and Carl exit the locker room. David glared at him across the gym. Carl flicked a glance his way, then branched off down the side of the gym. As Cillian walked out of the front door with a grim expression, David made a beeline to follow him.

'I think he's following me now, so check up on me in a bit, yeah? I've got that tracker on me, just in case.' Cillian ended the voice note and sent it on to his brother.

He walked down the road, passing Joe's small delivery truck. Joe was standing next to it with his head in his hands, looking distraught.

'Hey, what's up?' he asked, turning his body to casually check whether David had followed. As he asked, the door opened and David appeared, pausing just outside and pulling out his phone.

'I've gone and locked me bloody keys in the van, ain't I?' Joe groaned, his expression forlorn as he looked at them through the window. 'I'm gonna need to go all the way home now to get the spare set.'

'Nightmare,' Cillian replied. In his peripheral vision, he saw David tap on his phone – perhaps sending a text – then he slipped the phone back into his pocket. Cillian frowned and rubbed his head. 'Where do you need to go?'

'I'll have to jump on the train at Bethnal Green overground,' he said with a sigh. 'Don't suppose you're headed that way, are ya?' He gave Cillian a hopeful look.

David started walking towards them, shoving his hands down into his pockets.

'Yeah, I'll drop you,' Cillian replied. 'Come on – I'm up this way.'

Turning on his heel abruptly, Cillian marched towards his car. David was obviously following, but hung back. Likely because Joe was now with him, Cillian realised. He exhaled grimly and pushed forward. Was this just delaying the inevitable? Or was he imagining it all? David could just be going this way too. It was a free country. What could he really do to him in broad daylight anyway? Cillian was stronger and faster than he was. It wasn't as if the older man would be able to overpower him.

Joe fell in beside him and glanced back with a small frown. 'He's an odd one, ain't he? If I didn't know better, I'd say he was following us.'

Cillian looked at him, surprised that Joe had noticed. If it was that obvious then he couldn't be imagining it at all. Not sure how to reply, he just gestured towards his car instead. 'Get in.'

As he walked around to the driver's side, a feeling of exhaustion washed over him. He wiped his face with his hands and slipped into the seat, feeling suddenly like he hadn't slept in about a week. His limbs were heavy and he longed for his bed and Billie. Joe got in the passenger side and frowned at him in concern.

'You alright?' he asked.

'Yeah, fine. Just need to start getting some earlier nights,' Cillian replied.

He glanced in the rear-view mirror and saw David was still headed towards them, eyeing the car with a grim expression. Slipping it into gear, Cillian pulled out onto the road and started driving. Up ahead, the lights turned red and he squinted at them as they began to swim in front of his eyes.

'Mate?' Joe's voice sounded concerned now, and as Cillian turned towards him, a strange ache began to grow behind his temples.

'Shit, you don't look so good.' Joe's eyes widened in fear. 'Pull over.'

Cillian wanted to argue that he was fine, but the entire world started to spin as though he'd just downed half the whisky in Scotland, and he realised that he really wasn't. He pulled over to the side of the road, hitting the kerb with a jolt as he tried to move alongside it.

'Cillian?' Joe sounded scared now, but Cillian couldn't seem to answer him. His mouth was no longer connected to his brain. He felt himself sway and tried with all his might to stay focused. He saw Joe – or what now seemed like about three Joes – turn back and look through the back window, the worry on his face growing. 'Cillian, talk to me?' he begged.

Cillian tried to work his mouth but he felt it slacken, and the last thing he saw before he passed out was the reflection of David Higgs in the mirror, headed straight towards them with a look of dark determination.

THIRTY-ONE

Scarlet looked up at the tired-looking hotel with interest. Who was this girl that Lily was giving such a big chance? And why? There were plenty of people they knew in the local area who would jump at the opportunity to join the ranks of the notorious Drews. People who knew who they were and how the game was played. People who knew the city and their businesses.

Pushing her hands down into the pockets of her knee-length cream jacket, she entered the building and made her way up to the room as instructed by Lily. She stopped and knocked, waiting as a voice on the other side begged a minute.

As she waited, she thought over their plans. Really, she wanted to be the one following AJ. She knew he was behind the murder and the other kidnappings and she was desperate to find proof. But he knew her face, and with her long raven hair and pale-as-porcelain skin, she knew she would stand out too much to get away with it. He knew them *all* too well, for any of them to get away with it. Which was why Lily had come up with this new plan.

The door finally opened and she saw a young woman

smiling tentatively at her. 'Come in,' she said in a soft Mancunian accent.

Scarlet entered the bright, airy hotel room and crossed to the window, looking down at the busy, thriving market down below. The boys would be going around to pick up the cash from the stolen goods they'd pushed through it later, she thought idly. Turning back to the room, she assessed the girl in front of her critically.

Slight and on the shorter side, she had a friendly face, wide brown eyes and an easy smile, her skin dappled with pale freckles. Her blonde hair looked as though it was freshly styled and it hung around her face to just below her shoulders.

'I'm Scarlet,' she introduced herself with a quick smile.

'Isla,' came the reply.

'Yes, Lil's told me all about you. From what I understand, you're on our payroll now.'

'That's right,' Isla said, clasping her hands together in front of her.

'We don't usually have people working for us who haven't been known to us long,' she said frankly. 'So I was quite surprised to hear about you, to be honest.' She held the girl's gaze levelly, wishing she could see into her brain and read what she was thinking, what her true intentions were.

Isla nodded. 'That's fair. It's hard to trust anyone in this game, let alone a stranger.' She sat down on the end of the neatly made bed. 'Lily verified my history of course. But that doesn't guarantee anything, I know. All I can do is try to prove myself to you, over time.'

Scarlet nodded. 'Well, you can start today,' she replied. 'Lily says you can drive but have no licence, is that right?'

'Yeah, pretty much,' Isla replied. 'My dad taught me around our estate when I was fifteen.'

'Good. I'm going to take you out to a scrapyard we know. The owner has a car waiting there for you. It's unregistered but works fine, so it's not traceable so long as you don't get pulled over for some reason.' She eyed the girl. 'You do understand what's expected if you are?'

'I do,' Isla said. 'I found the car on a side street, door open, keys inside. Took it for a joyride. And I don't know no one here in the city.'

Scarlet nodded. 'Great. Make sure you remember that,' she warned. How far was this girl really prepared to go, for a firm she had no prior loyalty to? Would she endure or would she fold the moment she was questioned?

'This isn't my first job in this life – I know the score. And I'm prepared for it,' Isla said, holding Scarlet's gaze with confidence.

It was so genuine that Scarlet found herself liking the woman already, despite her resolve to stay wary. She could see what Lily liked in her. She was quiet and unassuming at first, but there was a strong confidence and an air of experience running just underneath the surface that was starting to show.

'OK. Once we've picked up the car, you'll follow me to a builder's yard. You need to stay out of sight, but keep watch for this man...' She pulled her phone out of her pocket and opened it to show a picture of AJ. 'We think he's kidnapped someone we know and we need to find out for sure. I'll give you his home address so you know where that is, but if he goes anywhere else, we need to know. Follow him to and from the yard over the next few days, as much as you can, but *do not* let him see you. Keep me in the loop, and if there's anything that looks off at all, you call me and I'll come to you. OK?'

'I can do that,' Isla replied. She stood and pulled a zip-up hoodie from the back of the desk chair. 'Are we going now?'

'Yeah, grab anything you need.' Scarlet waited while Isla filled her pockets with her essentials then followed her out of the hotel room. As they walked, she looked sideways at her. 'Lil says you cut ties with everyone back home.'

A shadow fell over Isla's face and her smile faded. 'Yeah,' she replied. 'I didn't exactly have many people. My parents died and then I fell in with a bad boy who wasn't the kind that was worth it. Only really had one friend left towards the end. And she's safer without me back there.'

The words were so bleak, Scarlet felt a pull on her heart. They were about the same age, born into the same life. It could so easily have been her, had she not had such a strong family around her.

'I'm sorry about your parents,' she said gently. 'I lost my dad last year. I know how hard it is.'

Isla gave her a sad smile. 'It's never easy. But at least they ain't here to see the bad bits. That's a small comfort.'

Scarlet knew only too well what Isla meant. She'd been glad a couple of times that her father hadn't been around to witness the things she'd suffered since his death. But that still didn't make up even slightly for the gaping hole his absence in her life had left. She couldn't image having to go through all that so completely alone.

'Once you're settled in and we've sorted this job, we'll go out for lunch,' she offered suddenly. 'I'll show you around a bit.'

'Yeah?' Isla's face lit up. 'That would be great, thanks.'

Scarlet nodded and pushed open the door leading onto the pavement. For now she'd just have to trust Lily's judgement on Isla, and hope that her own instincts were also on the right lines. But only time would tell whether this girl was a friend or foe. For all they knew, she could be infiltrating their firm on the orders of her old one.

For all they knew, Isla could be the Manchester firm's Trojan horse.

THIRTY-TWO

Connor dialled his brother's number, holding it to his ear and waiting for him to pick up for what seemed like the hundredth time. Again, it rang out to voicemail and he threw it down onto his wide grey settee in anger.

'Shit,' he cried. 'Shit, shit, shit!'

He sat down on the armchair that matched the settee and leaned forward, running his hands through his hair as he tried to think of any reason why Cillian might have suddenly stopped answering his phone.

Leaning forward, he picked the phone back up and dialled another number. It rang twice and was picked up.

'Hello?'

'Billie,' Connor said, clearing his throat and trying to make his voice sound more casual than he really felt, 'is Cillian with you?'

There was a pause. 'With me?' He could understand the pause. He'd never had to ring her to ask before. 'No, he went out early to the gym like always.'

'And he ain't come back to change or anything?' Connor pushed.

'No. He don't always, if he has early stuff on. Why?' she asked, her tone sharpening. 'Is everything alright?'

Connor closed his eyes and suppressed a groan. 'Yeah. Yeah, 'course. Bugger just ain't replying to my texts. He's probably busy. In fact he's probably down the market, come to think of it, making an early start.'

'But—'

'Look, I gotta go, Bills – I'll catch you later.' Connor quickly ended the call and stood up. He needed to get dressed. It was barely eight in the morning and he was still in nothing but a pair of jogging bottoms.

On his way through to the bedroom he turned on the tracking app linked to Cillian's chip. He held his breath for a moment as it searched the grids for him, then let out a small breath of relief as a small red dot appeared. But he frowned as he looked at the area. It was a long way outside of London and still seemed to be moving.

Quickly throwing on his clothes, Connor kept checking the dot every few seconds. As he laced his shoes, he tried to calm the racing thump inside his chest. They'd never been apart for long, he and Cillian. Not throughout their entire lives. They worked together, socialised together, plotted together, laughed together. They'd only lived apart for the last three years or so. Not knowing what was happening to him now, knowing that he was potentially in some very real danger, felt worse than anything he'd ever encountered.

He threw on a jacket and shoved his keys into his pocket after he locked the front door of his flat. Pausing by the lift for a moment, he decided to use the stairs. He didn't want to lose signal on the app for even a second.

He ran down the stairs as fast as he could safely run, glancing down at the screen on each floor. So long as he could still see where Cillian was, he knew that things would be OK. All he needed to do was get to Ray as they'd planned and the two of them would track him down, find Barnes, uncover David Higgs for who he really was and get everyone back to their rightful place. Except David Higgs. He would never be seen again after this.

He exhaled slowly, trying to focus. All they had to do was stick to the plan. Cillian had signed up for this. He'd probably played gullible and gone along with David for whatever fictional reason the other man had given him. Cillian probably still had his phone and just couldn't answer. That would be a reasonable assumption. Because he knew, of course, that Connor and Ray would be tracking him via the app, hot on their heels.

But as Connor burst through the front door and unlocked his car, the red dot in the app instantly disappeared.

THIRTY-THREE

Cillian drifted between wakefulness and sleep, feeling as though he was rocking back and forth on some sort of boat. The waves kept pulling and pushing, side to side, lulling him back into the dark fuzzy nothingness he'd been stuck in.

'Cillian,' came a low scared voice. 'Cillian, please wake up.'

Who was that? he wondered.

It was cold out here, he realised. Hadn't he got a jacket? How had he ended up sleeping on a boat anyway?

The rocking became more of a lurching as he tried to move. His head pounded and his limbs still felt heavy. Too heavy to lift. Why was that? That was right, he realised. He'd passed out in the car. David Higgs had been following him. Joe had been there.

'Cillian?' came the voice again. It seemed louder this time, though perhaps that was because he was beginning to feel more awake. 'Cillian, *please* wake up.' It was almost a sob. 'You need to get us out of this.'

Those words served to sharpen his focus. His brain still felt hazy but it was clearing a little more each minute. He tried to open his eyes and found that he could – though they felt tired still. There was no open sky above him as he'd expected. And as his attention centred on the grey concrete ceiling above, he realised the swaying was just his brain trying to fight through whatever it was that had knocked him out. There was a weak, ancient-looking light flickering away in the middle of the ceiling, and a long, thick wire ran down the curved wall.

'What the fuck?' he breathed as he tried and failed to understand his surroundings.

'Oh, thank God, I thought you were dead,' came the voice once more.

With difficulty, Cillian turned his head to the other side and saw Joe laid out on what looked like an operating table. His legs were strapped down with leather belts and his wrists tied to it with rope. Cillian moved with a start, only to find his own limbs were tied in a similar fashion. They hadn't been heavy from sleep after all, he realised. They were restricted.

'What the hell is this?' he asked, hearing the panic in his own voice.

'I don't know,' Joe replied. 'You passed out in the car and I was trying to wake you up when that coach who was following us opened my door. I turned to ask him for help, but then he smashed me around the head with something. Next thing I knew we were here.'

'Where is *here*?' Cillian asked, knowing even as he said it that Joe likely wouldn't know the answer.

'I have no idea. I've tried shouting for help and I've tried getting out but it's no use.' His voice wobbled and Cillian swallowed hard.

They were in deep shit. Of all the ways he'd suspected David was luring people away, something like this had never crossed his mind.

His eyes darted around the strange room. There were no windows. On one wall there was an old metal door, and to the other side was a black abyss where the room seemed to go on forever.

'I've never seen anything like this before,' he said.

'I think it's some sort of bunker. I visited one once as a kid,' Joe said.

'You mean like a war bunker?' Cillian asked. He'd never paid much attention in history class. He couldn't remember ever seeing one.

'Yeah, Second World War bunkers are still dotted around everywhere,' Joe replied. 'They're deep underground which would explain why no one heard me yelling.'

'Underground?' Cillian's heart turned to ice as Joe said this.

All along, the plan had been to get himself caught and taken temporarily so that Connor and Ray could track him down and rain hell on the person responsible. It was supposed to be simple. But now here he was underground, tied up, unable to move – and under a layer of thick concrete too, he realised. There was no way his tracking chip would be sending out a signal. No one would have any idea where he was.

He closed his eyes as the helplessness and the horror of the situation overwhelmed him. Why had he agreed to go along with this? It had been a terrible idea from the start. He should have paid attention to the warning bells that rang in his head when Ray had first suggested it.

'Can you try your binds?' Joe asked, pulling his spiralling thoughts back into the room.

'What?'

'Your wrists. Can you see if you can get out? I've tried – mine are too tight.'

Cillian pulled his hands and tested the ropes. One held fast, but he realised that the other was half tied over his watch.

'I think I might be able to get this one out,' he said quietly, still unsure whether anyone else was in hearing distance. Joe had said he'd shouted and got no response, but that didn't mean that someone wasn't in the shadows biding their time. Watching. Waiting.

He pulled against the rope. At first it held tight, but as he gently moved his wrist in small circles, the rope worked itself over the smooth metal of his watch and it slipped onto his hand. He released a small breath of hope, then pushed on, squeezing his thumb into his hand as much as possible. It was tight and for a moment he wasn't sure it would go, but after a few seconds, he pulled his hand free and let out a cry of elation.

'Got it!'

Pulling himself onto his side with difficulty, he reached over and began working the knots on the rope on his other hand.

'Hurry,' Joe whispered worriedly.

'I am, don't worry. We'll get out of this,' Cillian said, trying to reassure himself as much as Joe.

After what seemed like forever – but in reality was more like a couple of minutes – Cillian finally freed his other hand, then, ignoring the thumping pain still echoing through his brain, he sat up and unbuckled the leather straps around his ankles. He swung his legs down and – now that he was upright – took a second to look around again.

The weak, flickering light made it hard to see, but apart from the two beds they were tied to, there was a large wooden table at the edge of the room. Bundles of what looked like sheets took up most of the room, but as he squinted, trying to make out what else was there, Joe called his attention back again.

'Cillian, untie me!'

A noise echoed through the darkness beyond the door somewhere and they froze, staring at each other with wide eyes. Cillian jumped forward and quickly worked on the rope tied around Joe's nearest wrist. This didn't take long, and as one hand sprang free, he leaned over to start on the other.

'My feet,' he said urgently.

Cillian quickly unbuckled them, liberating his feet as Joe worked his other hand free. He helped the smaller man up.

'You OK?' he asked.

Joe nodded.

'Good.'

He looked into the dark abyss and then towards the metal door which stood partially open. At least they weren't locked in, he thought. That was one small thing that seemed to be working in their favour. He licked his dry lips nervously. 'Alright. Here's what we're going to do. We each need some sort of weapon. There must be something in here we can use.' He glanced around at a couple of piles of debris by the walls. 'Then we'll go through that door and search for a way out. We need to stay quiet and careful. Whoever's in here currently don't know we've got loose. That gives us a small advantage.'

He purposely didn't mention the many disadvantages that ran against them. There was no point scaring the other man further.

'OK.' Joe nodded and looked around, his eyes wide with fear.

Cillian felt a wave of guilt wash over him. Joe wouldn't be here at all if it weren't for him. The poor guy had been swept up in David's plan just for being in the wrong place at the wrong time.

'I'm gonna get you out of this, OK?' he said.

There was a load of empty rusting cans to one side of the room that might have contained food at some point in the past, some small bits of wood and a couple of broken tools. He picked up a half-rusted wrench and weighed it in his hand. It would have to do. He turned to see that Joe had found a large baseball bat and was testing his grip on it.

'Perfect. Just keep that held high, yeah? And if anyone comes close, you smash it down on their heads hard, OK? We don't know how many are here. He's probably not working alone.'

To have dragged two deadweight bodies in here would have taken a lot out of David. It could have been done alone, but Cillian would place money on him having an accomplice.

'OK, I can do that.' Joe practised swinging it a couple of times.

'Come on then,' Cillian replied, walking over to the door. 'We need to move.'

He peered around the door and found a long, wide hallway resembling the room they'd woken up in, a line of the same weak, flickering ceiling lights trailing off into the distance on one side and up to a corner on the other. The domed concrete ceiling had started to crumble in parts with large cracks showing here and there. Either side of the hallway were other metal doors, all the same as this one. Some were closed, some were open.

Cillian's jaw formed a grim line. His head still ached and his entire body felt exhausted. Whatever they'd given him was still running through his system. 'Come on then,' he repeated.

Leading the way towards the closer corner, he paused and looked round it cautiously. No one was in sight. The concrete turned to brick here and the hallway narrowed, showing multiple other hallways branching off. What he'd hoped was one small bunker had just turned into a giant maze.

'Fuck's sake,' he muttered. 'What *is* this place?'

A small sound, similar to the one they'd heard earlier, came echoing through the halls, this time a lot closer and, as they froze in fear, Cillian felt his hope swiftly fading.

THIRTY-FOUR

'Where's that coming from?' Joe whispered as the place once more fell into silence.

Cillian shook his head. 'It's hard to tell,' he whispered back. 'But we can't stay here, whatever it is.'

He started forward, his whole body tense as they moved quickly down the main brick hallway. There had to be an exit here somewhere. Maybe even more than one.

As they hurried along, a strange smell started to permeate the air around them; a cloying mixture that reminded Cillian of decaying food and sewage. The further they went, the sharper it got, and eventually he used his sweatshirt sleeve to cover his mouth and nose as he breathed.

'Christ, what is that stench?' he said, more to himself than to Joe.

'It ain't perfume, that's for sure,' Joe muttered through his own sleeve.

As they walked past doors and hallways, Cillian itched to check each one. Barnes was still in here somewhere. Cain hopefully too. He needed to find them. But first he needed to find an exit, a way out of all this, a direction in which to lead them when he did find them.

'I miss my mum,' Joe said forlornly.

'You'll see her soon,' Cillian promised, hoping he sounded more certain than he actually felt.

'She's all I got, you see,' he continued with a sad sniff. 'I'm all she's got too. Mary her name is. If something happens and you get back, but—'

'You're getting back,' Cillian said forcefully. 'Alright?'

'Well, it's better to be overprepared than under, don't you think?' Joe replied.

Cillian exhaled tiredly. 'I guess.'

There was a long silence before Joe spoke again. 'What about you? Who you got to get back to? Not that it's likely I'll get back and you won't, but... well. You know.' He shrugged and cast his eyes down miserably.

Cillian stopped himself from telling him to buck up. Joe wasn't like him, and tough love was unlikely to work. 'A few people. My girlfriend, Billie. Me mum, twin brother Connor, sister...' He reeled them off, almost feeling bad that he had so many people that cared about him in comparison to Joe.

'You're a lucky guy,' Joe replied with a weak smile. 'What's your girlfriend like?'

Cillian didn't want to chat right now – he wanted to focus on the task at hand. But Joe was clearly trying to distract himself to cope, so he indulged him. 'She's a firecracker. Beautiful, hard-working, not afraid to tell it as it is.' He smiled fondly as he thought of the woman he loved so dearly. 'And she'll probably have my balls for earrings when I tell her the trouble we got ourselves into today.' He'd not told Billie about the danger he'd put himself in. He'd known she'd worry too much.

'But it wasn't your fault,' Joe said with a frown.

They reached the end of the hallway and found it split off in two directions. Cillian paused and looked down each, hoping for something that might lead them in the right direction, but it all just looked the same. The smell was now overpowering and his eyes began to water. Whatever was creating the stench was close.

'This way, come on.' He turned left, blindly hoping it was the right path, no idea whether it was or wasn't.

The sound they'd heard before came again, closer this time. Walking down the hallway with the wrench clutched tightly in his hand and all the muscles in his body tense, ready to jump to action should anyone appear, Cillian picked up the pace.

They continued in silence for a few minutes, wary of revealing themselves. Door after door was passed. A couple were wide open, showing smaller rooms within. Some looked as though they'd maybe been offices, with old bare tables and wooden chairs. Some had rusting bunk-bed frames. None showed any signs of life.

'I can't work out how he drugged me,' Cillian whispered after a few minutes. 'He didn't even touch me.'

'I've been thinking about that,' Joe said heavily. 'When you were warming up, he wandered over to the bench where I had me stuff. He crouched right next to it and I thought he was just sorting his lace or something. I didn't think nothing of it, you know? Why would ya? But that can of drink I gave you was there. He must've seen me put them aside for you before. Maybe he wiped the rim with something, or I don't know.' He shook his head and pulled a face. 'I don't know how these things work, but I do know he was doing something right where I had that can.'

Cillian's forehead creased into a frown. David must have spiked the can somehow. It seemed crazy, but it certainly wouldn't be the craziest thing that had happened today.

Something caught his eye up ahead and he squinted. There were metal rungs on the wall. His heart began to lift in hope and he sped up to almost a jog.

'What is it?' Joe asked.

'I think it's a way out,' Cillian replied.

He reached the rungs and looked up. Sure enough, there was a hatch above and no sign of any lock. His face lit up in elation and he let out a huge sigh of relief.

'Go on then – you first,' Joe urged.

Cillian shook his head then turned and grasped him by the shoulder. 'No, there's something I need to do. Here...' He pulled at his waistband and quickly ripped apart the hasty stitching he'd applied that morning. The tiny chip fell into his hand and he placed it into Joe's. 'This is really important. You need to get up to the surface and throw this in the grass or bushes or whatever's up there, just in case you get caught. Then you need to run until you find a road or a building and get help.'

Joe looked down at the chip. 'What is it?' he asked.

'It's a tracker. It can't give off a signal down here, but up there it can. My brother's tracking it.'

Joe frowned, looking utterly confused. 'Why?' he asked.

'It's a long story, but I knew I'd be taken.'

Joe's mouth slackened and he looked at Cillian in horror.

Cillian raised his hands in a gesture of surrender. 'I know, I'm sorry. You were never meant to be part of this. I've been watching Higgs for a while. You were just... *there* when it came to a head.' He dropped his arms with a sigh.

'You a copper?' Joe breathed.

'No! Christ, no,' Cillian replied vehemently. 'But I figured out what he was doing. He took my mate Barnes, and some others. Look.' He pushed Joe towards the rungs. 'Just get that above ground so my brother knows where to search. He's got men with him. I need to go back and look for Barnes. Tell them to come in and find me if I ain't out by the time help comes. OK?'

Joe nodded, swallowing hard. 'OK,' he said bravely. 'Where you gonna start?'

Cillian looked back the way they'd come. 'When we turned left to come down here, there was another hallway going the other direction. I'll start down that end and work my way up here, then if I don't find nothing, I'll go back down the main hall and start the other way. But hopefully there'll be more of us by then. It's a maze down there.'

'It is,' Joe agreed. He stepped up the first couple of rungs. 'Go safe and hurry,' he urged.

Cillian nodded and turned with a deep breath. The last thing he wanted to do was wander these creepy old halls alone, especially knowing that he likely wasn't alone. But he had to find Barnes. He had to get him out.

At a brisk jog, he advanced down the hallway until he found the place where they'd entered it.

It wasn't as far back as he'd thought, though they'd been walking more slowly on the way up. It took him no longer than a couple of minutes.

He checked that no one was around the corner then hurried straight on, aiming for the other end so that he could start searching the rooms methodically. There was a small sound behind him somewhere, but he didn't pause this time. He needed to hurry and get on with it. The chip would be above ground by now and his brother would be searching for it frantically, so even should he come face to face with trouble, it wouldn't be long before Connor and Ray came to his aid.

Two more minutes of light jogging and he finally reached the end of the hallway. The smell that had hit them was now overwhelming and Cillian could barely breathe even through his sleeve. The putrid, cloying odour seemed to cling to the inside of his nose and mouth, and made him feel physically sick. Whatever it was, he was close.

He opened the first door, yanking it hard as it scraped the floor, having sunk with age. The room beyond was empty other than a tall metal filing cabinet in one corner.

He moved on but the next seemed little more than a cupboard with a long bench and an old shoe brush discarded on the floor.

The third opened up into a long, thin, tiled room, the small once-white tiles now grey from neglect and cracked with age. Along the long wall there were hooks and benches and the occasional sink.

As soon as he'd opened this door, he knew that this was where the smell was coming from. He balked as a concentrated wave of it hit him in the face and doubled over for a moment, sure he was going to be sick.

As he caught hold of himself once more, he peered in and looked down towards the end. The light barely reached it, but he could see that there was something down there. With his heart thudding in his chest, he pushed back down the wave of panic that threatened and stepped into the room.

Cautiously he crept towards the dark pile on the floor at the end of the room. A few steps in, his sight finally adjusted to the new level of darkness and he realised what he was staring at.

Suddenly, the careful hold he'd had over his stomach broke loose and he threw up, dropping to his knees with a cry of pain and horror. Under a circle of shower heads, in a slightly depressed area of the room, there were thick metal grates, and on top was a body laid on its side, almost as if he might just be sleeping. Except he wasn't sleeping. Dark stains – which even in the darkness Cillian recognised as blood – covered his torso, and his face showed the hollow grey marks of a death that had arrived long before today. His friend was gone. Jude Barnes, his warmth and jokes and the deep friendship he gave with no expectation, was gone.

A sob escaped Cillian's lips and he reached across the floor towards his friend, not quite able to bring himself to actually touch him. 'What did they do?' he heard himself wail, his voice cracking with emotion as hot tears began to fall down his cheeks. 'What did they do? I'm too late.'

Racking great sobs roiled up through his chest and came out of his mouth, much louder than he'd have dared to allow just minutes before. But he couldn't control them. This had floored him completely. He'd failed. He'd sworn to find Barnes and bring him home safe and he'd failed. Instead, he lay dead and broken in this hellhole of a place under the ground, God only knew where. He put his hands to the sides of his face.

'I'm too late,' he repeated, his broken voice shaking and echoing around the room. He squeezed his eyes shut as the world spun around him. The effects of the drug had been strong and he'd pushed through until now, but finding Barnes like this was just too much. He opened his eyes again and tried to calm his breathing through the tears. He needed to get out of there.

The smallest of sounds made its way through the ringing in his ears and he turned instinctively, but it was too late. Whoever it was was already upon him, and with a sickening crack as something was smashed around his head, the whole world once again went black.

THIRTY-FIVE

As she ended the call with Connor, Lily turned and kicked out at a filing cabinet with a ferocious cry of anger. The display was unlike her, and she caught Scarlet's expression widening in shock. She took a deep breath and exhaled, trying to collect herself. Her son had been taken and she needed to think clearly.

'Where's Connor?' Scarlet asked.

'Headed to Ray's,' Lily replied heavily. 'They're going to see what they can do about this tracker – see if there's some way they can still reach it.' She closed her eyes as fear and helplessness threatened to overwhelm her.

'So it was definitely this David Higgs?' Scarlet questioned, still sounding doubtful.

'It looks that way,' Lily replied.

'What do we do? What *can* we do?' Scarlet ran both hands back through her long dark hair, her expression as worried as Lily's.

Lily shook her head and tried to think it through, but for once her usually cool, calm head was whirling round and round with fear. Gary Oldham's body turning up in pieces in the river kept flashing to the forefront of her mind. She rubbed her head and tried to push the thoughts away.

'We, um...' She wasn't sure where to start.

Scarlet's phone began to ring, and she pulled it out of her pocket. She looked as though she'd been about to silence it, then her forehead creased into a frown and she answered.

'What is it?' Scarlet looked over to Lily and mouthed the name *Isla*.

Lily's attention sharpened and she waited to find out why the girl was calling. Scarlet's eyes widened and locked onto Lily's.

'Text me the address and stay out of sight. We'll be there as soon as we can.' She ended the call. 'AJ just left the site in a hurry, apparently jumped in someone's car and they drove off to an empty warehouse where they met another man and disappeared inside.'

'Where?' Lily asked, her sharp brain piecing everything together.

'About twenty minutes from here – she's going to send me the exact address.'

As if on cue, her phone pinged with a text from Isla. 'It's just outside the M25.'

'Connor said he looked like he was headed out of London,' Lily said, her hope rising. They stared at each other. 'Are you thinking what I'm thinking?'

'They're working together,' Scarlet said. 'He's AJ's inside man.'

Lily picked up her own phone and called through to Andy. The call was picked up on the second ring. 'Where are you?' she demanded.

'The pub,' he replied. 'George is on his way here too.'

'How soon can you be tooled up?' she asked. If they had a fight ahead of them, they needed to make sure they arrived with full force.

'George is grabbing everything now,' he replied. 'Connor already called.'

'Perfect,' Lily replied. 'I'll meet you there and we'll go together.' She grabbed her keys and marched out of the office, gesturing for Scarlet to follow. Now she had a goal, all her anger balled up in her very core and her focus sharpened dangerously. 'We'll find the bastards who took my son, and when we do, we will rain pain and hell down on them in ways they have never before imagined.'

THIRTY-SIX

The front door of the boxing club slammed back against the wall and Ray marched in with a thunderous expression. Connor followed directly right behind, along with two of Ray's men, his expression matching Ray's. Jimmy stood talking to one of the coaches and his eyes widened as he saw them both. He hurried over, his gaze flickering from Ray to Connor and back again.

'Ray, Connor, what a surprise,' he said warily. 'Everything alright?'

'No it most certainly fucking isn't,' Ray replied, his dark menacing gaze boring into the other man. 'Higgs – where is he?'

Jimmy blinked, confused, and looked over to where David Higgs stood by the ring. David looked back at him, apparently equally as confused. He raised his hand, slightly reluctantly.

Connor stepped forward. 'Give us your office, Jimmy,' he ordered in a low growl.

'Guys, this place is neutral ground – you know this,' Jimmy replied.

'Not today it ain't,' Ray replied. 'It's either your office or out here in front of everyone. Your choice.'

David paled, his gaze darting back and forth between

Jimmy and the angry men who looked fit to kill. Jimmy stepped back with a regretful sigh and nodded his agreement.

One of Ray's men went over to David and grabbed his arm roughly, marching him towards Jimmy's office. The others fell in behind him, but Ray looked around with a warning glare and leaned in towards Jimmy before he joined them.

'No one is to come into that room until I'm done. You hear me?' he said.

'I hear ya, Ray,' he replied, his expression grave.

'No matter what you hear.' Ray cast his gaze around the room at the young men who were there training. They stared solemnly back at him, none saying a word. They wouldn't be a problem. Each and every one of them knew who he was. He'd even trained here himself in his youth. His picture still hung on the wall among all the other champions of the past.

Hearing sounds that indicated that the conversation had already started without him, he turned and walked across the gym into the office.

David had been seated in one of the chairs in the middle of the room. Connor stood above him, red-faced and seething as he punched his face once more. Blood ran down from David's nose as Connor bellowed into his face and his head rolled back.

'Where's my brother? Come on – where is he?' Spit flew from his mouth, and a vein by his temple began to bulge as he neared the point of complete explosion.

Ray closed the door and locked his jaw, suppressing a sigh. Connor wasn't going to get anywhere by bowling in like a raging bull straight away.

'I told you—' David tried to speak, but Connor cut him off almost immediately.

'*Nothing.* You told me nothing,' he yelled.

'Connor,' Ray said curtly. He shot the younger man a hard stare. 'Let the man speak.'

He grabbed another chair from the side of the room and

turned it round, straddling it backward so he could leer in the face of the terrified, bloodied man. Connor looked as though he was about to argue, but after a moment he stepped back and took a deep breath, wiping his face with his hand.

Ray held David's gaze. 'Where is he, David?' Ray's words were quiet and calm in comparison to Connor's.

'I tried to say, I ain't seen him since he left this morning,' David replied, spitting a mouthful of blood to one side.

Ray turned to Connor with a look of disbelief.

'You want to play him that recording?' he asked.

Connor pulled out his phone and held it in front of David, playing back the conversation between him and his son that Cillian had sent him earlier.

'... *don't worry about it. He'll be gone soon, and then we can resume some proper training. Get you ready for the big fights.*'

'*I don't know.*'

'*Hey, don't you back out on me now, boy. The plan's already underway. We've got this.*'

David's jaw dropped open and he looked up at Ray. 'Wh-Where did you get that?' he asked.

'That's not really what matters here, David,' Ray replied. 'What did you do to him?'

'*Do?*' David asked, looking confused. 'Nothing. When I came out of the locker room, he was just leaving.'

'He told me you followed him,' Connor said.

'Followed him? I didn't follow him. I went out to buy some fags. I did see him. I mean, I was looking at him when he drove off, I guess, but only because he was with that weirdo who delivers the drinks,' David explained. 'I was surprised to see them together, that's all.'

There was a short silence as Ray searched the man's face. Men under this sort of pressure usually found it hard to stick to their story, stay calm and maintain a poker face. It was always the face that went first. But he looked like he was being genuine. Except that didn't add up. He scratched his head.

'Why'd you say all that to your kid?' Ray asked.

Immediately David's cheeks coloured and he looked over to Jimmy guiltily. 'He is my kid,' he admitted. 'I didn't want no one to know we were related, didn't want them thinking he'd be treated differently, you know?'

Jimmy just shook his head and looked away.

'I get it,' Ray said. 'If I had kids, I'd probably do anything for them too. I'd probably kill for them,' he added. 'That's why you got everyone out of the way, right? Barnes and the others.'

'What are you talking about?' David asked, his forehead crumpling in confusion once more.

'Oh, don't play dumb with me, David, eh?' Ray snapped. 'Drop the act.'

'It ain't no act!' David replied, frustrated.

'But you even talk about doing it to Cillian, on the recording!' Ray exclaimed. '*He'll be gone soon. The plan's underway.* We know your game, mate. It's over.'

'I just meant from the gym! He'd just kicked the *shit* out of Carl. I was saying that he'd be physically gone soon from the gym!' David cried.

'And what about the plan then, eh?' Connor asked, stepping towards him menacingly. 'We supposed to believe it was your *plan* for him to just leave the gym too?'

'No! Christ!' David cradled his head with a groan. 'You've got this all wrong. Carl was never going to compete when he first started training. He wasn't up to that sort of level. But then all those in his weight range who *were* going to compete kept dropping out or leaving. We talked about training him up properly for the fights and put a plan together. It was going to be tight, but I reckoned I could get him good enough in time for the season.'

Ray sat back and looked at Connor. If what David was

saying was true then they'd got the wrong man. But if that was the case, where was Cillian?

'You say you saw him get in the car this morning,' Ray said. 'Then what?'

'Then nothing. He, er...' He shook his head as if trying to recall the exact details. 'He got in the car with the drinks bloke, drove off, then pulled back over for some reason. I don't know, looked like they were talking about something. I went into the shop, got my fags. By the time I came out, he was gone.'

'Then what did you do?' Ray asked.

'I had a smoke and came back in here. I've been here all morning – I've had training sessions.' He looked at Jimmy and raised his eyebrows as if asking him to confirm his words.

Jimmy nodded and turned to Ray. 'It's true, he has been here all morning. He's had back-to-back sessions.'

'Well, if that's true, then...' Connor trailed off, his frown deepening as he turned to Ray.

Ray looked back at him with a grim expression. 'Who the hell has Cillian?'

THIRTY-SEVEN

From the back of the car George passed a handgun to Scarlet as they pulled to a stop. She quickly checked the magazine and took off the safety. 'Thanks,' she said quietly.

He nodded in reply, taking the safety off his own.

Lily was glad they'd not bothered with the usual – more cautious – level of baseball bats and knives. If caught with one of those, it could be fairly easily explained to an officer of the law. Being caught with a gun, on the other hand, promised a far-too-heavy prison sentence to risk usually. But they'd gone straight for the guns this time, knowing that when one of her boys' lives was in danger, nothing else came as a higher priority.

Scarlet pulled out her phone and called Isla, who was tucked away down a side street in her car. 'Hey, listen, go back to the hotel. Your job here is done,' she instructed. She ended the call and put her phone away, looking back to Lily with a grim expression.

'We'll leave the car here, sneak up the side path and see if there's a way in round the back. It's too open on the front,' Lily said, eyeing the building partially in view ahead of them.

'True. At least we can stick to those trees,' Scarlet added, looking at the bank of vegetation that fringed the path Lily was referring to.

'Let's go.' Lily's tone was filled with a vengeful anger.

The four of them left the car, keeping their guns concealed for the time being. It was the middle of the day and whilst this area seemed quiet enough, anyone could appear at any time.

As they made their way towards the old warehouse in silence, Lily couldn't help but think about all the terrible things that could have happened – or could be happening to – Cillian. Was he scared? He might be one of the hardest faces in London, but just because he never showed fear didn't mean he never felt it.

Had they hurt him?

She swallowed as an even worse possibility flooded her mind with pain. She saw Scarlet glance her way, concern in her eyes, and she forced herself to bring her anger back to the fore. Worrying wouldn't help anyone. But fury would.

They reached the side of the building and crept towards the back. There were sounds coming from within. Low voices and something heavy being moved. Rounding the corner first, Lily spotted a door that stood ajar. Two cars were parked nearby, but both were empty. She pulled her gun from underneath her jacket and pointed it steadily in front of her as she cautiously approached.

She strained her ears to hear as she moved down a dark side corridor that led into the main warehouse.

'Seriously, though, what are we going to do with him?' one gruff voice asked.

She held her breath and paused. Were they talking about Cillian?

'Make a fire,' she heard AJ reply, his tone bored. 'And get rid. The last thing we need is more evidence floating about.'

Lily felt her heart rate shoot up in alarm and she rounded the corner, ignoring Scarlet's desperate call for her to wait, fire blazing in her eyes and gun trained straight towards AJ's head.

'I don't *fucking* think so,' she roared as the others quickly joined her, fanning out to make sure they held everyone in the room at gunpoint.

Straight away, the two men with AJ dropped what they were holding and threw their arms up in alarm. 'What the hell!' one of them exclaimed.

'Where is he?' Lily yelled as she reached AJ. 'Where the *fuck* is my son?' She stopped a couple of metres away and cocked her gun, her face contorting in rage.

AJ pulled back, his eyes locking onto hers. 'What the hell, Lily?' he asked, staring at the gun. 'Put that fucking thing away!'

'Not until you tell me what you've done with my son,' she yelled. 'Where is he?'

She could feel her panic rising, now that they were here, now that she was faced with the man who had taken him. Cillian needed her – she could feel it. She had to get to him quickly. Where was he? What had they done to him? Were they already too late? All these questions swam around in her mind as she stepped forward again, forcing the gun closer to his head with a growl of frustration.

'I don't know where your son is!' AJ exclaimed. 'I ain't seen either of them in years!'

'You liar,' Lily spat. 'You've taken him, just like the others. I know you have. I know everything. So save yourself some pain and just *tell* me – or I swear, I will blow your *fucking* brains out!'

She could hear the shake in her voice, knew only too well that for the first time in her life she sounded desperate. But she *was* desperate. That was her son in there. Her firstborn, the one who'd entered this world just minutes ahead of his brother. He was everything to her, and she couldn't lose him. Not like this.

Suddenly the world seemed to still, and she zoned in on the man who stood between her and her boy.

'You have thirty seconds to tell me, or I will pull this trigger and be damned with the consequences.'

'Lily, I swear to you, I have no idea what you're fucking on about,' AJ said strongly. 'Listen to me. And look around you. I'm a dodgy cunt, I'll give ya that, but I wouldn't kidnap anyone. Least of all one of yours,' he added with feeling. 'I wouldn't kidnap one of your boys for all the tea in China. I actually value my life. Seriously, look at me.'

Lily searched his face. AJ was useless at hiding the truth when under pressure like this, that was something they all knew. Yet he seemed like he was telling the truth. But how could that be? She looked around the almost empty warehouse. The only thing of note in the wide space was a large crate full of old-fashioned furniture in the middle of the room. Her eyes moved to a small oil painting of a severe-looking Victorian man that one of the men had dropped to the floor. This wasn't a hold-up – this was the aftermath of a heist.

'That's who you were gonna burn?' she asked, pointing towards the painting, doubt creeping into her tone.

'Yeah, it looks like a family picture. Too distinctive. Didn't want to draw attention when we auctioned stuff,' AJ admitted. 'It was this old girl, you see. Did some building work a while back on her house. She called me back and gave me a key to add a new downstairs loo, then popped her clogs. I figured no one would miss the furniture.' His cheeks coloured.

Scarlet stepped forward. 'I ain't buying it,' she said in a steely tone. 'The others. Gary Oldham. I *know* you recognised that name when I came into your office. So don't play dumb with me, AJ.'

AJ blinked and frowned. 'What *about* Gary Oldham? What is it you're on about exactly?'

'His death,' Lily answered. 'He went missing, like some of

the others from the boxing club. Except he turned up a while later. Or parts of him did anyway, in a bag that had been weighted down in the river.' She watched as AJ paled, the shock on his face clear.

'And you think that was me?' he asked, flustered. 'Fuck me, Lily. I'm a lot of things, but I don't go round chopping people into bits.'

'But you did know him,' Scarlet pushed. 'So why did you pretend you didn't?'

AJ exhaled and shook his head, closing his eyes for a moment. 'I did know him, yeah. But it was a while back. I needed an extra couple of brickies for a big project I got. Put an ad out, two guys came forward, one local, and then Gary. Started the job, put in a couple of weeks' work, then the project was pulled. I was out of pocket big time and I was looking for anywhere I could claw some money back—' He grimaced.

'So you stiffed him,' Scarlet finished coldly.

'I couldn't do it to the local guy – he knew too many people on the workforce, but Gary... I can't remember where he was from but it weren't here. He was just here for the job, was a quiet geezer, hadn't really made friends. He came looking for his pay; I told him to fuck off. Threatened to tarnish his name with all the other builders if he kicked up a fuss. That was the last I saw of him. Got wind he'd found work elsewhere, but that was it. That's what I thought you were getting at the other day.'

Scarlet's lip curled and her gaze hardened with contempt. 'You bastard,' she said in a low voice. 'You know, I've heard it about you, seen it a bit, but hearing that...' She looked him up and down in disgust. 'I hope karma really does get you one day, you selfish, scummy piece of shit.'

AJ looked as though he might argue with her for a moment, but then his gaze flickered warily towards Lily's gun, still pointed at his head, and he closed his mouth.

Lily looked around the warehouse. AJ still might be pulling

their chain, he still might have Cillian somewhere else, but something instinctive told Lily he wasn't. She lowered her weapon and ran a hand back through her wild curls. If this was really it, then all the trails they'd followed had run cold. There were no clues, and there was no direction left in which to turn.

Which meant that Cillian was in serious, life-threatening trouble, and she had absolutely no way of getting to him.

THIRTY-EIGHT

Cillian's head pounded as he came back round, and he groaned. What was it with people hitting him over the head these days? It was amazing he hadn't suffered some sort of brain damage.

He tried to move and quickly realised he was back on the operating bed where he'd found himself previously with Joe. This time, though, he was face down. Ignoring his splitting headache with some difficultly, he turned his head slowly to look at the other bed. It was empty.

He closed his eyes and breathed out. At least Joe had got out. At least the chip would be above ground, and help would be on the way. That was one small mercy.

There was a low chuckle from above him somewhere, and he realised he wasn't alone this time. He strained to look up, a frisson of fear running down his spine. Whoever was there was just out of sight.

As he strained to see, Joe stepped out of the darkness towards him. Cillian looked up at him in relief. 'It's you. Untie me – quickly.'

'Oh yeah, right away,' Joe replied. He stared back at Cillian with a strangely blank expression.

Cillian frowned. 'Joe,' he prompted. 'The ropes.'

'You looked so glad, just then, to see that bed empty,' he replied, a small smile creeping up his face.

Cillian's eyes widened and his frown deepened. 'What are you doing?'

Joe chuckled once more. 'It always amazes me how people like you can't see what's right in front of your eyes.'

'What are you talking about?' Cillian asked. But even as he spoke, a cold sinking feeling began to settle in his stomach.

'It was so easy to convince you it was Higgs,' Joe said, stepping towards him. 'And I didn't even know you'd already pinned him for all this. That was a stroke of extra luck – though I have to admit, you surprised me with that. I know those notes I left didn't quite sit right with everyone, but that's OK – they were enough to stop the police taking things too seriously, which was the main thing. But *you*' – Joe shook his head with a smile that said he was impressed – 'you almost had it. I hadn't realised how close you actually were until you showed me that chip and came back for your friend. Hell, I didn't know you were looking for him *at all* until that point.'

'I don't understand,' Cillian replied, horrified by the details that were unfolding. How could he have been so wrong?

'I just thought you hated the guy,' Joe continued. 'Higgs, I mean. That's why it was so easy to act like I thought he was following us to the car. But you really thought he was after you even before that point.' Joe laughed loudly, tickled by this.

Cillian swallowed, his heart thumping hard in his chest. He was in a very bad position, and without the use of any part of his body, his only hope was to talk himself out of this. If only he could figure out where to start. The aching in his head was still so intense though that it was hard to think straight.

'The chip I gave you?' he asked.

'Smashed to smithereens,' Joe replied. 'I'm glad you let me

know about that,' he added sincerely. 'It could have really tripped me up if it had got above ground.'

Cillian swore inside, biting his tongue to stop himself groaning. 'Why did you kill him?' he asked, the image of Barnes's body seared into the walls of his mind. 'What did he ever do to you? Or *they* I should say,' he added, remembering Cain and Gary.

'Huh.' Joe pulled a face and gave a bitter laugh. 'What *didn't* they do? Guys like them. Big strong competitors. The best of the best. The popular ones. The *funny guys*. People like them have always treated people like me like we're nothing more than punchbags. Physically, emotionally, it doesn't make any difference. That's all we are to them.'

'That's not true,' Cillian answered.

'Yes it is,' Joe yelled back. 'You wouldn't have a clue – look at you,' he sneered, his lip curling in contempt. 'Big, strong, popular Cillian. You ain't had a day in your life where people who think they're better than you have pushed you around, shoved you down in shit, taunted you, laughed at you.' His face contorted maniacally, and he turned away with a short, bitter laugh. He put his hands on his hips and took a deep breath to calm himself. 'No, no, no. I ain't gonna let you get to me like that. You don't get to put me down anymore.'

'*Me?*' Cillian exclaimed. 'I've never done a *thing* to you. We got on, we shared jokes, we – we *talked*. I even offered to coach you, help you train!' He tried to form as strong a connection as he could to the guy, in the hope he could use this to his advantage.

Joe nodded, turning back to him. 'That surprised me, I have to admit. You're right, you're not...' He paused and scratched his head. 'You're not like the rest of them. But that don't matter now. I have orders to fill, and everything was already set up.'

'What do you mean?' Cillian asked, perplexed. 'Joe, *listen* to me...'

He licked his lips and tried to decide how best to proceed. He still had absolutely no idea what Joe was doing or why. All he did know was that the man was dangerous and evidently unhinged. The two bodies that had shown up so far were testament to that, along with the total sham he'd acted out before. But what *was* clear was that the man was desperate for someone to care.

'We're *friends*, you and me. And friends don't do this to each other.'

'*Friends*,' Joe said with a bitter laugh. 'What, because I gave you a few free drinks? That's the only reason you gave me the time of day.'

'Not at all,' Cillian argued. 'I got chatting to you because we always seemed to end up hanging around the same area at the same time. That's just natural progression, two guys hanging out.' He eyed Joe warily as the other man began to pace in agitation. 'I can buy my own drinks. It was *you* I wanted to chat to. It was *you* I enjoyed all that banter with.' It was a stretch calling their few exchanged comments *banter*, but it was all he had.

'Well, it doesn't matter now. I'd already spiked your drink before you offered to coach me.' Joe sighed. 'That did mean a lot actually. And it always will. I'll remember that.'

'You don't have to remember it, Joe. I'm gonna train you, remember?' Cillian pushed. 'Once you let me out of here anyway.'

Joe shook his head. 'No, you're here now. You've seen too much. And besides, like I said, I've got orders to fill.' He shrugged regretfully.

'What orders?' Cillian asked. 'What are you actually doing here, Joe?'

He looked around the room, his brain trying and failing to connect the dots. His gaze landed on the other bed. 'And what *was* all that before? Why did you pretend you were taken too? Why did you go to all the trouble of letting me get out and almost escape, only to bring me back here? I don't see the point.' He shook his head.

Joe grinned – a strange eerie grin. 'Couple of reasons really. *One*, because I needed to get you talking to find out who I need to write to. You find people are more open to talking about personal things when they're scared and under pressure and trying to distract a fellow victim. It's the best way.'

Cillian groaned as that part suddenly clicked into place. His mind went back to Barnes's letter. It had been to his mum, the only person he was close to. And he must have admitted he was single but not mentioned that he was gay, which led to Joe's cock-up about him finding a girlfriend.

'And also, just for fun. Watching you all panic and then try to work your way out, try to save me too.' His face creased up in mirth for a moment. 'I let you all get to the hatch, then when you start to climb, that's when I knock you all out – well, not actually you. All the others tried to go first, you see – that's when I knocked them out again. I'm actually a lot stronger than I look.' He puffed his chest out proudly. 'I'm wiry but I've got a strong back and plenty of practice carrying people through these hallways.'

Cillian was reminded of a cat they'd once had when they were kids. It used to play with its prey in a similar fashion, cornering mice and letting them search for an escape for a while for its own amusement, before it grew tired and bit their little heads off. He strained against the ropes again as Joe turned away, but they were much tighter this time.

'It's always fun. A little entertainment to liven up my day. It gets lonely here sometimes,' Joe finished glumly.

'You *live* here?' Cillian asked, wondering what dire circumstances could possibly have led to the man living in such a dismal hole.

When Joe didn't answer, he carried on, not wanting to lose

his attention. 'You say you've had plenty of practice. How many people have you taken here?' he asked.

'Oh, many,' Joe replied. 'Not for myself. Only a few so far for myself.'

He stared off into the distance, unseeing for a few moments, then seemed to snap back into the room. He moved to the other, now vacant, bed and pulled himself up to sit on it, facing Cillian.

'My stepdad was the one who first showed me this place. I was just a kid when he married my mum, then she died and left me with him. That's when he showed me. It's an old farmhouse, you see, and the entrance is hidden in a barn. He always kept it locked before, so neither of us knew it was here.'

He looked around as if admiring the dark, dank room under the weak, flickering light. 'When mum was gone, he told me I could earn my keep. Help out with his other business.'

'His other business?' Cillian asked.

'Women. Trafficking them. He was part of a chain. Someone would select a girl or young woman and gather information. Another person would take her and knock her out, then they'd bring them to us.'

Cillian felt the bile rise up in his throat. The Drews were criminals, there was no doubting that for a second. But even in the criminal world, there were levels that were unforgivable, and this was one of them. Human trafficking was one of the worst crimes imaginable. He cast his gaze away to try to hide his disgust.

'My stepdad used me to drag them through the halls to wherever they were staying, then we'd keep them drugged up there until the heat died down and their buyer arranged collection. I grew quite strong that way. Never put much weight on, as my stepdad, well...' Joe fiddled with the bottom of his T-shirt, reminding Cillian of a nervous child. 'He never gave me much to eat. He liked to keep me small and beatable.' His resentment shone through his words. 'But I grew strong anyway. *He* wasn't expecting me either, when I knocked him out and killed him.'

The eerie smile came back, and Cillian suppressed a shudder. 'And you're planning to kill me too?' he asked.

Joe nodded, not looking round.

'Why? What does that achieve? You keep saying about your orders – surely a dead man ain't much use to a human-trafficking ring?'

'I don't work with them anymore. They didn't trust me after Steve – my stepdad – disappeared.' He shrugged. 'But that was fine. I'd made my own contacts by then who wanted something a little different. Something that paid more.'

A chill rippled through Cillian's body. 'What?' he asked.

'Organs.' Joe smiled. 'They were paying a fortune to this doctor for black-market organs. And I managed to undercut him by quite a lot and still make much more than we did on the girls.' He shared this proudly. 'I taught myself how to harvest them using medical books. It's not that hard really when you don't have to worry about keeping the patient alive. Haven't mastered hearts yet,' he said regretfully, 'but kidneys are easy enough. Livers too.'

The dark bloodstains all over Barnes's top suddenly made sense, and Cillian's heart nearly stopped in horror.

Joe walked over to the table at the side of the room that held what Cillian had thought were bundled-up sheets. Now, watching out of the corner of his eye, from the awkward position he was strapped in, he could see that while there was a couple of sheets there, they were for the sole purpose of covering up a bulky leather bag. Joe opened this now and pulled out a rolled-up leather holdall full of tools. Small surgical knives, hooks, clamps and drills gleamed in the dull light. Cillian felt his panic reach a crescendo.

'Joe, stop and think about this,' he begged.

'I have,' Joe replied, running his hands over the selection of

tools. 'You're the perfect candidate. All of you were. Peak physical condition, no drugs, not too many legal toxins in your body
either, otherwise it would have affected your ability to compete.
I'll have to make sure I do a better job of disposing of you after
than I did Gary though. Clearly didn't weight that bag down
enough. That's why your friend is still here – I thought I'd
better let that all die down a bit first before disposing of him.'

'How can you do this to people?' Cillian cried in fear and
anger, no longer trying to keep a hold of his emotions. There
was no point. It seemed Joe wasn't going to listen to any kind of
reason.

Joe pulled out a pair of surgical gloves and a disposable
apron and set about putting them on. 'Easily,' he replied. 'It's
easier for me than it should be actually,' he said, in a matter-of-
fact tone. 'If I had to guess, I'd say there's something missing in
my head. I do feel some things. I mean, I get angry when
people treat me badly, and I feel excited when I play the
games, but when I actually do this' – he tilted his head to the
side as he considered it – 'I don't feel anything. It's funny
really.'

'No, Joe, it ain't funny at all,' Cillian argued, pulling against
his restraints with force, no longer caring whether or not Joe saw
him doing it. He bucked and tried throwing his body from side
to side, but the bed was sturdy and Joe didn't even bother to
look round.

'It's no use – you won't move it. Save your energy to try and
deal with the pain. I don't have painkillers. I could knock you
out again if you'd prefer?' He turned and lifted a questioning
eyebrow at Cillian. 'I'd kill you quick if I could, but I need you
alive for as long as possible. I only have an hour, you see, after
you die, to harvest them. After an hour of no blood flow, if
they're not out and on ice they're no longer useable. And I'm
not that fast yet, so...' He shrugged.

'You're a fucking *psycho*,' Cillian spat, now more terrified than he'd ever been in his life. He bucked and roared, to no avail. The bed hadn't moved, and the restraints held tight.

'Maybe,' Joe agreed calmly, walking back towards him with a scalpel. He looked down at Cillian with a sad smile. 'I really am sorry for the pain you're about to feel. You're an alright guy, compared to the others.'

Reaching down to fold the T-shirt up neatly upon Cillian's back, Joe cut down hard into his skin, and deep bloodcurdling screams began to fill the room.

THIRTY-NINE

Ray drove steadily down the windy country road as Connor stared at the small map on his phone. Two of Ray's men sat in the back, silent, as they all waited for Connor to direct them.

'Slow down – it's somewhere here,' he said.

'Where?' Ray asked, following his gaze across the fields and trees.

'Somewhere directly left of us, but I can't see a road that leads to it. We might have to go on foot.'

Ray's gaze narrowed as he peered further down the road. 'I think there's a turning ahead.' He sped up and then slowed as he reached an old rotting wooden gate that was closed across a dirt track. A muddied sign warning people to keep out hung across the middle. As they came to a stop, Connor wasted no time in getting out of the car and opening the gate so that Ray could drive through.

He pushed the awkward old gate quickly, not caring when he accidently stepped into a deep muddy puddle. All he could think about was getting to Cillian. They'd been lucky. The tracker only showed up on the app when it was transmitting, but by some miracle, he'd been watching the screen when it had disappeared. He'd quickly marked and saved the location and this was what they were going on now. They had no idea why the tracker had stopped or whether Cillian had since moved on, but it was all they had now. He just prayed that this wouldn't end up being another dead end.

Connor jumped back into the car and they carried on down the uneven dirt track until finally an old farmhouse came into view. Ray killed the lights and slowed to a gentle roll as they approached.

There were no lights on inside, and in this remote area there was no light anywhere else, other than the glow from the almost full moon. It wasn't until they were very close that the wooden planks that boarded up the windows and door became clear. No signs of life were visible at all.

Ray turned off the engine and they all stepped out. One of Ray's men opened the boot and took out a number of baseball bats. As he handed them out, Connor shook his head.

'I'm already tooled,' he answered, pulling out a hunting knife from inside his jacket. He preferred dealing with people at close range. Especially people who'd tried to hurt his brother. And whoever the hell had taken him had better not have *actually* hurt his brother, he thought darkly. Because they'd pay for that in the worst way possible.

He gripped the knife tighter as his anger began to rise, then forced himself to focus on the house. They actually had to *find* Cillian first.

'Connor, come with me. Al, Ben, you go round the other side,' Ray said quietly.

Connor forced himself to ignore the instinctive way his hackles rose at Ray's instruction. Every instinct was screaming at him to dig his heels in and refuse to comply. He didn't work for Ray. Ray was nothing to their firm or to any of them except Lily, so it grated to be ordered around in any fashion by him. But right now his aversion to the man wasn't important. They were in this together, and they were stronger as a team. All that mattered was the end goal of finding his brother.

They slipped around the edge of the farmhouse, searching for any kind of entrance. The whitewashed walls were dirty and neglected, cracked and crumbling in parts. It didn't look as though anyone had lived here in a long time. They reached the back in a matter of seconds, meeting the two men who'd scaled round the other side. They held their hands out to the side, indicating that they'd found nothing either.

Connor walked back the way he'd come and pulled at the wooden planks at every window, then the front door, but nothing budged. His forehead creased and he stepped back, craning his neck to look upwards in case there was a way in above, but the first-floor windows were too high to jump, and there was nothing on the walls that would make it easy to climb. He rejoined Ray and the other two, who were eyeing up the two large barns past the bottom of the garden.

'Maybe they've got him in there,' Al said, looking to Ray for further instruction.

Ray nodded. 'They wouldn't be the first to have a barn as a safehouse.'

Connor agreed with a nod. They had bought a couple of barns themselves to commit dark deeds and hide hot goods.

They moved quickly over to the barns and once again Ray instructed Al and Ben to check one while they approached another.

As they neared the entrance to the larger of the two, Connor paused. Tyre marks ran off the main track and up to almost right outside the door. He clicked his fingers to get Ray's attention and pointed down to them. Ray's jaw locked in a grim line, and he tilted his head to signal that they should try the door.

Connor stepped forward and gently pushed the door. It opened a few inches with a horrible creaking sound that sent a frisson of alarm up his spine. He cringed and then pushed forward into the room in one swift move, deciding he might as well go for it now that they'd all but announced their presence. Ray came to his side, his bat held high in the air, but as their eyes adjusted, they could see that they were still alone.

There were no lights on, just like in the house, the moon-light shining down through a wide, gaping hole in the roof. Grey, brittle straw littered the floor, and the edges of the room were cluttered with old farm equipment and broken bits of furniture. Connor scratched his head, perplexed. What *was* this place?

'Come on, maybe there's something in the other one,' Ray said, turning to leave.

'No, wait,' Connor said, holding his hand out to stop him. 'What's that?'

Partially hidden behind a rusting tractor hood there was a raised concrete slab with some sort of metal drum on top of it. It wasn't so much this that had caught his eye but the turning wheel above it. It looked as though it was some sort of handle. He moved closer, and as he rounded the tractor hood, he realised it was a round wide metal hatch. His heart lifted in hope and he beckoned Ray over. Together they pulled open the top, finding it unlocked, and he peered down into the shaft below.

'There's a ladder,' he whispered.

'And lights,' Ray added.

They exchanged a glance. Behind them, Al and Ben returned and joined them at the open hatch.

'Jesus,' one of them whispered with a frown. 'What is it?'

'No idea but I guess we're about to find out,' Ray replied.

Connor tried to gauge how far down the floor was. He could see it, in the eerie flickering light below, but it was hard to tell exactly. With a deep breath, he lifted his leg over the side and found the top rung, carefully lowering himself down step by step. He heard Ray instructing Ben to stay up and guard the hatch, then he began to climb down after him.

Moving as swiftly as he could, Connor's heart began to beat faster as he thought about how exposed he was. For all he knew, he could be backing straight into the enemy when he reached the lower level. They could be lying in wait. There was no way to see.

He swallowed and tried to focus on getting down as quickly and quietly as possible. It didn't matter what was down there – he had to go no matter what. Because whatever happened, he could not leave this place without his brother. And it was looking more and more likely that they'd found the spot where Cillian had been taken.

Reaching the bottom rung, he jumped away from the wall, tensed and ready in a half crouch, his knife brandished. Ray jumped down next to him, followed by Al. He looked around, his head switching from side to side as he tried to make sense of what he was looking at. They were standing in the middle of a long, grey concrete hallway with half-rusted metal doors leading off of it here and there. The place was huge, and it was the last thing he'd expected to find under the barn. It must stretch on for miles, he realised in dismay.

'Jesus Christ,' Ray muttered.

'We should split up,' Connor suggested, thinking of nothing else but finding Cillian as quickly as possible.

Whatever this place was, it wasn't good. He could feel the dark weight of something sinister settling into his bones the moment his feet had touched the ground, and there was also an overwhelming smell of something rotten and foul coming from somewhere.

'No,' Ray said, shaking his head. 'We have no idea what we're dealing with – we need to stick together.'

'But we don't have time—' Connor began to argue.

'Time won't matter at all if we find we're outnumbered and

get picked off one by one down here – nothing will. We're stronger together,' Ray replied firmly.

Connor sighed in exasperation and wiped a hand down his face. 'OK,' he snapped. 'Just...' He trailed off and looked around, trying to decide which way to go. 'Let's go down here.' He pointed to their left, but as he did, Al's hand shot up to silence them.

'Did you hear that?' he whispered.

Everyone turned silent and Connor strained to hear beyond the low buzz of electricity from the dull lights overhead. After a couple of seconds, he heard a sound. It was faint, coming from some way in the distance, but it was definitely there and it chilled him right down to the bone. Quiet as it was, it was still completely unmistakable. Nothing else in the world sounded anything like it. And he knew this first hand, having been witness to such sounds on many occasions, when he and his brother had been set to the task of paying back physical debts.

It was the sound of a man screaming in agony.

FORTY

John yawned and glanced at his watch, surprised at how late it was already. He'd been in the office for nearly fifteen hours. Half of his team were out on a stake-out, and tonight was the night that they should finally get the man they were after. He and the rest of the team would be here until they got the call to say they had him, even if that took all night.

He scrolled down the list of hotels he'd been looking at on his computer, but none were catching his eye. With a small sigh, he picked up the half sandwich he had left over from lunch and bit into it, his attention once more on the screen. These hotels were OK, but he really wanted to find something special. Scarlet deserved special at any time, but this coming weekend in particular he wanted to surprise her with something spectacular. She'd seemed distracted and irritated lately, unable to sit still for very long. He guessed it was something to do with work but hadn't asked her what it was, and he knew she wouldn't volunteer the information either.

It was hard, having this unspoken distance between them when it came to work – something that was such a big part of both their lives. They couldn't confide in each other, and this was incredibly frustrating at times for them both. Hopefully a weekend away somewhere by the sea with a spa where he could spoil her with all sorts of relaxing treatments would take her mind off whatever was bothering her.

He clicked onto one hotel and began scrolling through the pictures. It looked very plush, the rooms large and bright with creams and golds.

'Oooh, *fancy*,' came a voice from behind him.

He jumped with a start. He hadn't realised anyone was there.

'Ah, Jenny, hi,' he said, forcing a smile while cringing inside. He hadn't wanted anyone to see this – least of all Ascough.

'I've heard of this place – it's supposed to have an amazing spa,' she said, standing next to him and looking down at the screen. 'You thinking of going?'

'Er, yeah, I was actually.' He decided it was better to stick as close to the truth as possible to avoid slipping up on lies later. 'I've got the weekend off so I thought I'd treat myself to some R&R.'

'Nice!' she replied. 'You going with anyone?' The words were casual but he knew she was fishing.

'Nah, just me. I like to get away on my own now and then. Peace and quiet, you know?' he lied.

'Yeah, I get that,' she said with a nod.

It was a plausible situation. They dealt with so much stress as police officers, it was quite common to need to get away from everyone and everything to recharge.

'You alright?' she asked, her keen eye piercing into his. 'That last one, the woman under the train, it was a hard hitter.'

John offered a placating smile. 'I'm fine. Honestly.' They had to keep an eye out for each other in this game. Mental health was a big issue in the force, with the horrors they dealt with on a daily basis. So he appreciated her asking, even if she was barking up the wrong tree. 'Just tired.'

Ascough's gaze rested on his and she smiled warmly. 'I bet you are.'

There was a long silence and John began to feel slightly awkward, trying hard not to break eye contact in case he looked guilty somehow.

'What about you?' he asked. 'What are you up to at the weekend? You're off too, right?'

'Yes, I am actually,' she replied brightly. 'Though not sure what I'm going to do yet. No plans, though it's supposed to be a really warm weekend. Should probably try to make the best of it. Maybe take a leaf out of your book.' She gestured towards his screen.

'You should,' John agreed. Ascough was the hardest-working member of his team, and he knew she was probably close to burnout herself with all they'd been juggling lately. 'You should get away too if you can. Maybe try some sea air in your lungs.' He grinned. 'Before we fill them back up with all the smog and soot of our great city again.'

She laughed. 'Grime and crime – it's what we signed up for, right?'

'It is.' John nodded and glanced back towards his sandwich pointedly. He wanted her to go so that he could book the hotel. He didn't need her seeing him book it for two people. That would raise questions, and he didn't want to have to lie in response to them.

'Anyway, I'll let you get back to your food,' she said, turning away after one last smile.

'Catch you later,' he called after her, making sure she was out of view of his screen before he clicked on the booking page.

―――――

Ascough watched John in her peripheral vision as she sat at her own desk and moved her mouse to wake up her computer. Sure enough, he glanced over again, and a thrill shot through her. They'd had another moment just then, a long silence as they'd held each other's gaze. It was subtle, so subtle that she could just be imagining moments like these. She'd tried to be sensible, told herself that it was only she who had romantic feelings for him. But was it? These lingering stares and the fact they got on so well, could there be more to it on his side too?

They spent so much time together, she and John, both on the job and travelling to and from work. They did most things in pairs, professionally speaking, and nine times out of ten, he would call on her to join him rather than one of the others when he had to go out and about. She'd always tried not to read too much into that.

Inhaling deeply and trying to calm the questions that were running around her head, she pulled out her phone. Scrolling through her texts, she found the one she'd received from her neighbour just a couple of hours before, inviting her for a coffee the next day.

Would love to. Same place?

Almost immediately after she pressed send, the three dots at the bottom flashed up, indicating that a reply would soon be forthcoming.

Great. See you there.

She locked the screen and slipped her phone back into her bag, smiling across the office at John as he stole another look her way. They were ideal for each other, she and John. But was she right about all these little moments, or was she just creating something that wasn't there? For the first time in her life, she found herself totally unable to read the person she was trying to analyse. She was too close to the situation to dissect everything rationally. Perhaps this predicament was one for the girlfriends in her life. She might be the policewoman, but there was nothing more analytical than a girlfriend when it came to working out a bloke's intentions.

She'd bring it up at her coffee tomorrow and get a second opinion. And for now she would just have to push these romantic dreams of herself and her boss aside and get back to focusing on her work.

FORTY-ONE

Brandishing the knife, Connor ran full pelt down the hallway, towards the sound of his brother's screams. Every second of Cillian's pain was like a spear through the gut, as though he felt everything his twin was enduring. He had no idea what was happening – all he knew was that he needed to get to him and stop whatever was causing his agonising screams.

He ignored Ray's low warning calls as he struggled to keep up. He didn't care what Ray thought; he didn't care for caution or safety – he *had* to get to his brother.

The passage seemed to stretch for an age, and when he reached the next turn, he almost shot straight past the main hallway. He slammed on the brakes, slowing to an abrupt stop and turning round, but this gave Ray the extra couple of seconds he needed to catch up. He grabbed Connor by the lapels, forcing him against the wall. Al caught up just behind and bent over, holding his knees as he gathered his breath.

'Get off me,' Connor growled, keeping his voice low as he glared at Ray furiously.

Ray kept him pressed hard, his face just inches away from Connor's. 'Calm down,' he hissed. 'We have no idea what we're running into. I'll let you go but we need to *stay together*. You got that?'

'Fine,' Connor replied as Cillian's agonising screams reached new heights. 'Just let me go,' he begged. 'Now!'

Ray released Connor, propelling him forward, and fell in beside him with Al just behind. Connor reluctantly slowed just marginally in order to stay together, though even doing this pained him. Luckily they didn't have far to go, and as they reached the room the screams were coming from, Connor's heart leaped into his mouth. What was in there? What were they doing to his brother to make him scream in such a feral way?

The door was ajar, and as he pushed it open, the sight that met him shocked him to the core. Cillian was strapped to a table, face down, his torso covered in blood and some sort of clamp holding a wound on his back open as a weedy-looking man calmly stood watching them. This man looked surprised, but no fear crossed his strangely vacant features. Blood dripped off the table onto the floor beneath, and what looked like a cool box stood to the side, his brother's blood spattered all over this too.

It took Connor only a millisecond to process all this – the slightest hesitation as the shock hit – then he ran forward around the table with a roar and kicked the man assaulting his brother hard in his core. He'd been holding a scalpel, and he lashed out with this as Connor approached, but Connor dodged it easily, sending the man flying back into the rear wall. His head hit the wall with a sickening crack and he crumpled to the floor.

Ray and Al ran over to secure him as Connor flew to Cillian's side. His hands hovered over his brother's mangled form, shaking, as he tried to work out what to do. Everything was such a mess, he was scared of making things worse. Tears streamed from Cillian's eyes, his cries still coming, but weaker now as his eyes started to roll back.

'What did he do to you?' Connor cried, his voice almost as shaky as his hands.

Ray joined him and pushed him aside. 'He's lost too much blood. *Fuck!*' he exclaimed.

Grim-faced Ray started to undo the clamp, which roused Cillian once more. His cries grew louder and Connor felt his heart break in two as he watched his twin suffer.

'That's making him worse!' he cried.

'It *has* to come off so we can close this up or he'll bleed out within minutes,' Ray argued. 'Even then—' He closed his mouth, focusing on getting the clamp off as quickly as he could.

Connor bent over and gripped the side of the bed, his face stricken as he watched and tried harder than he'd ever had to try in his life to keep himself together.

'It's gonna be OK, Cillian. You hear me?' he said, dipping his face towards his brother's. He had no idea if Cillian could hear him anymore. His screams were horrifyingly pitiful, and his face was ashen, pressed as it was into the filthy operating bed. 'Hold on. *Please*,' he begged. 'Just hold on, yeah?'

'What shall I do with *him*?' Al asked from behind.

Connor turned around, almost glad of the distraction from his brother's pain. His chest rose and fell as he heaved in deep angry breaths. 'Who the fuck are you?' he asked, his fury making his voice tremble dangerously.

The man had come around and was now holding his head where it had hit the wall. He looked up at Connor and narrowed his eyes with a humourless smirk. 'Me? No one really.'

Connor marched the few steps over to him and kicked him hard in the side. 'I said, *who – the fuck – are you?*' he bellowed.

'Joe,' the man managed to mutter resentfully as he cradled his side.

'Al, pass me that sheet,' Ray said behind him. 'We need to wrap him as tight as we can.'

Connor glanced back to Cillian, naked fear on his face as he saw how quickly his brother was declining.

'We've got your brother,' Ray said, catching his indecision. 'You deal with him. We can't leave him here or he'll be gone.'

Connor nodded, turning back around. Ray was right. They couldn't leave him and they didn't have time to take revenge in the slow drawn-out way this man had earned. He needed to be dealt with now. Quickly, so that they could get Cillian above ground and to a hospital.

'I liked your brother, you know,' Joe said, almost conversationally.

Connor stared at him for a moment, tensing his jaw as he tried to keep himself in check, then he turned and took Ray's baseball bat from beside the bloodied bed. He didn't want the sharp efficiency of his knife this time. He wanted something that would spend his rage.

'Anyone else in here?' he asked, though he doubted it. There had been no one at the farmhouse, and if there had been anyone else here, they'd likely have come to his aid already.

'No, this place is all mine,' Joe said proudly, looking around the room with a half-smile.

Connor nodded and stepped forward, raising the bat high above his head. Joe turned and caught the action just before Connor swung it down, shock and then fear finally flashing across his features.

'Wait, what—' Joe began.

But Connor smashed the bat down hard into his face, cutting him off. His nose immediately caved in from the force, and his words turned into a bloody gurgle of a scream as Connor raised the bat again and smashed it into the same place a second time, the hands Joe had raised no match for the furious force behind the swing.

Connor swung the bat again and again in fast, hard succession, beating the man who'd done such horrifying things to his brother until his head was nothing more than a smashed bloody pulp. He wished, as he did this, more than anything, that he could have kept him alive and meted out the worst punishment he'd ever inflicted on anyone. That he could spend all his hurt and rage until it was gone. But time was ticking and that was more important for Cillian right now.

'Connor,' Ray said urgently.

Without a second's pause, Connor dropped the bat and turned, grabbing his brother's feet when he saw that Ray and Al had linked arms under the top half of his body.

'This ain't gonna be easy, mate,' Ray said nervously to Cillian. 'But we need to get you out of here fast.'

Cillian made a small sound of what could have been agreement, then Ray and Al lifted him up. Connor adjusted his grip on his brother's legs as Cillian screamed out once more, and clamped his jaw hard to stop himself from faltering. Cillian was in a bad way. Worse than Connor had ever dreamed they could find him in. And he knew without needing any doctor to tell him that his chances of pulling through this weren't great. He'd lost too much blood. His twin was dying, and Connor had no idea whether they would make it to hospital in time to save him.

They moved as quickly as they could, all falling silent as they carried Cillian through the dark, eerie halls of the old forgotten bunker. No one said a word as he finally passed out being carried awkwardly up the shaft to the hatch. And no one said a word as Connor openly wept over Cillian's deathly quiet form in the back of the car while they sped towards the nearest hospital.

FORTY-TWO

Lily ran up the stairs and down the hallway to where Connor had told her to meet them. They'd arrived at the hospital only a few minutes ahead of her.

Turning a corner, she let out a desperate cry of fear as she saw Connor and Ray standing there outside the room. They were covered in blood, the pair of them. Their clothes were a mess, their expressions drawn and haunted. Was she too late?

'What happened?' It came out as a panicked scream as she flew towards them. 'What happened?' she repeated, grabbing Connor as she reached him.

He took her hands and squeezed them gently but firmly. 'He's in a bad way.' His voice broke and he turned back to the small window in the door.

Lily pushed him aside and looked through the glass, gasping when she saw her other son on the bed inside. A handful of doctors and nurses were rushing around him, one holding up some breathing apparatus by his head.

'What the fuck happened?' she asked in barely more than a whisper. She turned to Ray, her face ashen. 'Tell me!'

He looked at her with sorrow and guilt and ran his bloodied

hand through his messed-up hair. 'Lil, I'm not sure you can take the details right now—'

'Just *tell me*,' she screamed, anger now making its way through the haze of fear.

Just then the door opened and a doctor rushed out of the room. 'Who here is family?' he demanded.

'I'm his mother,' Lily said, her voice shaking.

'Brother,' Connor added.

Ray was about to speak, but the doctor held his hand up to cut him off. 'OK, all of you please come through here – this is urgent.'

They followed him across the hallway to a small sitting room and waited as he shut the door. The little room felt almost as dismal as Lily felt herself. The pale blue paint was faded and worn, the matching blue chairs saggy in the middle from use. One bookshelf sat under the window with a selection of dog-eared books, some held together by Sellotape. Lily wasn't sure why she was noticing such trivial things at a time like this, but she was grateful for the fact they were filling her head for the brief few seconds before he talked and were stopping her from screaming.

The doctor stood in front of them and began to talk. 'Cillian has lost a lot of blood – too much blood. He's also lost a kidney, but that's not as urgent a priority right now.'

Lily heard a sharp gasp, and it took a moment to realise it had come from her own mouth. How could he have lost a *kidney*? She felt Ray's arm around her shoulder and she sagged into him.

'Cillian needs an urgent blood transfusion—'

'Do it – you have my permission,' Lily jumped in, cutting him off.

A brief smile flickered across the doctor's face. 'Luckily as he's not a minor we were able to start the process without your consent,' he said gently. 'They're prepping him now.'

Lily shook her head at her own stupidity. She wasn't thinking straight right now. All she could see in her mind was her son's broken body in the other room. It didn't matter how old he was, to her he'd always be the six-year-old child who'd fallen off his bike at times like these. 'Of course. Go on.'

'Cillian has a rare blood type – are you aware?' the doctor asked.

'Yes,' she replied, nodding. 'He's AB negative.'

'Right. AB negative people can only receive the same blood type, O negative or A negative,' the doctor explained urgently. 'Right now, we have very little compatible blood on site. Other hospitals do have some and we are blue lighting some over, but Cillian is in a very bad way and I worry it won't arrive in time.'

'Take mine – we're identical,' Connor said quickly. 'Can you do that? Can you take—'

'No,' Lily interrupted, feeling her body turn cold as the implications of what she already knew began to race through her brain. 'You can't. You're B positive.'

'What?' Connor swivelled to face her. 'How?'

'It... You were a very unusual case,' Lily said, the memories all flying back to her. 'When you were born, the doctors said it was so rare only a few cases had been documented. They wanted to do a study on you, but I said no.'

She closed her eyes and rubbed her head, her heart beginning to hammer in her chest as if it were an animal in a cage. Her breathing spiked and the world started to spin. She broke free of Ray's grip and sat down.

'And you?' the doctor prompted.

'B positive,' she whispered.

'So we need Dad,' Connor said in a low, resigned voice.

Lily shook her head and opened her mouth to speak, but he cut her off. 'I know you don't want to hear this, but I know where he is.'

Lily's head shot up, and she looked at him in horror. 'What?' she asked faintly.

'Cillian and I, we hired someone a few years ago to track him down. We half hoped he was dead so we could tell you, but he wasn't.' A flash of disgust crossed his face. 'We never approached him, but he ain't actually far from here. I could go and—'

'No,' Lily said forcefully, standing back up. The hammering in her chest grew stronger and began to fill her ears as the world she had so carefully constructed over the last few decades started to crumble.

'If it's the only way to save Cillian, I have to try,' Connor argued.

'I said no,' Lily replied, her voice beginning to tremble.

'I'm not sure we'd even have time—' the doctor said quietly.

'Mum, I have to try!' Connor snapped, his voice angry now. 'I'm going!'

'It won't do you no good,' she said, raising her voice to meet his. The hammering reached a crescendo in her head and she put her hands up to hold it.

'Why are you arguing this?' Connor yelled. 'He's our *dad*, and I know he's a bastard, but if his blood can save Cillian's, it's worth a try.'

'His blood *won't* save your brother,' Lily cried, releasing her head as her heart all but stopped and the one small lie she'd kept from them all these years finally broke free of its bindings and grew into the giant monster it had always really been. 'He can't help your brother because he ain't the one who passed down that blood type.' She clasped her hand over her mouth, wishing she could undo the words, but there had been no choice.

There was a millisecond of silence as Connor stared back at her, stunned, and in her heart of hearts, she wished more than she'd ever wished for anything before that she could stay right there in that moment forever. The moment before their entire world imploded. But time, in its cruel way, moved forward, and the realisation dawned on his face.

'You mean...' Connor breathed.

'He's not your dad.' Lily lowered her hand and felt the heat of shame and fear warm her cheeks as her secret was finally laid bare.

'Then who?' Connor asked, his face falling into an expression of devastation. Devastation, she guessed, not because of who his father was not, but because he'd just discovered the person he'd trusted more than anyone had been lying to him his entire life.

Part of her wanted to walk out of this room and refuse to ever share more on the subject. But she knew she couldn't do that. Her son's time was running out, he needed blood and she knew that by damning herself further, she could deliver it. And that was all that mattered.

Her entire body began to shake as she turned and rested her eyes on Ray's horrified face. Letting her mask drop completely, she nodded back to the question in his gaze.

'They're yours,' she uttered in barely a whisper. 'They're your sons.'

FORTY-THREE

Lily sat on the sagging blue chair nearest the window and stared out of it, one arm crossed over her middle, her other fist raised to her mouth. The only sound in the otherwise empty room was the incessant ticking of the cheap white clock hanging above the door. Every tick tore through her nerves and made her want to smash the damn thing into bits, but she kept her cool, reminding herself that each tick was one more second of blood being pumped into her son.

The urgency of the situation had meant that Ray barely had time to react to the bomb she'd dropped before he was being asked to give blood to save Cillian. Stunned, he'd just nodded and followed the doctor out to be prepped for the transfusion. She'd never been more grateful for anything in her life than for the fact that Ray was around right now. He'd always been there when she needed him, and today was no exception. Though whether that would continue after today's revelation, she was no longer sure.

She hadn't planned for things to go the way they had. But back then they had been so very different.

Ray had been her first love. Her *only* love throughout her life, even whilst she'd been married to Alfie. She'd been young, just a teenager when they'd first met. Ray had been older, full of life and grand ideas and a thirst for carving his own way in the world that reached far beyond the constraints and rules of society. He was everything she was trying to be herself. But she was hindered in ways that Ray wasn't. Her brother Ronan was still so young, and he'd needed her to be stable and consistent as his only parental figure, so she'd had to adjust the way she climbed the ladder towards the future she wanted.

Ray had lived his life loudly and wildly, and she'd been part of it for a while, when she could or on the sidelines. She loved him deeply, and they connected in ways that neither of them ever had or would with anyone else in the world. She'd thought that he too realised that what they had between them was something special, the kind of connection people don't often find once, let alone twice in a lifetime.

When she'd neared her eighteenth birthday, she'd gathered her courage and asked if they could move in together, the three of them. To her surprise, he'd refused and backed away, later telling her he wasn't ready to settle and that they should see other people for a while.

It had blindsided her and smashed her young, vulnerable heart into a thousand pieces. Just a few weeks later, after Ray had distanced himself and begun seeing other girls, she'd missed her period and went on to discover that she was expecting the twins.

The door opened and Scarlet walked in with two steaming Styrofoam cups of coffee. She handed one to Lily and sat down in the chair opposite.

'I realise it looks like drain water, but I promise it did say latte on the machine,' she said with a small apologetic smile.

The corner of Lily's mouth twitched upwards in a ghost of a

smile in return. 'Your dad always used to think they purposely only sold crap coffee so people would go home and not clog up the waiting rooms.'

'Well' – Scarlet looked down into her cup and then took a sip with an expression of resentment – 'they ain't getting us out that easily.'

Lily sat the cup down to the side, unable to put anything into her churning stomach just yet, and they fell into a stressed but companionable silence. She was grateful for Scarlet being here right now. Scarlet knew what had happened – the shocking truth that had come out – but she hadn't said a word. She'd kept her opinions to herself and her expression neutral, in the way she always seemed to do whenever there was conflict within the family. The subtle show of support had not gone unnoticed.

The door opened and Ruby walked in, her expression as worried as the rest of them. She made a beeline for her mother, ignoring her cousin seated in the other chair.

'What's going on? What happened?' she asked, sitting down next to her.

'Turns out it wasn't Higgs *or* AJ who took those men from the club,' Lily replied. 'It was a black-market organ dealer. He took the bait we laid for Higgs and actually managed to take a kidney before Connor and Ray got there.'

Ruby's eyes widened in horror.

'He's OK. Or at least he should be,' she continued. 'He's lost a lot of blood; he's having a transfusion now. So long as it takes alright, he should be fine.'

'Christ!' Ruby exclaimed. 'What about his kidney?'

'The doctors have operated on the area, patched him up. They say he'll be fine with just the one. He just has to make sure he's careful that he doesn't do any damage to that one.'

Lily pulled a face and Ruby mirrored it. Telling Cillian to be careful was like telling a fire not to burn.

Ruby looked around the room, once more ignoring Scarlet. Lily noted this. Nothing had improved between them it seemed, despite her urging each of them to try.

'Where's Connor?' Ruby asked.

'Down the hallway in the next waiting area,' Lily replied, her heart sinking once more at the mention of her other son.

Ruby frowned and gave her a questioning look.

'He's not talking to me right now.'

'What?' Ruby asked, shocked. Her forehead creased into a deep frown.

Lily wasn't surprised at her reaction. This would be the first time Ruby had ever known one of her brothers to be so angry with their mother they'd dared to give her the cold shoulder.

'So...' For the first time since she'd entered the room, she looked over towards Scarlet, the silent question there, before turning back to her mother. 'What happened?'

Lily paused; it was the last question she wanted to answer right now, especially from Ruby. Ruby was unpredictable. She had no idea how her daughter was going to take this news, and she didn't have the strength right now to deal with her potential reaction on top of everything else going on.

A knock sounded at the door and it opened, the face of a friendly nurse popping round with a smile.

'Ms Drew?' she asked, looking at Lily expectantly.

'Yeah, that's me,' Lily replied, her hope rising at the sight of the smile on the nurse's face. 'Ruby, I'll talk to you in a bit. Your brother will fill you in.'

She shifted her gaze and stood up with a feeling of relief. No doubt Connor would give Ruby the worst version possible, but at least she could avoid having to deal with the fallout a while longer.

She walked out into the corridor, closed the door behind her and turned eagerly to the nurse.

'He's come around?' she asked, her tone as hopeful as her expression.

'No, I'm sorry, he's still out at the moment. But that's to be expected for a little while longer,' the nurse answered gently.

Lily's hope faded, and she swallowed the lump of worry that resurfaced in her throat. 'Alright. But everything is going OK?'

'Everything has gone really well. He's still got a while longer to go with the transfusion as it needs to be introduced into his bloodstream slowly, but he's out of danger and I know the doctor already told you that they've patched up the area around his kidney nice and neatly. He should come round and be up for visitors in an hour or so,' the nurse explained.

'And the blood loss. He was out for a while before they got him here,' Lily said, her fear beginning to creep into her voice. 'Will that have caused any long-term damage to anything else, like his brain?'

'Oh no.' The nurse was quick to reassure her. 'He didn't pass out because of the blood loss – he most likely passed out from the pain. There...' She hesitated. 'There were no painkillers in his system.'

Lily drew in a sharp breath as she realised what that meant. He'd suffered having his kidney removed feeling every single moment of it. Her heart ached as though someone was crushing it with their fist, and tears stung her eyes. She blinked them away and cleared her throat. 'OK. Thank you for letting me know.'

'I'm sorry,' the nurse said softly. 'That can't be easy to hear. Cillian's blood reached a critical condition around the time he arrived. He'd been bleeding out for a while. A few minutes later, they might have been too late, but they got him here in time. And that's what we should hold on to and be grateful for.' She grasped Lily's hand and squeezed it. 'You'll see him soon. But in the meantime, there's someone else asking for you.'

The nurse led Lily towards the room Ray was recovering in, and her heart dropped like a stone at the thought of the conversation to come.

FORTY-FOUR

Ray was sitting on the edge of the bed fiddling with the button on the cuff of his shirt when they walked into the room. Lily watched him warily as she entered behind the nurse. He pointedly ignored her while the nurse was present, but she could feel the silent anger radiating from him underneath the cool, polite mask fixed upon his face.

She watched him struggle with the button. Any other time she'd have stepped forward to do it for him, but she knew how close to explosion he must be and decided it was wiser not to. Instead, she sat down on the visitor's armchair in the corner of the small private room and waited.

'Are you feeling OK now, Mr Renshaw?' the nurse asked. 'No dizziness or anything?' She cast her gaze over him critically.

'No, all good,' he replied. 'That sweet tea and toast fixed me up a treat.'

'OK, well, take a while longer to rest on the bed. You gave a lot of blood so the doctor will want to come and check you over before he can sign you off,' she said, checking his clipboard. She looked up at him with a smile. 'And well done. You saved your son's life today.'

Ray's fixed smile wavered, but he just about kept it in place. He nodded instead of replying, and the nurse quietly left the room, shutting the door behind her. His smile dropped, and he turned to glare at Lily with a mixture of accusation, pain and pure fury.

There was a long silence as Lily held his anguished gaze, unsure exactly how to start. Eventually Ray shook his head and made a sound of exasperation.

'You've really got nothing to say?' he asked in disbelief.

'I'm sorry,' Lily answered.

'You're *sorry*?' he bellowed. He took a deep breath and exhaled it slowly before continuing more quietly. 'You're sorry?' he repeated. 'I have two sons, two *grown fucking men* as sons, with the woman I have loved my whole life, who let me believe they were someone else's, and you're *sorry*?'

His voice shook with emotion, and for a moment – to her alarm – Lily thought he was going to cry. Instead, he sniffed and balled his fists in his lap, the heat of his gaze burning into her like a branding iron of fury.

A lump of pain rose in her throat, and for a moment she couldn't get the words out as she saw the raw wounds she'd inflicted burst open in front of her. Raising her head, she looked at him and took a deep breath. It was time to explain – and defend – her actions.

'You remember that day when I asked you to move in with me?' she asked, her own voice shaking now.

'Of *course* I remember that day,' he cried. 'I've regretted that decision every day of my damn life – I have *paid* for it every day of my damn life. Lily...' He reached up and grasped his hair in both fists with a look of pure frustration. 'I was a fool, I've told you this time and again, but I didn't deserve *this*!'

'You *were* a fool, yes,' Lily cried back, pulling herself up to her full sitting height. 'But it wasn't *you* who had to pay for it back then, it was *me*.' She jabbed her finger hard into her chest.

'You'd ended things. I came to find you, to tell you I was pregnant, and I found you that night in the Rose and Crown with Shelley Bassett. I thought maybe you might have been missing me, maybe you hadn't meant what you'd said, but that cleared up my delusions. You'd moved on.' The memory was a harsh one, and she took a deep breath.

'Shelley *who*? I don't even remember a Shelley,' Ray argued.

'Of course you don't,' Lily replied. 'But I do. She was the first in a long line of short skirts.' Her bitter expression turned cold. 'All dispensable. None of them lasted much longer than a couple of weeks, but that was what you wanted back then. Remember?'

Ray glared at her but grudgingly nodded. 'It was. I was young and an idiot. But if you'd just *told* me—'

'You'd have what?' Lily cut him off. 'Shown me pity?' She looked away and shook her head, biting her lip to stop her rising emotions showing too clearly.

'I'd have looked after you. All of you,' Ray replied.

'Out of *pity*,' she said, looking back at him. 'Out of duty. I loved you, Ray. And I wanted us to be a family, but I'd already offered that to you and you'd run a mile. I may not have had much else back then, but I had my pride. I wasn't going to force myself on you as a weight around your neck you didn't want. I couldn't have borne looking at you every day, knowing I was that.'

One hot tear escaped down her cheek, and she rubbed it away angrily. These jagged memories were ones she'd buried at the bottom of her heart many years ago, but they tore just as cruelly as they were dredged up now.

'Did Alfie know?' Ray asked.

'No.' Lily shook her head. 'After you'd gone, he took his chance. Told me he loved me and asked me to go out with him. I needed someone to pin the pregnancy on.' Lily watched as Ray winced, but she didn't want to sugar-coat her words. There was no point changing history now that it was out. 'So I said yes. The twins went pretty much full term but came out small, so it was easy to pass them off as early births.' She sniffed and blinked back the tears, the bittersweet joy of meeting her sons mixed with the sadness at lying about their parentage coming back to her.

'*Him*, of all people,' Ray snarled, punching the bed next to him.

'He was the only option I had,' Lily said, lifting her chin defiantly. 'They needed a dad who didn't look at them like they were the reason all their life's dreams had been crushed. And I know you, Ray. That's how you'd have seen them.'

'And Alfie was *better*?' Ray asked in angry disbelief. 'Don't give me this shit – I know you can't actually believe that.'

Lily looked away for a few moments. Ray had always hated Alfie. He was someone on the very outer edges of their circles, someone who'd made himself useful from time to time but who never actually stepped a full foot into the underworld they thrived in. He was just a straight shooter who sometimes helped not-so-straight friends for some extra cash. His day job was boring and safe and had held zero opportunity in terms of career advancement. No one had much respect for him, but mostly people liked him, although even those who liked him laughed at him behind his back for his lack of gumption. Sometimes even to his face. He was everything Lily had never wanted, but at that time in her life, he'd been everything she needed.

'Nothing was ever going to be *better* than us, Ray,' Lily said quietly. 'But you'd destroyed that. And Alfie was safe.' She looked up at him. 'Dependable.'

'Yeah, till he ran out the *fucking door* and left you and your kids for a younger bit of fluff,' Ray said with a sharp sting of his tail. He immediately stopped and breathed out, shaking his head. 'I'm sorry – that was uncalled for.'

'No, go for it,' Lily replied sharply. 'Get it out, if it makes you feel better. You reminding me that a husband I never loved, who I saddled myself with because you broke my heart, ran out when he couldn't cope with us all, is *not* the thing that's gonna hurt me today.'

Ray's anger seemed to intensify. 'You don't get to turn this around, Lil,' he snapped. 'I hurt you back then, I know I did. I've tried to make up for that for decades. But you kept my *children* from me. I have spent all these years without a family when I had one *all along*! You could have told me later, after he left. You could have told me any time.'

'What – and screw up my children even more than they already were after Alfie left?' Lily replied indignantly. 'Not bloody likely. *They* were my priority back then, Ray, *not* you. And don't forget Ruby. How was I supposed to tell them they had different dads, eh? How exactly would you have put that?'

'I don't know, Lil, but I would have fucking tried,' Ray yelled, no longer caring who heard them. 'We could have made a go of it, Ruby and all.'

'You didn't even *want* a family, Ray,' Lily argued.

'Yes, I *did*,' he shouted back. 'Not at first, no, but later I *begged* you to be with me full-time, to marry me, to move in, so many times over the years.'

'Later, yes, but not when they were young,' Lily reminded him. 'And honestly, Ray, you don't get to pick and choose like that. They were kids – they're *people*. They can't be messed around and pushed from pillar to post whenever we feel like it because *you* finally grew up and changed your mind. You don't get to choose when their existence is convenient.'

'Except I never got the *choice*,' Ray roared at her, his face red with anger.

Lily stared back at him, the air between them thick with emotion. He was right. It wasn't fair on him. But it hadn't been fair on her either, back then. She took a deep breath, and when she spoke, it was calmly and quietly.

'I can't change the past. I don't regret the way I did things, because it was the best I could do with the situation I was in at the time. And I don't regret keeping it from you all these years either, because, honestly, I'd have let you all go to the grave before willingly causing my children the pain and suffering that this revelation now has. But I *am* sorry that my choices have hurt you. I love you as much now as I did then. And I always will. Nothing will ever change that.'

Ray looked at her, his pain open and raw. 'I used to think that nothing could ever change how I look at you, Lily,' he said, anger mixing with the pain in his tone. '*Ever*. Right up until today.' He shook his head and lowered it into his hands.

Lily felt a cold spear of ice pierce her heart. His words were so defeated and so final that she knew they came straight from the heart she'd just broken. Everything had changed today. Lines had been revealed, and they were so far over them they could never cross back. What that meant to their reality, only time would tell now.

'I need you to leave,' Ray said, his voice quiet and his tone hollow.

Lily stood up, her whole body feeling strangely numb as she moved slowly to the door. She paused and looked back at him. 'My children always have and always will come first. But next to them, I love you more than anything else in the world, Ray Renshaw. And even if you never speak to me again, I always will.'

She bit her lip and sniffed, fixing her hard, impenetrable mask back in position to hide the pain, then slipped out of the room, closing the door behind her.

FORTY-FIVE

Ruby looked down at her brother lying so peacefully on the bed. Or at least he could have looked peaceful, were there not all sorts of tubes coming out of him and machines surrounding his body, beeping away. But the beeps of the heart monitor were at least a soothing sound. A sound that confirmed his body was holding on and fighting back towards life. She reached for his hand and squeezed it, relieved to find it warm.

'You gave everyone quite a scare,' she said quietly. She studied his face, the strong jaw and stress lines on his forehead. The long dark lashes that fringed his closed eyes, and the full lifeless lips she recognised better curled into a cheeky grin. He was always so upbeat, her brother. To see him like this was harder than she'd thought it would be.

She moved her gaze back down to her hand in his, and the bracelet around her wrist caught her eye. It was the most thoughtful present she'd ever received in her life. The warm gold with the understated stone was exactly her style, and she cherished the effort Cillian must have put into finding it. She squeezed his hand a little tighter.

Cillian had always believed in her, even when she'd put

the family through the toughest of times. He'd always seen her, encouraged her and been there for her. She didn't deserve such a great brother, but he'd always been one anyway.

'Hurry up and get better, yeah?' she whispered.

The door opened and Connor walked in, looking at her with surprise. 'Oh, sorry. Didn't realise you were in here.' He began to retreat.

'No, don't go. Come, – sit.' She gestured towards the chair on the other side of the bed and Connor walked over to it.

He pulled it closer to the bed and sat down, his shoulders slumping defeatedly. Ruby studied his haggard face. His bloodied clothes had been discarded and replaced with one of Cillian's tracksuits that Billie had had the good thought to bring along when she'd been told what had happened. They fitted him perfectly of course, being Cillian's.

It was always remarkable to Ruby that her brothers were so similar in every way, down to the size of their clothes and the styles they favoured. Even despite the fact they were identical twins, what life threw at them and the choices they made should have rendered *some* variation. But there was barely a pound's difference in their weights or a visible blemish on their complexions that placed them apart. They were identical in every way. Or at least every way except their blood.

Ruby saw the misery on Connor's face and the way his gaze flickered resentfully towards the drip that was slowly transferring Ray's blood into Cillian's body.

'Where's Billie gone?' Connor asked.

'To see if Mum's OK and to get some food for us all,' she replied.

Connor made a sound of bitter amusement. 'To see if *Mum's* OK,' he repeated. 'She ain't the one lying here in a hospital bed, or who's found out their whole fucking life was a lie.'

'Your whole life ain't been a lie,' she replied. 'You can't think of it like that.'

'No?' Connor looked up at her. 'I just found out the man she's been seeing on the casual basically our whole lives – who we *hate*, by the way, in case you forgot – is our fucking dad. Honestly, I always thought we couldn't have been less lucky being born by that loser Alfie, but here I am proven sorely wrong.'

Ruby pulled a face and looked back to Cillian. She could understand his feelings. She'd be fuming too, if it had been her in this position. More than that, she'd have been horrified. For once she was actually glad that the deadbeat dad she couldn't even remember was hers. For she hated Ray even more than her brothers did.

'It was a shitty way to find out,' she offered.

'I don't think there would have been a non-shitty way to find something like that out,' he replied glumly. 'I mean...' He made a sound of exasperation and pushed his fingers back through his hair. 'Why would she *do* that? Why keep something that big, that important, a secret all these years? Our whole life he was right there, and it's just...' He trailed off, shaking his head with a look of complete disbelief.

Ruby bit the inside of her cheek. She could guess, to an extent, why. She didn't know the ins and outs of their relationship when they'd been young, but she had overheard a conversation between her mother and her aunt Cath once, referring to a time when Ray had broken her heart. Knowing Ray, she imagined he would have been pretty wild and unpredictable in his youth. Perhaps Lily had just been trying to protect them.

'I don't think she did it with bad intentions,' Ruby said.

Connor stared at her. 'Are you really sticking up for her?' he asked incredulously.

'I'm not sticking up for anyone,' Ruby replied with a defensive frown. 'I'm just saying, I don't think she meant harm. You know what she's like. Everything she does is for the good of the family. Maybe this was too.'

'Well, this really weren't *good for the family*,' Connor shot back resentfully. 'It weren't for the good of anyone but herself. And you say that our lives ain't a lie, but who are we, Rubes? Me and Cillian, who are we?'

'You're *Drews*,' she replied firmly.

He shook his head and opened his mouth to argue but she cut him off. 'No, seriously, Connor. Listen to me. None of us have ever credited Alfie for who we are as people. He didn't raise us, he had no influence as we grew up. We didn't even keep his last name. We formed our identity through what we had. Through Mum and each other and our way of life. *That's* what made us who we are, nothing else,' she said, her eyes beseeching him to listen. 'So nothing has changed. Not really. I know it's hard, and you have every right to be angry about it, but you are no different today than you were yesterday. *He* makes no difference. He's no one. Blood or not, he ain't your family. *We* are. Me and Cillian and Mum. That's it.' She knew, as she said the words, that she was trying to console herself, as much as Connor. The news that her brothers were only her half-brothers had knocked her for six.

Connor closed his eyes and exhaled slowly, looking as though he had the weight of the world on his shoulders. Just as Ruby thought he might try to argue with her again, he nodded.

'I appreciate that, Rubes,' he said quietly. 'I just don't know how to get my head around this right now. Or how the hell I'm supposed to tell Cillian when he wakes up.'

Ruby's gaze shifted back to Cillian's face and she pursed her lips.

'I'm surprised you're so calm about it all,' he continued. 'I mean, this affects you too.'

Ruby nodded. Ray was the person she hated most in the world, and now it felt as though he'd half taken her brothers away from her. And it felt like this was all their mother's fault, a betrayal in its purest form. But she also knew how hard life could be when you were vulnerable and alone, and so she tried to remind herself that she couldn't blame Lily for something that she didn't understand and that had happened before she was even born. Lily had been protecting her family from outside dangers, the same way she always had. And Ray would always be an outside danger.

At the thought of outside dangers, her mind returned to John. He was another one. But she was already dealing with that. She'd been setting it all up so carefully, eager to strike but cautious enough to make sure it happened in a way that looked organic. But perhaps she'd been too cautious. Perhaps she'd waited long enough.

'Mum was just trying to protect us all,' she replied, looking up at him, her eyes turning hard as her decision to make her final move cemented in her mind. 'Sometimes we have to do some dark things that people don't like in order to keep them safe. Sometimes that's the only way.'

FORTY-SIX

Scarlet walked up the path towards Lily's house and glanced grimly at the closed curtains in the kitchen window. In all her years coming to this house, she'd never once seen those curtains closed in the daytime. Cath locked the car and hurried after her, balancing a wide tray covered in foil under one arm.

'Christ,' she muttered, eyeing the curtains. 'This is worse than we thought.'

Scarlet opened the front door and walked in, turning towards the kitchen. Lily was seated at the small round table under the window, smoking a cigarette and staring off into the distance. Her eyes were tired and her face was drawn. She looked as though she hadn't slept.

'Lil?' Scarlet said, frowning with concern.

Lily seemed to realise they were there at the sound of her name and roused herself, sitting upright and stubbing the cigarette out in the nearly full ashtray in front of her.

'Scarlet, Cath,' she said hoarsely before clearing her throat. 'Can I get you a coffee?' She stood up and rubbed her eyes.

'Have you been here all night?' Cath asked with a disapproving purse of the lips. 'You sit back down – I'll get the coffee.'

'What time is it?' Lily asked, lowering herself back down in the chair.

Scarlet reached past her and opened the curtains. 'Gone ten,' she replied. 'You OK?' It was a stupid question really. Of course she wasn't OK. She kicked herself for not staying over with her aunt the night before. She'd offered, but Lily had declined, and she'd backed off to give her some space. Looking at her now though, she realised she should have insisted.

'I'm fine,' Lily replied, wincing at the sudden daylight. 'I'm just tired. Couldn't stop thinking about Cillian.'

Scarlet and Cath exchanged a knowing glance. Lily had no doubt been thinking about a lot more than just Cillian, with all that had come out the day before.

'I've made you a lasagne,' Cath said, pointing to the covered dish she'd placed on the side. 'Should keep you guys going a few days. Plus, you know what they say. Home-cooked food does wonders for the soul.'

The corners of Scarlet's mouth turned up fondly. In her mother's eyes, food solved everything. Especially her lasagne.

'Thanks, Cath,' Lily answered.

She stood up and took the ashtray to the bin, emptying it and then rinsing it out in the sink. Sitting down again, she looked at Scarlet critically, back from whatever dark place she'd been dwelling in before they came.

'Did you get that address I asked you for?' she asked, lifting one eyebrow expectantly.

'I did.' Scarlet reached into her pocket and pulled out a scrap of paper, handing it to Lily. 'Miranda Hartley, forty-eight, one divorce, no children, likes to bet on horses. That's her office address – she'll be there today until two.'

'Good work,' she replied with a look of approval.

Cath walked around the kitchen island and leaned back on

it, looking at her sister-in-law with an expression of concern. 'Do you want to talk about it, Lil?' she asked.

'Talk about what?' Lily replied a little sharply.

'About Ray. About the boys,' Cath responded, not put off in the slightest.

'There's nothing to talk about,' Lily said, her words clipped. She stood and brushed down her black dress. 'What's done is done – I can't change the past or the choices I made any more than I can stop the sun rising in the sky.'

'But the boys – do you want me to talk to them? Maybe I can—'

'No, Cath,' Lily cut her off. 'There's nothing you can do. They have every right to be angry. As does Ray.' She shrugged, her expression heavy. 'We all have to pay for our sins eventually. The boys will come back when they're ready. If they ever are.' Her eyes glazed over for a moment, then she sniffed and walked over to the counter and picked up her handbag.

'Of course they will be,' Cath replied. She looked as though she wanted to say more, then decided against it.

'Do you want me to come with you?' Scarlet asked, seeing that her aunt was getting ready to leave.

'No, get in touch with Connor and help him get round everything today. And if Ruby comes down before you leave, tell her we need her back in the factory this afternoon to start payroll,' Lily ordered. 'I'll catch up with you when I'm done with Miranda.'

She left the house, and Scarlet watched through the window as she made her way down the path towards her car. The strength her aunt possessed never ceased to amaze her. Lily's entire world was falling apart and yet still she just carried on doing what needed to be done for the good of the firm. The events of the last twenty-four hours would have floored most people, but not her. Never her. She was their rock. The cornerstone of their family, through thick and thin.

'I'd better get going,' Cath said behind her, and she turned. 'I need to get to the salon. Where do you want me to drop you?' she asked. They'd come in her car.

'Don't worry, I'll get Connor to meet me here,' Scarlet replied, walking over to the coffee machine that Cath had turned on a few minutes before and checking the pot.

'OK, love,' Cath replied. 'I'll catch you later.' She kissed Scarlet's cheek and left her to it.

Scarlet poured herself a coffee and perched on one of the stools at the breakfast bar, pulling out her phone to text her cousin.

I'm at your mum's. She's not here but can you pick me up?

She pressed send as she heard Cath start the engine and pull off the drive outside. Her phone beeped as the sound of the engine faded into the distance, and she looked down at the screen.

OK. Be 20 mins.

Scarlet locked the screen and brought the coffee cup up to her mouth, savouring the rich smell and the silence around her for a few moments before taking a sip. She rarely had time to just sit and do nothing, so she appreciated these stolen moments between the different chapters of her chaotic day.

The silence was short-lived though, as was the feeling of peace, as Ruby trundled down the stairs and into the kitchen, rubbing the sleep from her eyes. As the two women clocked each other, there was a mutual flash of annoyance across both faces.

'Where's Mum?' Ruby asked.

'Gone out,' Scarlet replied curtly, taking another sip of her coffee.

'Good,' Ruby replied, walking over to the coffee machine. 'We don't have to keep up the pretence that we can actually stand each other then.'

She looked Scarlet up and down rudely as she passed, and Scarlet felt a fresh flare of resentment rise up. She clamped her jaw and looked away, not interested in getting into it with Ruby today.

After pouring herself a coffee, Ruby opened the fridge and pulled out some ham and a block of cheese. She found a chopping board and a knife and began slicing off thick chunks of cheese.

'So *why* are you here?' she eventually asked in a withering tone. 'Getting kinda tired of finding you in my house. You do realise you don't live here, right? That you ain't actually a part of this side of the family.'

Scarlet balled the hand in her lap into a fist and glared at Ruby. 'I had business to discuss with Lil. Not that it's any of *your* concern.' She let her cold gaze travel over her scruffy cousin as rudely as Ruby's own gaze had before. 'It was more management stuff. She said to remind you to start payroll this afternoon though, once you're actually up for the day, that is. And the only person confused about who's part of this family tends to be you, Ruby. I mean, you *were* actually the most recent one to join it, despite the fact you were born into it,' she added scathingly.

'Huh.' Ruby let out a humourless laugh. 'Is that what it is?' she asked, pointing at Scarlet with the knife, her eyes flashing dangerously. 'You can't stand it, can you? That you're just the niece, not the daughter. A secondary position, when you feel like you deserve to be first.'

'What the fuck are you on about, you crazy bitch?' Scarlet exclaimed. Something inside her finally snapped, and the words she'd held back for so long all came tumbling out. 'Honestly, you're a joke. You think I want to be *you*? Really?' She raised her eyebrows and laughed. 'I wouldn't change my family for the world. And I don't feel my *position* is anything other than alongside Lil, running this company and looking out for our family, because that's exactly what it is.'

Ruby rounded the counter, her face filled with a dark thunder, the knife still pointed out in front of her towards Scarlet. She tilted her head. '*What* did you just call me?'

Scarlet's gaze slipped down to the knife and then back up to Ruby's face. Her cousin was trying to intimidate her. Well, it wasn't going to happen. Not now. Not ever again. She'd spent years as a child being pushed over and tripped up by her older cousin. Having her favourite dolls' heads ripped off and her homework scribbled on in spite. Being taunted and having mud slung at her dresses. She'd spent years hiding her tears from the incessant bullying in the dark under the covers, because Ruby had told her that she was weak and not a Drew if she couldn't handle it. Ruby had been threatened by her ever since she could remember, and Scarlet had paid for it tenfold. She wasn't going to continue doing so for the rest of her life.

She stood up and stepped towards Ruby, a cold threat behind her grey-blue eyes. 'I called you a crazy bitch,' she repeated in a low voice. 'Because that's what you are. I am *done* with your shit, Ruby. I put up with it for years.'

She took another step closer and looked down at her cousin. She was taller than Ruby, towering over her now they were both adults. 'I sat there as a kid and let you make my life hell. Then I ignored you as we grew older, as you continued your little digs. And when you finally fucked off – shooting that shit in your arm and disappearing down your little spiral of self-destruction away from the rest of us – when you finally just left us to live in *peace* – do you know what I did?' She raised an eyebrow, pushing her face closer to Ruby's. 'I rejoiced,' she whispered.

She couldn't move any closer now, the knife in Ruby's hand

almost touching her stomach. Ruby shook with rage, her face turning red.

'*I* made *your* life hell?' she cried. '*You* were the one who pushed me out of the way at every opportunity you could get. Parading around, getting the better of me at every single turn possible.'

'You're *deluded*,' Scarlet shot back angrily. 'I was a *child*. A child much younger and smaller than you, and you pushed me around like the vicious little bully you are. And you know what? I don't give a shit anymore. I grew up. Life goes on – for those of us who actually *have* a life, that is. But pathetic cows like you – the kind who spend their whole life playing the victim and leeching off everyone else – can't get past the issues of childhood I guess.'

Her expression turned to one of disgust as she looked down at her cousin. 'You're a waste of space, Ruby. You always have been. You've toed the line these past few months, but we all know that won't last forever. You'll fuck up somehow and run off to whatever little hole you have waiting as your plan B.'

'It ain't *me* who's fucking up right now though, is it?' Ruby yelled, spittle flying from her mouth as she shook with rage. 'It's *you*. You and that scumbag pig you go to bed with every night.'

'You don't get to say a *word* about John, you spiteful, self-centred liability!' Scarlet screamed back at her, seeing red. She pushed forward, grabbing the knife out of Ruby's hand and throwing it back behind her into the kitchen. It dropped with a clatter to the floor, and Ruby made a sound of pure hostility as she shoved Scarlet back hard with both hands.

'You know *nothing* about me, or the things I've been through,' Ruby spat. 'You stupid, pampered little princess.'

Scarlet righted herself and flew at her cousin, pushing her back with force. Ruby grabbed the kitchen island to stop herself falling and picked up the utensil holder, throwing it at Scarlet's head. Scarlet just managed to dodge it, leaning to the side as it hit the wall and fell to the ground, its contents spilling everywhere.

'That's *it!*' she screamed and dived at Ruby with a roar.

Ruby leaped at her too, and the pair fell to the floor, hitting and kicking and grabbing each other viciously as they knocked over one of the bar stools.

'You don't get to say jack shit about my life. You don't even deserve to be here,' Scarlet screamed. 'You bullied and stole and lied your way through this family on every level. I watched as you hurt everyone, time and again. And I was the one left picking up the pieces you left behind. You're not worthy of the chances you've been given after all you've done. You and I both know it's just a matter of time before you fuck everything up again, and because of that, I will *never* accept you as part of this firm.' They struggled, each caught in each other's grasp.

'You don't get to choose. You ain't actually part of this family – you're just a fucking extension. This family is my mum, my brothers and me. You're a no one to me. A sad clinger-on desperate to be part of someone else's life. A life you then threaten by sleeping with the fucking enemy. You've brought danger into our home, into our— Argh!'

Scarlet caught her chin with a sharp blow, and Ruby grabbed her hair in return, yanking it down hard.

'You psycho!' Scarlet yelled. 'Get off me!'

'What the *fuck* is this?' bellowed a deep horrified voice.

It was enough to shock them both into a momentary pause, and Connor took the opportunity to drag them apart on the floor.

'Jesus Christ!' he exclaimed. 'I know you hate each other, but for fuck's sake, do you really think this is the time?' He glanced from one to the other, pure disbelief written on his face.

Scarlet looked around in shame. Utensils and stools lay all over her aunt's floor in disarray. One side of her crisp white shirt had pulled loose from her cigarette trousers and the collar stuck up awkwardly, pushing into her neck. One of her shoes was a few feet away from her. She couldn't even remember it coming off. All she could remember was seeing red and going for Ruby, as the final straw was laid on her back.

'I...' She tried to find the words but couldn't.

Ruby stood up and backed away from her, straightening her pyjamas and trying to smooth her wild hair. Her face was still red, and the anger still burned in her eyes. She glared at Scarlet with a level of venom she had never seen in her entire life, and for a moment it shocked her even more deeply than the state they'd got themselves in.

'You've crossed the last line you ever will with me, Scarlet,' Ruby warned, her voice low and full of threat. 'You're gonna pay for this, and for everything else you've done. And much, *much* sooner than you think.'

Her gaze bored into Scarlet's for a moment longer, and then – with those final menacing words – she melted away into the hallway and was gone.

FORTY-SEVEN

The reception desk sat to one side of the white marble waiting room, with the glass coffee table and four chairs placed in the middle of a wide-open space that was otherwise so empty that the constant flow of clicks and clacks that came from the receptionist's keyboard as she typed echoed around the room. Lily sat on one of the black leather chairs, and as she looked over now, she could see the serious-looking woman eyeing her around the side of the monitor, her typing not pausing for a moment. She pursed her lips and looked back to the screen, and Lily turned away, pulling a face.

Another ten minutes passed and the typing finally stopped. The receptionist stood up and walked over with a fake practised smile. 'Ms Hartley will see you now. Please follow me.'

They walked through a door and down a long, carpeted hallway with glass-walled meeting rooms on each side, until they came to the last one. The receptionist slowed and opened this door, moving aside to let Lily through.

'Ms Drew for you,' she announced to the well-dressed, severe-looking woman sitting at the table.

'Thank you, Anita,' she replied in a haughty, bored tone.

Anita left and Lily assessed the woman curiously. 'Do sit down, Ms Drew,' she continued. 'And then tell me what it is I can do for you.'

She wore an expensive and elegant yet casual-looking three-piece suit in green. The rings on her hands were emerald to match, as were her earrings. Lily smiled and took a seat.

'Beautiful earrings,' she commented.

'Thank you. A favourite of mine,' Miranda Hartley replied, watching her curiously.

'Beautiful but not expensive,' Lily continued. 'They're created emeralds, not natural. You can tell by the depth of the colour.'

Miranda's eyebrows shot up in disbelief. 'How observant. And rude,' she replied.

'I apologise,' Lily said. 'I just know a woman who has a more expensive taste than her wallet allows when I see one.'

Miranda laughed, clearly amused by this. 'I can afford to buy whatever emeralds I want, but thank you for the concern,' she said. 'Now, I don't know who you are, or why you're here, but if it is for any reason other than just to insult me then now would be the time to talk. I'm a very busy woman and I will not be wasting much more time here.'

'It would be nice though, wouldn't it? Not to have to choose the cheaper earrings, so that you had more money to play with at the racing,' Lily continued.

Miranda paused, her cheeks turning pink as she stared back at Lily. 'Who are you? Do you work for my ex-husband? Because I have told his lawyer—'

'I neither know nor wish to know your ex-husband. I just want to make you an offer. A good one,' Lily replied.

Miranda's curiosity began to show, despite her wariness. 'Go on.'

'You dabble in all sorts of businesses, I've discovered. Mainly charities. Charities that pay well, that is.' She watched

Miranda's gaze narrow slightly, but the woman didn't try to deny it. 'I imagine when you bought Repton Boxing Club you thought it wouldn't just make you look good, taking care of all those unprivileged young boys, but that it would be a decent earner too.'

Miranda sighed. 'If this is about the club, you're sadly far too late. I'm in the process of arranging its sale with a local building company.'

'Actually, AJ Conway will be pulling out of that sale,' Lily informed her.

'*What?*' Miranda asked, her face aghast. 'No, you're wrong. He wouldn't,' she argued, shaking her head. 'He's already invested a lot of time and effort into these plans.'

'He did,' Lily agreed, nodding seriously. 'You know, it struck me as odd at first, that AJ would be smart enough to have someone in planning in his pocket. The man is a bull. No finesse at all. He don't possess the kind of smarts needed to smooth his way into that kind of relationship.'

Miranda's face fell, and although she tried to keep it together, Lily knew that she'd already guessed where this conversation was going.

'It made much *more* sense, once I discovered who was handling the plans and his relation to you. It really didn't take much digging either. It was all there online. Your dating history, pictures, everything.' She folded her hands in her lap and waited for Miranda's response, knowing by the look on her face that she'd got her – hook, line and sinker.

Miranda shook her head and glared at her. 'So what do you want?' she asked in a bitter tone. 'Clearly, you're here to blackmail me, so go on, name your price.'

Lily frowned. 'You know, if I really was here to blackmail you, you're not doing a very good job of negotiating. You should at least try to pretend you have some kind of upper hand in that situation.'

'Thanks for the tip,' Miranda replied icily. 'Now, I'll say it again: what do you want?'

'To offer you a fair price for the club,' Lily replied.

Miranda blinked. 'Oh. I see.' She shifted in her seat, and Lily could almost see the cogs turning in her brain as she tried to work out where this was all going. 'You wish to take over where AJ is pulling out?' she asked.

'Not exactly. That amount was far too much over value,' Lily replied.

'You're joking?' Miranda retorted, frowning. 'It was significantly *under* value, considering the profit that can be made from the flats. I dropped the price for a sale that was supposed to be no hassle.'

'It *would* have been under value, if those plans were still on the table. But they're not. In fact, none ever will be.' Lily reached into her bag and pulled out a folder of papers, sliding them across the desk. 'The building is now protected, due to the discovery and official documentation of a very rare plant on site.'

'You can't be serious—' Miranda spat, grabbing the folder off the table and ripping it open. Her eyes scanned the first page of the report and widened in horror as she saw that Lily was, in fact, very serious. 'This is absurd,' she cried. 'It's not real.'

'It's very real. Feel free to check the government's conservation lists. This building cannot be torn down and is protected from any future plans to build on the land,' Lily said calmly. 'And with that in mind, I'd like to make you an offer.'

Miranda looked up to her, her eyes burning with fear and anger. Lily smiled.

'You need the money tied up in that place. You don't want to keep on such a financial burden. Without planning to change anything, that place is worth maybe eight hundred thousand. I'll give you nine, if the deal is signed and completed within a week. After that, my offer drops back down to eight.'

'But it was about to be bought for three million,' Miranda said, her hope dying with each word.

Lily shrugged. 'That's life for you. What something is worth one day is not necessarily guaranteed the next.'

She stood up. 'My details are in that folder. If you want the full nine, I suggest you get the paperwork drawn up and over to me quickly. It's the best offer you'll get.'

The defeat was already clear in Miranda's eyes, and Lily turned to walk away, the dark smile of triumph hidden as she made her way out of the building.

FORTY-EIGHT

Cillian shuffled up in the bed, wincing as the action pulled at his internal stitches. He'd been awake for a couple of days now, and with each passing hour, his recovery was improving.

Waking up in itself had been an eventful experience. The last thing he could remember was being down in the bunker, the pain of having his body cut open and operated on by a complete psychopath without even a painkiller to take the edge off. He remembered trying to fight and eventually giving up as the hopelessness of the situation overwhelmed him. He remembered realising that he was going to die down there, cold and alone. And as he drifted into an agonising, light-headed darkness, he remembered seeing Connor. He'd thought it was his imagination, some comfort offered up by his subconscious brain in his last few minutes of life. Except Connor hadn't left him to slip peacefully away, holding his hand as he went. They'd forced him to move, the pain excruciating as they dragged him through the halls. That was the last thing he could remember.

When he'd woken up in hospital, he'd been on high alert, assuming he was still there, assuming that he'd only blacked out for a few moments. He'd cried out in panic, scared and confused, but Connor had been there right by his side. He'd calmed him and told him he was safe, and he'd never been so glad to see his brother in his entire life.

Connor had quickly told him to play dumb and pretend he remembered nothing just before the doctors swooped in, alerted by the change in his monitors. Ray and Connor had told the police they'd known nothing of what had happened, only that they'd received a call from Cillian begging for help and to be picked up on a quiet country road somewhere. This road was strategically far away from the bunker so that they would never find it and the horrors it housed. So that they would never find Joe's body, his skull caved in by Connor's bat.

Since then, after getting the full story, Cillian had spun a tale – half lie, half truth – to cover their tracks. He told the truth that he'd been drugged and taken unexpectedly, but he pretended he didn't know who had done it. And while he couldn't pretend he didn't remember being cut open, he told them he'd been blindfolded and then driven around before being dumped on the roadside, luckily with his phone. It was a tall tale, but while he was in this state and as long as he stuck to it, there wasn't much the doctors and police could do but take him at his word.

'You OK?' came a soft voice from his side. Billie touched his arm and reached up to adjust his pillows. 'Here – let me do it.'

He allowed her to help him, grateful that she was there. Between her and Connor, they hadn't left him alone since he'd awoken. His mother had been in of course, but he'd sent her away after she'd told him about Ray. Shock didn't quite cover the first reaction that had hit him when she'd laid the truth bare. Disgust, horror, rage, none of them quite fitted, but it was somewhere in that ballpark. He wasn't quite sure how to process it. How to process *any* of the last few days. So much had happened all at once, and although physically he was healing well, mentally he was still reeling.

Connor walked back into the room juggling an armful of canned drinks and crisp packets from the vending machine. ''Ere we go,' he said, dropping them on the bottom of the bed. 'Got your favourite.' He handed Cillian a Dr Pepper, and he was rewarded with a tired grin.

'Thanks.' This had been their favourite pop when they'd been teenagers. 'So what's going on?' he asked.

'What do you mean?' Connor asked, opening a bag of crisps and popping one in his mouth, gesturing for Billie to help herself to the pile on the bed.

'With the firm. Life outside this place. You guys must be really busy without me.'

Connor looked out of the window, crunching another crisp before he answered. 'Nothing much. Ain't nothing we can't handle. You just need to rest.'

'To be honest, I'd welcome the distraction. At least update me, so I know where we are when I get out of here,' he asked. He didn't want to think about what he'd been through. He didn't want to think about what Lily had admitted either.

He balled one fist and flexed his arm, looking at the veins that ran beneath the surface of his skin. Hating that Ray's blood was now running through them. Hating that Ray's blood always *had* run through them. Billie squeezed his other hand, and he forced his body to relax.

'I'll update you whenever there's anything to tell. You know about the club. Hopefully we're buying it. Scarlet says *she* has plans to turn it into more of a moneymaker, while keeping it the safe haven it always has been. But I dunno what they are yet. I ain't exactly gonna ask her,' he said gloomily.

'Come on, guys,' Billie said, interrupting. '*She* has a name. She's your mum.'

'Right now she's just she,' Cillian replied firmly.

Billie exhaled loudly through her nose and looked at both

brothers. 'Look, I know you're still coming to terms with everything she's told you.'

'Yeah, just a bit,' Cillian snapped sarcastically.

'And you've every right to be pissed off,' Billie continued placatingly. 'It's a lot to take in. But remember, she's still your mum. She did what she felt she had to do at the time, for her own reasons, and I'll bet they were because she was trying to protect you, the way she always does.'

'It don't excuse it, Billie,' Cillian argued.

'I'm not saying it does. And if she was a mum like mine, who didn't give a shit enough about you to even bother being in your life, then I'd say crack on. Condemn her if that makes you feel better. But she ain't. She's a diamond, your mum. She ain't perfect, but she has *been there*. For the highs and lows, for the everydays, for the bigs and the littles. And she has never let you down. So all I'm saying is try to remember that too. Because she, more than most people, deserves a fair trial when you're holding court in your heads.' She eyed them meaningfully, each in turn.

Cillian looked down and clamped his jaw. He knew she was right, to a degree. Lily had always gone above and beyond as a parent. Annoyingly so at times. And to Billie – whose mother was actively absent and more interested in playing games than being a parent – this was more precious than gold.

But Lily had betrayed them. Not so much by hiding them from Ray, but by continuing to hide the truth from them for all these years. He felt betrayed by the one person he'd always trusted most in the entire world. By the one person he thought held back no secrets from him. And he had no idea how to move on from that. Neither of them did.

He patted Billie's hand and chose not to reply. Connor was also tellingly silent, and he knew the same thoughts were likely running through his mind.

'I've gotta shoot. I just wanted to pop in to make sure you

were OK. Do you need anything?' Connor asked, standing up and straightening his suit jacket.

'Nah, all good. I'll see you later,' Cillian replied.

Connor nodded to Billie and then left, so they were alone once more.

'I'm sorry,' she said, after a few moments. 'I didn't mean to make him leave.'

'You didn't,' he reassured her. 'He really does need to go. Without me, there's double the work to keep up. And he ain't gonna ask for help right now.'

'Scarlet would give him a hand, wouldn't she?' Billie asked, pushing her sunshine-blonde hair back behind her ear with a concerned look. 'Or is there anything I can do to help?'

'Yeah, Scarlet's around. And Rubes. He's alright, don't worry. Besides...' He looked down to her hand in his. 'I could do with you here,' he admitted quietly.

He wasn't sure what it was about Billie, but almost from the time they'd met, he'd been able to pull his guard down around her. More so than he even did in front of his family. They were two of a kind. Polar opposites, yet similar souls, and these souls connected in a way he'd never known was even possible before her. She was his one. He knew that as certainly as he knew his heart was beating. And nothing else mattered.

'You're still there, in that room?' she asked, her bright blue eyes piercing into his intently.

'Every time I close my eyes,' he admitted.

Whenever he tried to sleep, he was back there, tied down to that table, feeling the agony of the tools Joe had used to slice through his flesh. Each time he grew so weary that he let go of the mental armour he protected himself with, he was trapped. He woke screaming and sweating, back here in this hospital bed and then, awake, he was once again safe. But sleep could not be avoided for long. And it was always there, waiting. It helped to know Billie was there, to feel her pull him awake when the nightmare got too much and his screams spilled out into reality.

'I ain't going anywhere,' she replied, settling back in her chair.

Cillian nodded.

There was a knock on the door, and he looked up to see Ruby enter. He smiled, glad to see her. 'Well, if you ain't a sight for sore eyes,' he said warmly.

'Back at you. It's good to see you awake. You're boring as hell to talk to when you're under anaesthetic, I tell ya,' she joked.

'Charming as always,' he replied drily.

She grinned and pushed her wild red curls back off her face, and her bracelet glinted in the light.

'You're wearing it,' he remarked, gesturing towards it.

'Yeah, 'course,' she replied, looking down at it and then back up to him, clamping her mouth shut.

'I'm gonna go grab us a coffee. Do you want one, Ruby?' Billie said tactfully.

'Nah, I'm good. Thanks,' Ruby replied.

Billie smiled and stood up, then left the room and closed the door quietly behind her.

'So, you holding up OK?' she asked, her eyes looking over him critically.

'I'll get there,' he replied. 'Another couple of days and I should be out. Apparently despite the fact a psycho hacked me up for parts, I was sewn back together quite easily.'

'Hacked up for parts,' Ruby repeated with a roll of the eyes. 'Honestly, it was one kidney – you do exaggerate.'

They both grinned, and Cillian narrowed his eyes at her. 'So funny, ain't ya, little Rubes?'

'I think so,' she replied. 'Nah, but seriously, you all good?'

'Yeah. I lost a lot of blood, which was actually more of a worry to them than the kidney. But of course...'

'Yeah, I know.' She looked away and bit her lip.

'So that's all good now,' he said, moving swiftly on. 'Just need a couple more days' rest then I'll be back up and running.'

'You won't be back to work though, will you?' she asked, surprised.

'No reason why not.' Cillian sniffed and looked out the window. 'I'll never compete at boxing again,' he admitted. A stab of anger hit him in the gut. It wasn't that he even wanted to compete, particularly. But he felt angry that he no longer had the choice. 'Life don't change that much with one kidney, but whereas before if something happened, I'd have one to fall back on, now this is it. Have to be forever careful not to be punched too hard in the remaining kidney or I'm fucked.' He pulled a face. 'Not ideal. But there we go.'

'No, that's really not ideal in our line of work,' Ruby said with a frown. 'Kickings are pretty regular for you, aren't they?'

'Hey,' he said, pointing his finger at her. 'We dish 'em out – we rarely get them.'

'Fair enough. You can still train though, can't you? Ain't that your thing anyway? The fitness side of it all.'

'Yeah. I did like to spar though. Me and Barnes...' He stopped as the memory of Barnes's body hit him full force and closed his eyes for a moment.

It was the only thing that bothered him about the fact the police would never find that place. Joe's body could rot down there for all eternity, for all he cared. But Barnes had deserved so much more than he'd ended up with. He'd been a good man with family and friends who'd loved him. But instead of being laid to rest the way he should, he was still down there slowly rotting in the dank darkness of that horrifying place. It just wasn't right.

'I know Connor and Billie have you covered, but if there's anything else you need, like, you know. Well, let me know, yeah?' Ruby offered.

'Ah, thanks, Rubes. Look at you looking out for your brother, eh? It's usually me looking out for you.' He gave her a wink and smiled.

'Half-brother now, I guess.' She looked down but not quick enough for him to miss the fleeting lost look that crossed her face.

'Hey,' he said sharply. 'Look at me.' He waited for her to do so. 'I'm your brother. There ain't no "half" about it. That's the way it's always been and always will be. Blood may be thicker than water, but roots are thicker than blood. And ours have grown together, intertwined at every turn. There ain't nothing that can change that. You hear me?'

For a moment, he thought he saw her eyes glisten, but she blinked and her composure returned. 'I hear ya,' she said. 'Anyway, like I said. Anything you need.'

'I'm OK. Just keep me in the loop with what's going on in the firm.'

''Course.'

Her phone beeped, and she pulled it out of her pocket and glanced at the screen. 'I've got to go – there's an issue at the factory.' She stood up to leave.

'Look after everyone for me, Rubes,' Cillian said with a half-smile. 'Keep 'em all safe till I get back, yeah?'

A strange look crossed her face. 'Oh I will, Cillian. I plan to do exactly that.'

FORTY-NINE

Saturday morning came around quickly for Jenny Ascough. All week she had plotted and planned, packed and repacked and been in and out of the salon making sure her nail and wax game were on top form. Her hair was freshly washed and styled, and her make-up was perfect – as it should be, after spending over an hour on it. She'd been up since just gone five, unable to sleep, and now, at nearly eleven, as she downed the last of her third service-station coffee, her satnav told her that she was only a couple of minutes away from her destination.

She drove on down the long straight road, flat green space spanning out endlessly to one side and towards the sea on the other, and the hotel came into view. She pulled in a breath, her heart doing somersaults as she realised how close she was to her goal. It had been a long time coming, and now it was almost in reach, she wasn't quite sure what to do with herself.

She hadn't been sure that she was reading the signs right at first, but then she'd talked it all out with her neighbour over coffee, and she'd realised that she had. It was all there. He'd laid the path before her, shown her the hotel, given her a long mean-ingful look as he suggested that she too should take a weekend off by the sea. He'd practically begged her to take the first step. What other explanation could there be? As her friend had said, there was no smoke without fire. And if she didn't take this chance now, she'd end up regretting it.

The road split, and she took the fork that led down towards the large regal-looking hotel on the cliff. It was such a romantic spot. This was certainly going to be a story to top all stories. She let her mind wander, imagined them at parties, people asking them how they'd got together. They'd laugh and look at each other, then trip over each other's words as they described the way it had all come together.

The picture in her mind shifted to an image of them a few years older, telling the story to their kids at bedtime, their hands clasped together over the covers as they tucked them in and read a bedtime story.

She shook her head with a laugh. She was getting ahead of herself. This might never get that far. Most relationships didn't, statistically. But part of her thought it might. After all, something that started off in such a grand way as their relationship was going to would surely be something worth keeping and building on, wouldn't it?

She parked the car and took a deep breath, trying to calm her racing heart. 'Time to be cool, Jenny,' she whispered to herself. 'Time to be calm.'

Was she doing the right thing? Was she crazy, doing this? She could still have been imagining it. But it didn't seem imagined, the moments between them, the way he'd shown her the hotel, told her he was going alone and then suggested she should get to the sea this weekend too, all while holding her gaze. Her friends had confirmed her thoughts too, both her neighbour over coffee and her best friend from back home over text. Surely all three of them couldn't be wrong.

'This is nuts,' she muttered to herself with a giggle.

She got out and retrieved her bag from the boot, then made

her way up to the entrance and into the lobby. Here she looked around cautiously. This wasn't how she wanted their meeting to be, her feeling all sweaty from the drive and with her bag in hand. She wanted to go to the room and freshen up. The spa was where she hoped she'd find him. She'd gone all out on her new bikini and matching sarong and for once felt rather glamorous. It was a blue-and-red pattern, a red that matched her hair and the lipstick she'd bought just for the occasion. In her mind, she'd glide into the spa area, a bright vision next to the pool, and he'd see her and his eyes would light up.

But then again, that could just as easily not happen at all. He might be out taking a walk along the cliff or down on the beach or even just asleep in his room, making use of the down time. Either way, it didn't hurt to try. If he wasn't there, he would probably turn up at some point – what was the point of booking a spa hotel if you weren't going to use the spa? – and if for some reason he didn't, she'd try her luck in the dining room at dinner time.

She checked in and went up to her room, then spent some time admiring it, along with the view. John had come down the night before, and she had considered doing the same, but one night had cost her an arm and a leg already.

Half an hour and an outfit change later, Ascough was ready to go. She looked in the mirror one last time and checked her deep red lipstick, then pulled the hotel-room robe around her and made her way down to the spa. The hotel was bigger than she'd expected, as was the spa, but eventually she found her way through to the pool area.

Walking in nervously, she looked around. John wasn't there, as far as she could see. She pulled off her robe and laid it down on one of the loungers on the side of the pool and then wandered around checking it all out. A walkway arched over the pool and she followed this, realising that there was also an outdoor pool and jacuzzi just beyond. As her gaze swept over this, she noticed a mess of brown hair poking over the top of a lounger facing away from her outside.

Her heart rate immediately quickened and she stopped dead in her tracks. It was him – she was sure of it. She swallowed and forced herself to stay on mission, despite the fact her nerves made her want to bolt back to her room and hide. This was what she'd come here for. This was what they both wanted, even if he hadn't been brave enough to say it out loud. The conversation she'd had about it over coffee came back to her now as her nerves started to wobble.

How much clearer can he be, Jenny? You spend all your time together, you make each other laugh, you have these moments where you just stare at each other. He's definitely into you. And this weekend is basically an open invite. He's begging you to take the leap. Maybe he feels that he can't, being your boss.

Maybe... she'd replied.

If you don't go, you'll have missed the chance of a lifetime. In fact, I order you to go. I'll come and help you pack and then you are getting in your car and driving down there to tell him how you feel.

But what if—

What if nothing. There is only one reason all of this would come together the way it has. This is your chance at happiness, Jenny. Only a coward would shy away from this chance. And you are not a coward.

She took a deep breath and lifted her chin, forcing her shoulders back. Her friend was right – she needed to be brave. It was now or never.

Finding the strength from somewhere, Ascough forced one foot in front of the other, her heart beating so fast she thought it might actually break through her chest. She reached the glass doors that led outside and stepped through them into the bright sunshine beyond. Turning towards the head she'd seen, she felt a small thrill shoot through her as his whole side profile came into view. It was definitely him. He was lying back with his eyes closed, soaking up the sun, his face more relaxed and boyish than she'd ever seen it at work. She smiled at this. He was even more handsome without the day-to-day stress they handled creasing his frown.

As she began to walk towards him, something seemed to alert him to her presence and he opened his eyes and turned towards her. As his eyes met hers, her whole world seemed to freeze in place for a moment. For one tantalising, perfect moment. This was it. This was the moment they would talk about for the rest of their days together. Their perfect beginning. Her heart sang and her spirits soared as she smiled at him and took one step closer.

Recognition registered in his bright green eyes and they widened just as she'd anticipated, but the elated smile she'd assumed would accompany that wasn't quite there. Instead, in its place was an expression of something like horror. Her own smile began to falter as confusion set in.

Oh God, had she been wrong? She couldn't have been, could she? He'd told her to get away to the sea, hinted that he wanted her there. Practically begged her with his eyes... But suddenly she wasn't so sure. All her doubts came rushing back in at once.

Her smile turning sheepish, she started to form the apology in her head, hoping that if she just told him the truth that he'd find the whole thing funny and rather cute. It could still be salvaged. But as she drew closer and opened her mouth, someone else caught her attention. A young woman, just stepping out of the pool nearby. It wasn't the fact she was out there; there were other people too, but something about her caught Ascough's eye. Something familiar.

She stopped and looked at the woman, her brow puckering as she tried to place her. She was beautiful and striking with her long raven hair and pale flawless skin. As she walked up the pool steps, her lithe body glistened with droplets of water, giving her an almost ethereal glow. Her movements were graceful, and her black two-piece was timeless and elegant.

John still hadn't moved, frozen in his seat, just staring at her with wide-eyed horror as she watched the other woman walk over to him. As she watched the woman lie down on the lounger that was pushed up close to his, and as her hand reached out to touch his leg.

The realisation hit her like a truck. They were together.

She swallowed, feeling sick, a roaring sound filling her ears as she realised in blind panic what a fool she'd been. Suddenly, the bikini she'd picked out with such care seemed garish, and the red lipstick on her face cheap and tacky. Her body confidence plummeted and she wished she'd kept her robe with her – wished the ground would just swallow her whole, or that time would reverse so she didn't need to be here at all, watching him stare at her in the way he still was. Watching the beautiful creature by his side.

The woman stirred, asking him something, and when he didn't answer, she looked around, her gaze following his. And as her cool grey-blue eyes met Ascough's, it finally clicked who she was.

She was Scarlet Drew. The woman who'd got away with murder, who'd walked out of their station a free woman despite being known as guilty, because the evidence in the locker had disappeared the night before her trial.

Suddenly, with sickening clarity, it all clicked into place. And as her gaze moved back to John's, she finally understood the root of the horror on his face.

They were together. He'd taken the evidence.

Stepping backward, desperate to get away from this nightmare, she turned and fled.

FIFTY

'Shit, shit, *shit!*' John paced the hallway just outside the spa, trying and failing to work out what to do.

Scarlet came through the door, looking up and down the hallway until she saw him and then hurried over. 'Where is she?' she asked.

'I don't know – I lost her,' he said with a groan, rubbing his face with both hands before dropping them to his hips.

He'd been floored when he saw her approach outside. It had been the last thing he'd expected to see in a million years and he'd floundered, taken by surprise. Scarlet had been in the pool, and as much as he'd wanted to move, to do or say *anything* that would stop that car crash of a situation happening, he couldn't. He'd just had to sit there and watch as it all unfolded, as Ascough saw her and the recognition dawned. Then he'd watched as her shock turned to horror, as the penny finally dropped, the way they'd all hoped would never happen.

She'd run out, and it had taken a second for him to slip on his shoes and grab his shirt and make his way after her. He'd called out as he entered the indoor section of the spa and she'd opened the door at the other end. She'd turned at her name, and as their eyes had met, he'd seen the devastation and accusation there, before she slipped through the door and out of sight.

'What shall we do?' Scarlet asked, running her hands through her hair. 'We need to find her. Shall we split up?'

'Yeah, you search this floor. I'll try everywhere else. Listen' – he grabbed her arm as she made to move off – 'if you find her, call me. She won't listen to you.'

Scarlet pulled a face of exaggerated agreement. 'No shit,' she said sarcastically. 'Don't worry, I'll call you.' She waved her phone in front of him then jogged off down the hallway and around the corner.

He turned the other way and put one hand to his head, stressed. Where would she go now? To her room, he guessed. Somewhere she could lock the door and be alone to take all this in and work out what to do. He set off towards reception.

Why was she even here? He kicked himself for being so stupid as to let her know where he was going this weekend. But never in a million years had he imagined she'd follow him down here. Who did that kind of thing – turned up unannounced on someone else's weekend away?

Luckily there was no queue at reception and the girl who'd checked them in the night before was waiting with a smile. 'Can I help you?'

'Yes. Please,' he said urgently. 'There's a guest here by the name of Jenifer Ascough. Could you tell me what her room number is please?'

The woman frowned slightly. 'I'm sorry, sir, I can't give out room details. I can call up to her room for you though, if you'd like me to pass on a message?'

'No, no, thank you,' he replied quickly. 'I um...' He considered pulling rank, using his police status to get what he needed, but this would just cause more of a damning trail than there already was, down the line. 'I'll find her later.'

He turned away and walked outside, pulling out his phone.

He called her number, but after two rings, the call was cut off. He tried a second time, and she cut him off again. Making a sound of exasperation, he headed over to a bench to the side of the door and sat down, putting his head in his hands. After a few seconds he called Scarlet.

'Have you found her?' she asked hopefully.

'No, they won't give me her room number. I'm guessing she's not still down here either,' he replied.

'Not that I can see,' she responded. 'I've done a lap but no sign. Listen, John...' She hesitated before continuing. 'We need to go home. I know you need to speak to her – maybe you can even reason with her – but we need to get out of here and go underground until we know what's happening. And we need to call Lil. We need to prepare for the fallout – make a plan.'

She was right. He eyed the car park and his gaze landed on Ascough's car. She would probably be thinking along the same lines. She wouldn't want to stay here now, after what she'd just seen.

He nodded. 'OK. Can you head to the room and start packing up? I'm going to stay here for a bit, see if she leaves. Cut her off on her way to the car.'

'Good idea. I'll call Lil while I pack. Keep me updated.'

The line went dead and he slipped the phone back into the pocket of his shorts. Realising his shirt was still undone, he quickly fastened the buttons and started turning the situation over in his head. This was the exact outcome they'd been avoiding. He still couldn't understand how it had all happened this way, but it had. And now they were in deep shit.

They'd hidden their relationship so carefully, to make sure no one ever discovered what he'd done to save Scarlet from prison. But now Ascough knew. And it had taken her barely a few seconds to make the connection. He'd seen it. She would report him and he would be investigated and most likely jailed himself. He'd be stripped of his career and could serve years behind bars for this. And that would put Scarlet at risk too. He put his face back in his hands, feeling the overwhelming burden of what was happening begin to crush him from within.

He needed to speak to Ascough, beg her to keep their secret. Beg her, basically, to go rogue. Even as he thought this, he knew she'd never agree. It wouldn't matter what he offered, or what Lily was likely to offer, she was a woman of her word. She'd taken an oath which she would uphold to the end. He would have upheld that oath too once. Before all this. Before he met Scarlet. But everything had changed since then. Love sometimes did that to a person.

The main doors opened and he looked up to see Ascough charging through with her bag. She'd thrown on a dress and had rubbed off her make-up, her cheeks red and flustered. She looked like a completely different person from the one on the deck ten minutes before. He stood up, and she glanced at him, her gaze angry and hurt, and he realised she'd been crying.

'Jenny, please—' he started, walking after her as she yanked her bag down the steps.

'No,' she shouted, carrying on. 'I'm not interested in hearing your lies.'

'I'm not going to lie to you,' he replied, despite knowing that was exactly what he would have to now do. He jogged in front of her in an attempt to block her way. She just circled around him. 'Please, just listen. It's not what you think.'

Now she stopped and turned abruptly to look at him. 'No? It's not you and Scarlet Drew out here on a secret romantic getaway? The same Scarlet Drew you stole evidence for, so that she wouldn't go down for a murder she one hundred per cent *did* commit?'

'I, look—' He exhaled heavily. 'Yes. That is Scarlet, and yes, we're here together. But this is a new development.'

'Oh, please,' she scoffed, turning to continue towards her car.

He hurried after her. 'Jenny, it really is. We bumped into each other recently, we got chatting on a personal level and it just happened. This wasn't going on back then – this has *nothing* to do with that.'

'Do you *really* expect me to believe that?' she exclaimed, stopping and turning to him once more. 'You expect me to believe that this abomination of a relationship is brand new, and there just happened to be someone else in the station last year that cared enough to risk their own neck to steal evidence for her. Yeah? That's what you're telling me?' she asked with frank disbelief.

'I know it's a lot to take in, but yes, that is what I'm telling you. And I really need you to believe me,' he pleaded desperately. 'I really need you to remember who I am. You know me.'

Ascough stared at him for a few long moments, misery and accusation in her eyes. 'Well, I *don't* believe you,' she said brokenly. 'And I don't think anyone else in the station will either. I mean, *Scarlet Drew*?' she asked, her tone bruised and incredulous. 'Really? Sure, she's beautiful,' she added bitterly, 'but she's a *murderer*, John. A genuine, solidly proven murderer, from the top ranks of a known criminal firm. And you got into bed with her. I thought you were better than that.' She closed her eyes with a look of grief. 'God, I can't believe I was so *stupid*.'

'What do you mean?' he asked.

'I thought...' She shook her head and then looked up to the sky with a humourless laugh. 'Ah, I thought you had feelings for *me*. I thought there was something between us.' Her cheeks reddened as she laughed again, that hollow bitter laugh.

John frowned. 'Is that why you came here?'

'Yes. That and because my neighbour egged me on,' she said irritably. 'God, I feel like an idiot.'

'What do you mean she egged you on?' John asked, confused.

'My neighbour – she moved in about a week ago, introduced herself as new to the area and asked if I could show her around. We got talking about guys...' Ascough reddened and shook her head with a sigh. 'I told her about *you*, that I thought there might be some spark between us, and we got into it and she got me all hyped up – and then when I told her about you saying I should get away, she said it was a sign that you wanted me to come here. Which was clearly completely off the mark and I don't know why I got so caught up in her excitement.' She closed her eyes briefly. 'But I did.'

John frowned. It didn't make sense to him at all. Why would some new neighbour be so hooked on setting her up in a situation like this without really knowing anything about them?

As if following his thoughts, Ascough swiftly moved to excuse her. 'It's my fault, not hers. She was so excited and certain, I just allowed myself to get swept up in it all like an idiot. I guess Ruby's just an old romantic at heart and wanted to see something here for me that wasn't really there.'

John's whole body tensed as she uttered the name. 'Did you just say Ruby?' he asked.

'Yeah, that's her name.'

He felt a coldness trail down his spine. 'What does Ruby look like?'

Ascough frowned. 'Small, pale, red curly hair.' She looked him up and down, her fury and the betrayal she felt still bubbling just underneath her embarrassment. 'But that's really no concern of yours. Get out of my way, John. I may have been a fool coming here, but I'm certainly not fool enough to stay and listen to any more lies.'

His heart dropped like a stone as he realised with sickening clarity what had happened. He remembered the calculating way Ruby's dark eyes had stared at him across the table at the Sunday lunch as he'd told them all about Ascough – as he'd given her all the information she'd need to use her against him.

He'd told her of Ascough's feelings, her desperation to create something more between them. He'd told her they worked the same shifts, even that she lived in Tooting. All she would have had to do was follow her back and play to her kindness to get close enough to bring him and Scarlet down. He'd been such a fool.

He turned and wiped both hands down his face, reeling. How was he going to tell Scarlet?

Ascough moved off once more and unlocked her car. They had reached it now. He moved in front of her again.

'Jenny, she's not who you think she is. She's Scarlet's cousin.' He watched as Ascough's jaw dropped and she stared off into the distance for a moment. He grimaced. 'It's complicated. Look, she's—'

But Ascough cut him off with a bitter laugh and a piercing look. 'Honestly, at this point, finding out she's not really my neighbour and that I've been played is the least surprising thing I've discovered today. You guys obviously have some enemies that want to see your secret uncovered.' She threw her bag in the boot and slammed it shut.

'Jenny, please. You can't tell anyone about this. If you care about me at all—'

'*If* I care about you?' Her eyebrows shot up, and she shook her head. 'I think we both know I *care*, John. That was my mistake.' She looked at him, and her lip wobbled for a moment.

He watched her deliberate, saw her waver for just a fraction of a second. 'I'm sorry,' he said softly. 'I care about you a lot too, as a friend. I have never wanted to hurt you. And—'

'That's all great, John,' she cut him off. He saw his window of opportunity close as resolve formed on her face. 'But at the end of the day, whatever *you* are now, I'm still a police officer. And I have a duty to uphold.' She opened her car door and steeled herself. 'For the sake of the friendship we had, I'll give you the rest of the weekend to get your affairs in order. But first thing Monday morning I'll be reporting everything. And you *will* be arrested pending investigation.'

She got into the car and shut the door, then started the engine and pulled away. John stood back and watched her leave – watching the last chance he had of saving himself and Scarlet drive off towards London.

What the hell was he going to do now?

He turned and looked back to the hotel. What was Scarlet going to make of this?

He started to walk back, then paused as another thought hit him. What were Lily and the rest of the firm going to think of this? Ruby he couldn't care less about. She'd made her choices and she could deal with whatever came back on her because of them. But Ascough? He glanced back towards the road, suddenly worried for her. Because she now held knowledge that could destroy one of the Drews, and Scarlet was on the phone right now telling Lily all about it. Telling the head of the family. The very deadly, very serious head of the firm, who abided by no law made by man. What was *she* going to do about it? Was Ascough now public enemy number one? Was her life now in danger?

FIFTY-ONE

Ruby watched her phone ring out once more, ignoring it as she had the last five times. It was Ascough. She had no more use for the woman, and she certainly wasn't going to waste her time explaining herself. Jenny Ascough had been nothing more than a stepping stone. A tool she had used to get the ball rolling in the right direction. And judging by the frantic number of calls, it looked as though her plan had worked.

It had been so easy. She'd followed John and Ascough back from work the day after he'd given her the idea. She'd watched as the lonely young woman's spark died a little when they parted, and as she walked home alone to her little block of flats. The buzzer was broken, so she'd been able to walk in and out of Ascough's building as she pleased. She'd been there, the next morning, bumped into her in the hallway as if by accident as Ascough left for work. She'd spun the woman a tale of a girl coming to the big city for the first time, someone in need of a friend. They'd had drinks that night, and Ruby had made sure to secure another couple of coffees in the coming days.

At first, she'd expected this to be a long play. She'd thought it would take time to gain enough confidence from Ascough to be able to sway her, but then the perfect opportunity had fallen straight into her lap. The weekend away. Ascough had already half convinced herself that John was hinting for her to go. She wouldn't have actually gone on her own, but considering the desperation her heart was already mired in, it hadn't taken too much to push her over the edge. Ruby had put on a good show of excitement and confidence, spinning her a tale of perfect fairy-tale romance. She'd insisted on Ascough going, becoming downright pushy at one point. She'd expected some resistance, assumed that this time would be more a test of how far she could go in pushing the other woman. But Ascough had just been so eager to believe her words – to believe that they were true – that she'd not stopped to consider that Ruby was still basically a stranger.

Ruby had invited herself in, helped her pack her bags and waved her off as she drove away to her doom.

Now, her phone rang again, but this time as she looked down at the screen, she smiled coldly. On the third ring, she picked it up, put it to her ear and waited with anticipation.

'You bitch,' Scarlet spat down the phone. 'You stupid, reckless, psychotic *bitch*.'

'Hello to you too, cousin,' she responded, her smile clear in her tone. 'Having a bad day?'

'How could you do that?' she demanded. 'Seriously, what the fuck are you playing at?'

'Playing at?' Ruby asked. 'Nothing. I'm not *playing* at all. In fact, I've actually taken all this quite seriously.'

'You are an *idiot*, Ruby,' Scarlet shouted, enraged. 'This isn't a game; this is my *life*. *John's* life. You've put us in serious danger, do you not understand that? Do you not understand what you've done?'

'I understand completely,' Ruby said, standing up and looking out of the window of the small flat she'd rented to use as a hiding place whilst the storm she'd created raged. 'I've done what was necessary for the family.'

'For the *family*?' Scarlet exclaimed. 'This has *damaged* the family.'

'No, it's damaged *you*,' Ruby replied in a matter-of-fact tone. 'It's damaged the outsider *you* brought in, the *threat* you brought in to this family. He'll pay his price and be gone, and hopefully you will too. I did warn you, Scarlet. Remember?'

There was a short silence on the other end of the phone, and she used the opportunity to hang up. Scarlet had made her bed, and she'd made her enemies. She'd put herself in this position.

She sat down in the armchair in the middle of the room and folded her hands in her lap. Her work was done. And now all she had to do was stay here and wait for the fallout to be over and done with, so she could re-enter their world a harsh but necessary hero.

FIFTY-TWO

Scarlet pulled up to her aunt's house, and as she and John got out of the car and walked up the drive, the door opened and Lily appeared. Lily's gaze swept the street and she ushered them inside.

'Get in – quickly,' she ordered.

'It's OK, she's not saying anything until Monday,' Scarlet replied in a stressed, tired voice.

'So she says,' Lily said wryly. She closed the door behind them and led them through to the lounge, where Connor, Andy and George had already gathered.

'Run through everything that happened again,' Lily instructed, sitting down and gesturing for them to sit on the remaining empty sofa.

Scarlet sighed heavily and took her place, squeezing John's hand as he sat beside her. 'We were there enjoying the sun and the pool and then suddenly she just appeared out of nowhere. She recognised me straight away. It would be hard not to. I was news of the week throughout the station when they had to let me go.'

'And then what?' Lily pressed.

'She bolted. We ran after her, lost her, then John found her and tried to reason with her.' Scarlet held her hands out help-lessly and shook her head. 'She's a straight shooter. We're lucky she's given us till Monday.'

'I don't understand. Why was she there?' Connor asked. 'Did she already suspect? Was she trying to catch you out?'

Scarlet exchanged a look with John. It was only after her initial call with Lily that John had told her about Ruby. Enraged, she'd finished packing, got in the car and called Ruby from there. She'd been too furious to call Lily back, deciding instead to tell her in person.

'No. She didn't suspect. No one did – we were careful,' Scarlet said. 'It was Ruby.'

Everyone in the room frowned and looked at each other.

'Ruby?' Lily questioned, astonished.

'Ruby used everything John shared about Ascough that Sunday at lunch. She followed her home, pretended to be a new neighbour, befriended her and set us up,' she said. 'I rang her on my way here – she confirmed it. Quite proudly actually.'

'Surely not,' Connor replied, shocked. 'She's a lot of things, but she wouldn't do that. Would she?' He looked to his mother.

Scarlet stared hard at Lily, the weight of her accusation naked in her eyes. None of them had mentioned hers and Ruby's fight earlier in the week to Lily. She'd kept her mouth closed out of concern mainly, not wanting to add to Lily's burdens. She imagined Ruby hadn't said anything, fearful of any comeback. But this she couldn't keep back. Ruby had purposely sabotaged them, and Lily needed to see it for what it was.

'I told you something would happen,' she said in a low, heavy voice.

'You did.' Lily's answer was clipped but she didn't argue.

Scarlet couldn't fully blame Lily for bringing Ruby back into the fold. She knew the situation played on her one weakness. Lily had been in the impossible situation of having to choose between protecting her daughter and protecting her family from her daughter – but her daughter *was* family. They were one and the same.

But now here they were, stuck in this nightmare of Ruby's making, just as Scarlet had predicted. Stuck in a place that there was no way back from. And it was she and John who would pay the price.

Lily turned to John, her expression heavy and weary. 'This woman. She said she won't say anything to anyone until Monday. How much do you trust her to keep to that?' she asked.

'Explicitly,' he replied. 'She's a good person and sticks to her word. It's what makes her a good copper.'

Scarlet heard the sadness in his words and felt for him. He'd valued Ascough as a friend, she knew. She thought back to the look of hurt that had passed the other woman's features by the pool as her eyes had rested on their clasped hands and felt a flood of pity. She clearly loved him, and seeing them together must have hit her hard. And as much as she joked about Ascough's crush on John, she wasn't so heartless that she'd wish that feeling on her.

'Do you have her address?' Lily asked, her dark brown eyes watching him carefully.

John immediately tensed. 'Why?' he demanded.

Lily and Connor exchanged a look. 'Because we need to make sure she never tells anyone,' she replied evenly.

John's frown deepened. 'And how are you planning on doing that? I won't let you kill her,' he said fiercely. 'It ain't happening.'

'Whoa, who said anything about killing her?' Connor exclaimed.

'We're not in the business of killing coppers, John,' Lily replied. 'Or anyone we don't have to, for that matter. Christ, who do you think we are?'

He raised his eyebrows at her, and Lily just shook her head. 'We're not looking to kill her. But we do need to speak to her. Maybe there's something we can offer her in return for her silence.'

He shook his head. 'No, you don't understand. She's as straight as they come. She's got personal reasons for that too. If you try and bribe her – or threaten her,' he added, picking up where the conversation was headed to next, 'it will just make her more determined to do it.'

'So what do you suggest?' Lily asked. 'You know her. What can we do?'

There was a long silence as everyone in the room watched John, waiting for him to answer. Scarlet stared at him too, trying to decipher the strange mixture of emotions contorting his face. He looked at her and she saw the inner struggle and defeat in his eyes.

'I have to go down,' he said eventually, his voice devoid of any hope.

'*What?*' Scarlet cried. 'What are you on about?' She felt her heart begin to thud uncomfortably against the wall of her chest. 'No. There has to be another way. Right, Lil? Come on, John, just... keep thinking.'

'Could you turn this on her somehow?' Lily asked. 'Make out she made it up, some desperate revenge accusation because you turned her down or something?'

John shook his head wearily. 'No. I've had time to think this through on the drive back. There's no other way. It's a bad enough accusation to have me arrested and investigated at once, and when they start to scratch beneath the surface, they'll find evidence of us everywhere. Not on the phones perhaps because of the burners, but in every camera at every hotel we've been in, ANPRs on the roads, DNA at my flat...' He trailed off and turned to her with a hopeless look. 'It's no use. There's no way out of it.'

'No,' Scarlet said, though no strength lay within the word. 'That can't be it.' She turned to Lily, her eyes beseeching her to tell her there was a better way. 'It can't.'

John twisted his body towards her and took her hands in his. 'Whatever we do now, there will be an investigation, and when they find the evidence of our relationship goes back to before the evidence disappeared, it will be enough to put me away,' he said heavily. 'There's no way out of that for me. But as long as I say nothing and give no confession, and as long as they don't find the missing evidence when they search all your premises – and they *will* – then they still can't touch you. And that's what we need to focus on now.'

Hot tears stung Scarlet's eyes as the full weight of the situation hit home. She'd clung to the hope that when they got here, Lily could find another way. But that hope had now died. She gripped John's hands hard and shook her head, her breath catching in her throat.

'No,' she said. 'I won't let that happen. We *can't* let that happen. You saved me. You got me out of there and risked everything for me. We can't just let you go down now in my place.'

Lily cast her gaze down and wiped a hand over her face, and Connor looked away to the window. No one said a word. No one had the answer she was looking for.

John pulled his hand out of hers and touched her face, his sombre expression softening. 'I got you out of there because I wanted to and because I *could*,' he said. 'I know you want to get me out, but you can't. And it's OK. I knew the risks I was taking. And while I can't pretend I don't wish this had gone differently, I am going to accept it and do it knowing that at least I'm still keeping you safe.'

'But, John, you're a copper,' she replied, wiping her tears away with her hand, not caring who was watching her cry. 'You'll get a rough time of it inside.'

'He won't,' Connor chimed in. He looked over to John. 'Look, I know we gave you a hard time, but you did save Scar from prison and it looks like you'll be doing it again. We know enough people inside – we'll get word out that you ain't to be touched. We'll pay for your protection too.'

John nodded. 'Thank you. I appreciate that.'

'There is possibly another way,' Lily said slowly, rubbing her hand back and forth over her bottom lip as she thought it through.

Scarlet's hopes began to lift and she turned her attention back to her aunt. 'What are you thinking?'

'I need to talk to someone, but there's a possibility I can smuggle you across into Europe,' she said. 'You'd have to ditch your identity and start again. You'd never be able to come back. But you'd be a free man.'

John considered it. 'Where would I go?'

'That would be up to you,' Lily replied. '*If* I can pull this off, it wouldn't be easy at first. But we'll give you enough cash to set yourself up somewhere. Maybe in time we could organise a new ID, but that would be down the line – it's not a quick process.'

'If I did that, they'd focus harder than ever on you guys. On trying to trip you up about the evidence,' he said.

'They're going to do that anyway. But like you say, without the evidence or a confession, they can't touch us. That might give them enough evidence for you, but a relationship on its own ain't illegal for Scarlet,' Lily replied.

Scarlet looked down at his hand holding hers and felt her heart ache deeply. She was going to lose him, the man she loved with all her being, because of the petty cruelty of her sadistic cousin. There were two options ahead of them now, and they both resulted in the same loss.

'If Lil can arrange it, you should do it,' she said quietly, not able to meet his eyes. 'It's better than you rotting in jail. Because they'll throw away the key for that.' Another hot tear ran down her cheek. 'And even with our protection, you'll be at risk. We have friends but we don't control everyone in there. And you're still a copper. There will be vendettas waged against you. And your life is worth too much to be taken that way.'

She felt John squeeze her hand in agreement.

'Lil' – she looked up at her aunt – 'try and arrange it. Tonight. Right now, we're going home.' She turned to John. 'We're going home to spend one last night together.' She saw the tears finally well up miserably in his eyes too. 'And then tomorrow we need to get you out of here and somewhere safe.'

She stood and pulled John up with her, looking back at her aunt again before they left, all the hate and anger she felt for Ruby pouring into her words. 'And you'd better hope you find Ruby before I do. Because I promise you this, Lil – I don't care what you have to say about it anymore – as I live and breathe, if I find her before you... I'll kill her.'

FIFTY-THREE

Lily stepped out of the taxi and looked up at the name above the door of the heaving club. Club Anya was the third place she'd tried tonight in her search for Freddie Tyler. She'd been tipped off at the last one that he should be here, and she fervently hoped that this information was right. Time was of the essence – she couldn't afford to waste a moment more than she had to. Saturday night was a big night in the West End though, the area of London that Freddie's firm ruled on high. He was a busy man and really could be anywhere.

There was a queue but she ignored this and walked straight over to the bouncers. She didn't recognise them but tried her luck anyway. 'I'm here to see Freddie,' she said, tipping her chin upwards.

'Who's asking for him?' the first one asked, eyeing her hard.

'Lily Drew,' she replied, holding her gaze.

Instantly, the other bouncer tapped his arm and made a sound that clearly meant she was approved. The first one stepped aside and opened the rope for her. She moved through and into the heaving club beyond.

Inside, her eyes were instantly drawn towards the large

stage in the middle. Two dancers hung suspended from ropes, arching and twirling in the air as everyone in the crowded room watched in awe. Inhibitions were left at the door; loud music played, people danced, drinks flowed. She circled around the main floor and headed for the cordoned-off VIP area, where she knew Freddie would be, if he was onsite.

The first person she recognised was Anna, his partner, and part owner of the club, laughing and talking to some friends. They all held glasses of champagne, and the atmosphere in their group seemed relaxed. It was an evening off, and not work. She felt bad for intruding on their downtime, but in this instance, she had no choice.

As she drew nearer, she finally clocked Freddie, sitting in one of the rounded booths talking with his brother Paul and Bill, one of their mutual friends. She stopped just short of the rope and it was Paul who saw her first. He frowned, then smiled and tapped Freddie on the arm, gesturing towards her. She saw the recognition and then the concern before he also smiled and walked over to her. Anna caught on as he passed and joined him as he pulled back the rope between them.

'Lily, what a surprise,' he said, moving aside to let her in. 'Come, join us.'

'Yes, please do,' added Anna with a polite, controlled smile. It wasn't unfriendly exactly, but it was calculated. Lily wasn't put off by this, however – she was used to Anna's ways by now and respected the sharp guard she kept up. She smiled back.

'Thank you. I won't keep you long. I'm sorry to interrupt your night,' she said to them both.

Immediately Freddie's sharp gaze locked onto hers. 'What's wrong?' he demanded.

'Is there somewhere we could talk?' she asked.

'Use my office,' Anna offered.

'OK.' Freddie looked back towards Paul with a tilt of the

head. He immediately got up to join them, and Freddie led the way through the heaving crowd to Anna's office at the back.

Paul shut the door to the cosy room. The sounds beyond immediately dulled to a quiet hum, and Lily could once again hear herself think. Paul sat down on a small terracotta-coloured sofa on the side wall, and Freddie took Anna's seat behind the desk. Lily sat opposite him and moved the chair back so that she could address them both.

'What's going on?' Freddie asked. 'Is this anything to do with Ray?' He exchanged a look with Paul.

Lily frowned. 'Why would it have anything to do with Ray?' she asked. There was an awkward silence and the penny dropped. 'Ah. Good news travels fast, as usual,' she commented wryly.

Freddie gave her an apologetic grimace. 'To be fair, I always thought they were his anyway,' he said with a shrug. 'I'm surprised that he didn't clock it years ago.'

Lily blinked, amazed at how keen his observations had been. 'Well, he didn't. And as far as I know, you're the only one who guessed.' She cleared her throat. 'No, this is something else. Something that needs to stay between us.'

'You know everything we talk about stays between us,' Freddie replied. 'Come on, what's up?' He watched her carefully, his greeny hazel eyes unwavering as he waited.

'You remember how Scarlet was up on charges for Jasper Snow's murder a few months back?'

'Yeah, she got off though, right? Not enough evidence was there?' he recalled.

'Actually, there was. There was concrete evidence. She was set to go down. Our lawyer even suggested she plead guilty in the hope it might lessen her sentence,' Lily replied.

Freddie's eyebrows shot up, and Paul whistled through his teeth.

'How'd she get out of that one?' Paul asked.

Lily took a deep breath. 'She'd been dating a guy, who, until that point, she hadn't realised was Old Bill.'

'Jesus,' Freddie said. 'Undercover?'

'No, that was the joke of it all. They didn't know who each other was at all before that point.' She watched their frowns deepen and hurried on. 'We thought he was, at first. Figured he was lying. But then she was set free, no explanation. And turns out he'd nicked the evidence so she wouldn't go down. It wasn't an ideal situation, but we owed him and he came onto the payroll.'

'And Scarlet?' Freddie squeezed his gaze.

'Continued dating him on the quiet,' Lily admitted. 'We weren't happy about it, warned her of the risks. But' – she held her hands out and grimaced – 'now they've been seen. By one of his own team. It's all happened today, and come Monday morning, she's gonna hand him in.' She held back the details of Ruby's involvement. She could barely get her own head around that betrayal, let alone explain it to anyone else.

'Where he'll be investigated for the missing evidence and sent down for tampering,' Freddie said, catching on.

'Exactly,' Lily replied.

There was a long silence.

'He's willing to go down and has sworn to protect her at all costs. But we owe him more than that,' she said quietly.

Freddie nodded and looked over towards Paul, an unreadable expression on his face.

'I want to try and give him a fresh start over on the continent,' she continued. 'But I need to smuggle him out of the country.'

'And you want me to do that,' Freddie observed. He scratched his head and sighed. 'This is a mess.'

'It is,' Lily agreed. 'And I wouldn't ask if I didn't have to. But I have no way of doing it myself.'

'Who else knows about him?' Freddie asked.

'Other than the family, just Ray.' She cast her gaze down. 'I know he has certain resources in that area too, but we ain't exactly talking right now. So I've come to you.'

Freddie nodded and pulled his cigarettes out of his pocket. He offered one to Lily, who accepted, then chucked the box over to Paul.

'Anna will kill you for smoking in here,' Paul reminded him.

Freddie shrugged. 'She'll understand. Plus, she has a sneaky one now and then. She still thinks I don't know.' He grinned at Lily and his eyes sparkled mischievously. 'I let her think she's kept her secret.'

He lit his and Lily's cigarettes then took a deep drag and sat back, blowing smoke out high into the air.

'I have a small tug going across the channel tomorrow night, smuggling a small but very expensive package into Spain. If you can have him at the docks by nightfall, he can go on that.'

'Thank you,' she said in a heartfelt tone, blowing out her smoke. 'I owe you one.'

'You owe me a big one,' he said seriously. 'I wouldn't do this for anyone but you, Lil. Smuggling bent coppers ain't my game.'

'I know,' she replied. 'I really appreciate this.'

'It's a small tug and there's little cover. Dress him warm and waterproof, and anything he takes needs to fit in one bag, ideally a backpack,' he warned.

Lily nodded. 'Thanks.'

She'd go now and fill his one bag with money, as much as they could fit. It was the least they could do for him. He would just have to survive in what he wore until he could buy what he needed over there.

'I'd better go, see to everything,' she said, standing up. 'We'll be there. And thank you – again.'

Freddie nodded. She smiled at them both, stubbed out her cigarette in the mug Freddie had placed between them as a makeshift ashtray and left the office. She made her way back through the heaving club towards the front door, thinking over all she still needed to do.

That was the plan sorted, but there was still more to do before she could rest. Including finding Ruby. Because she'd seen the look in Scarlet's eyes earlier when she'd made her threats. The icy-cold look of resolution. She'd meant every word she'd said. And this time Lily would not be able to stop her. Which meant if Ruby was going to come out of this unscathed, she needed to find her problematic daughter – and quickly.

FIFTY-FOUR

Cillian woke abruptly to the sound of the door opening and his mother's voice.

'Cillian, please wake up,' she said, her tone urgent.

He prised open his eyes, and as they landed on her, he felt the newly familiar surge of anger and hurt arise. 'What do you want?' he asked flatly.

'I know you don't want to talk to me right now, and that's fine, but I need to find your sister. Urgently,' she said.

He looked at her face, at the dark circles that ringed her eyes and the drawn look that told him she hadn't been to bed since the day before.

Connor stirred in the chair next to him. 'What's happening?'

'I need to find Ruby. Where is she? Come on – one of you should know surely?' she continued.

Cillian pulled himself up gently in the hospital bed, ignoring the drag of his stitches, and rubbed the sleep from his eyes. He glanced at the clock. It was nearly ten in the morning – they must have overslept. Connor had told him everything that was going on the night before, including Scarlet's threats.

'Come on – surely you don't really think Scar's going to do anything, do you?' he groaned.

'Yes. I do,' Lily replied. 'Especially as she's out looking for her right now, while John's packing up his flat. She was deadly serious, Cillian. And part of me can't even blame her. If this had been anyone but Ruby, we'd have been out there on the warpath with her. But it *is* Ruby. I need to get to her before your cousin does. So if either of you know where she is, speak now.' She eyed them hard.

Neither answered, and after a few moments she sighed. 'Fine. But if you hear from her, you call me. Understand? 'Cos she ain't answering my calls, and her safety is more important than whatever argument's going on, OK?'

''Course,' Cillian replied with a nod. She *was* right, however angry he still was with her.

'Yeah,' Connor muttered in agreement.

Giving them both one last look, she turned and left them to it.

Wide awake now, Cillian rubbed his eyes again and sighed heavily. 'We need to find her,' he said.

'Tell me where to look – I'll go now,' Connor replied.

Cillian shook his head. 'She won't talk to you. She'll want to talk to me.'

Connor looked as though he might argue it for a moment, then conceded with a tilt of the head. They both knew Cillian had the stronger bond with Ruby.

'Help me get dressed,' he ordered, gently easing his legs out of the bed.

Connor frowned. 'You ain't supposed to be discharged until tomorrow,' he said, uncertainty in his tone.

'Tomorrow's too late,' he replied. 'Come on. Help me up. I'm OK,' he insisted.

Connor helped him get dressed and then he sat down, a

wave of dizziness passing through him. He closed his eyes and waited for it to pass.

'I don't think you're up to this,' Connor said gently.

'I'm fine. It's just because I've been lying down for so long, that's all. Go get one of those wheelchairs. If anyone asks, just say you're taking me for a short walk. They love all that fresh-air-therapy bollocks around here.'

He closed his eyes as Connor left and tried to draw up all the strength he had left inside for the next few hours. Ruby needed him. He had to be strong.

Twenty minutes later, they were in the car, the hospital far behind them. Cillian directed Connor towards the place he was certain she was hiding out. She thought no one knew about her little one-bedroom flat on the edge of the estate. But Cillian had eyes and ears all over that particular area, and he'd known from the moment she showed an interest. She'd rented it a few months ago, and he'd quietly waited and watched from the sidelines, wondering what her plan was for it. He'd come up with a few ideas over the months, but he'd never guessed it would be a hideout after something like this.

He picked up his phone and dialled her number, not really expecting her to pick up. When she did, he pulled a face of surprise. 'Well, if it ain't the wanted family felon,' he said wryly. 'Everyone's looking for you.'

'I know,' she answered nonchalantly. 'How's your wound doing?' she asked as if nothing else had happened since she'd last been in to see him.

'Oh, you know. So-so,' he responded. 'Scarlet's planning on killing you apparently,' he continued in the same casual tone she'd adopted.

'So she tells me,' Ruby replied, nonplussed. 'But she'd have to find me first.'

Cillian pointed to the entrance of the housing estate he'd been directing Connor to, and Connor pulled in. 'Why'd you do it, Rubes?' he asked.

'To rid our family of the pig in our midst,' she replied. 'I mean, come on. What other firm do you know who lets its members date the people who are trying to bring us down? Eh?'

There was a clanging sound, and Cillian narrowed his eyes as he tried to mentally place it.

'I know you agree with me,' she continued.

'Do you?' he asked.

'I've seen the way you look at him. You hate him just as much as I do and for exactly the same reasons.'

'Well, he ain't my favourite person, but that still don't warrant this,' he replied, pointing to a parking space.

Connor pulled up and opened the car door. There was a pause on the end of the line as he gently got out, gripping the door frame, and then let the door close behind him.

'You're not in hospital,' Ruby observed.

'Nah, thought I'd go for a little drive. Come and talk to my little sister. Try and work out what the hell we're gonna do now that she's totally fucked the family over.'

He gestured for Connor to stay there, then made his way slowly towards the front door.

'What?' Ruby asked, sounding shocked. 'I haven't fucked the family over, I've *saved* it,' she cried. 'I thought you of all people would understand that. Sometimes you need to get your hands dirty to get the job done. Well, that's what I did. I got the job done – I got rid of him.'

'You got rid of a man who had Scarlet's back when she was about to be sent down. A man who *saved* her and who was under the protection of this family, whether we liked him or not. A man who was *with* Scarlet. Who she loves,' he replied.

He leaned heavily on the handrail as he climbed the stairs to the first floor, where Ruby's flat was tucked away. Thankfully it wasn't any further up, or he wasn't sure he'd have made it. He reached the landing and leaned against the wall, closing his eyes for a moment as he caught his breath.

'I can't believe I'm hearing this from you, Cillian,' Ruby replied, her tone full of hurt. 'I did this for us, for all of us. *Our* family. You, Connor and Mum.'

'And what about Scarlet?' he asked. 'She could have gone down in this mess too. She still could, if everything goes south.'

'She made her bed,' Ruby spat.

'Rubes, none of this is OK. No one in this family is thankful for what you've done. For the mess you've made.' He shook his head with a sad sigh. 'You've really fucked up this time. And now we need to work out what we're gonna do.'

'That's right,' Ruby shot back bitterly. 'Turn on me. Turn on me like you lot always do. Protect princess fucking Scarlet while she topples our whole family down in flames, then turn on *me*, the person trying to protect you all from *her*. It's always the same, ain't it? Nothing's changed. I'm still the scapegoat.'

'Ruby, you brought this on yourself,' Cillian insisted. 'Now, I love you, we all do. But that don't mean you can just ignore the rules and do whatever you want. It don't mean you can go round destroying things – destroying *people* – this way. You need to come with me now, so we can figure out what to do about all this.'

'Ha!' She shot him a bitter laugh. 'I don't think so, Cillian. I'm not gonna toe the line anymore for people who can't see me for who I really am.'

'Actually, yes you are,' he said curtly, growing tired of the conversation. This excursion had taken more out of him than he cared to admit, and he needed to get it over and done with so that he could rest.

'Oh yeah? And how's that gonna go then?' she asked.

'Like this.' He'd reached the door of the flat and tried the handle. It opened easily and he walked in. There was an old armchair in the middle of the otherwise empty lounge and a couple of takeaway bags next to it. He quickly checked the bedroom and bathroom, but they were equally as empty.

'Did you really think I'd still be there once I heard you in a car? I knew that you knew about it. Saw your little minion watching me from the corner. Nice try though,' she said.

The line went dead and he cursed.

'I really thought we were on the same page, me and you,' she said from behind him in the hallway. He swivelled round to look at her. 'I really thought you actually cared.'

'Ruby, I *do* care. Why else do you think I'm here?' he argued.

'To pick me up, so you can deliver me back to Scarlet and Mum to pay for my sins,' she said sourly as she backed away from him, a look of hurt in her eyes. 'Which is exactly what you just tried to do.'

'No, Ruby, listen—'

'No, I don't think I will actually. Goodbye, Cillian. You could try and catch me, but looking at how long it took you to climb these stairs and the way you're clinging to your wound now, I don't think you can.'

Cillian exhaled in frustration, knowing she was right. He should have let Connor come up with him.

One arm outstretched, he begged, 'Ruby, come here. Please.' He could see the look in her eye and recognised it all too well. It was the look she always adopted when she'd given up on doing things the right way and given in to the chaos that reigned inside her.

'I really did try to be a part of this family, you know.' Her voice broke. 'But it's never enough. I'm not *Scarlet*.'

As he took another step towards her, she turned and ran down the stairs. With a shout for her to stop, he tried to follow, but it was no use. He felt too weak. He couldn't keep up.

He made his way slowly and painfully back down to the car, where Connor waited, leaning up against it with a cigarette.

'You didn't see her then?' he asked.

'Ruby?' Connor said with a frown. 'I thought she was up there with you.'

'No,' Cillian said grimly. 'But if I know her at all, I think I know where she's headed next.'

They pulled up on Lily's drive just before her car slid in alongside them. They all got out, and she looked at them with a frown of concern. 'What's going on?' she demanded. 'Cillian, you should be in hospital still.'

'There's no time to explain,' he replied as they made their way into the house.

Connor reached the study first, and his groan told Cillian all he needed to know. She had already gone.

He walked in after his brother and his eyes landed on the open door of the family safe. All the money they stored inside for a rainy day – a considerable sum, even by their standards – was gone. She'd taken the lot.

He shook his head, about to turn away, when something at the bottom of the safe glinted in the light and caught his eye. He reached in to pick it up and his heart sank to the bottom of his stomach as he recognised the gold-and-ruby bracelet. Ruby was gone, and she had left every last connection to the family behind her.

FIFTY-FIVE

Four men stood together under one of the weak lights that were dotted along the dock. Smoke rose from their cigarettes in swirling clouds that disappeared off into the darkness above. Their faces were hidden by shadows, and the evening mist shrouded the area behind them in a thin grey veil.

Scarlet clutched John's arm tightly as they approached them, wishing – the way she'd wished every moment since they'd made this decision – that this wasn't really happening. She still couldn't wrap her head around it all. Just two days ago she'd been living her life, fitting their relationship around all the challenges they quietly faced, the way they always had. Dreaming of future scenarios where they would find a way to live freely together. Because she knew, despite her lack of experience in long-term relationships, that what they had was something truly special. It wasn't easy, the situation they'd found themselves in, but they'd made it work because the way they felt when they were together – the way they just clicked in every single way – was wonderful and rare.

Now, all that was ending. And not because either one of

them wanted it to. Not because they'd had a fight, or one of them had wronged the other in some way – but because Ruby had engineered it. And that was something she couldn't forgive or forget. Not ever. Ruby had disappeared, along with a large chunk of the firm's cash. She had slithered away under some rock somewhere to ride out the storm, no doubt planning to return when there was calmer weather. But there would be no calm weather. Not from Scarlet. She wanted revenge, and that was the only thing that was going to keep her going after tonight.

Because tonight she was losing John. Once he stepped off this dock, she would likely never see him again. She'd never know if he was OK, or whether he'd succeeded in making himself a new life. She'd never know when the moment he chose to move on would occur, or who that would be with. These thoughts all speared her heart with hot jagged darts, but she couldn't not think them. They were just there. And they weren't going away.

They reached the group of men, and Scarlet stopped, allowing Lily to overtake her and John from behind and greet them.

'Freddie, Paul,' Lily said, nodding to them both in greeting. 'Thank you for this.'

'No problem, Lil,' Freddie said quietly. 'Alright, Scarlet?'

Scarlet forced a thin smile through her pain. 'This is John,' she said, her voice wavering slightly. She wasn't up to this. She couldn't do it. She looked down and squeezed her eyes shut for a second, trying to pull herself together.

'This is Mick and Rod,' Freddie said, subtly stepping back to allow her some more space to compose herself. 'Rod is taking the boat over tonight. I'll leave you to say your goodbyes.'

The four men and Lily walked off to one side and left the young couple alone.

Tears began to fall unchecked down Scarlet's cheeks as she realised that this was it. It was time for them to part ways for good. She turned to face him and wrapped her arms around his waist, burying her face in his chest with a sob.

'Hey. Hey, no,' he said, lifting her chin to force her to look at him. She stared up into his bright green eyes, now more greyish in the dark light. 'Listen to me. Please. It's going to be OK.'

'It's not,' she said brokenly. 'It's not OK.'

'It's not what we'd planned,' he admitted. 'I love you so much. And it breaks my heart having to leave you like this.' He pulled her face up and kissed her hungrily, urgently. 'I don't want to let you go,' he continued, pressing his forehead to hers. 'I hate that we have no choice. But you know what, I wouldn't change any of it. If I could go back, I'd still take that evidence and I'd still spend every second I could with you. Being with you has been a gift. And I'll carry that with me,' he said, looking into her eyes intently. 'And I need you to carry us with you too.'

'Of course,' she said, crying openly now.

John glanced over at the group of men and Lily. 'I need you to stay smart. I need you to stay on top. I know you want to hurt Ruby, and I know there's no point me telling you not to—'

'You're right, there's not,' she said, a spark of anger colouring her words.

'But remember who she is,' he whispered. 'Stay *smart*. Stay safe. That's all I ask of you. Don't lose through anger.'

Scarlet gripped his hands and pressed herself against him harder. 'I want to come with you,' she said.

She felt him shake his head.

'It's no life if you've got another choice. Plus, two of us on the run they'd find a lot easier. You need to stay and ride it out, and then live your life. And look after your family. Who knows, maybe one day...' He trailed off, clearly knowing he couldn't finish that sentence.

Scarlet reached up and kissed him long and hard, trying to

savour the feeling of his lips on hers and the warmth of his breath on her face. She squeezed him hard one last time and then let go, stepping back. It was the hardest step back she'd ever taken, but somehow she forced herself to do it.

'I'll be OK,' he said. 'And so will you.'

Rod, the man Freddie had said was taking the boat, stepped onto the small tug floating beside them by the dock. John stepped on after him, his eyes never leaving Scarlet's as Rod untied the rope and started the engine.

Scarlet wrapped her arms around her middle and sobbed, the sound carrying broken and empty over the top of the bubbling engine. She held his gaze as the boat pulled away, not daring to blink for fear of missing even a second. And then as the mist wrapped its embrace around the boat's end, John was gone.

———

Lily's heart broke for Scarlet as she watched her niece cry from a distance. She looked away sadly and caught Freddie's sympathetic gaze.

'Poor little thing,' Paul said quietly.

'She's certainly had a lot of heartache, for her tender years,' Lily agreed.

'I'll send word to confirm he arrived OK. And I'll keep tabs, try and get that ID sorted for him, like you asked,' Freddie said.

'Thank you. I'll not tell her that you know where he is,' she added. 'It would only make it harder to bear.'

Freddie nodded. 'Take as long as you need here,' he said. 'We need to shoot. Stuff going on in town that needs dealing with.'

'Yeah, of course,' Lily replied. 'Thanks.' She watched Scarlet as the younger woman wiped her tears and tried to calm herself down.

Freddie squeezed her arm. 'Stay safe, Lil.'

She watched them walk off and then made her way slowly over to Scarlet. Her shoulders rose and fell in sharp jerks as the tears still silently fell. Putting her arm around her, she gently pulled her niece, away. 'Come on, Little Doll,' she said gently. 'Let's go home. I've got you.'

FIFTY-SIX

Jenny Ascough stared out of the window at the weak morning sun, her eyes red-rimmed from crying. She'd barely slept, tossing and turning all night, the same way she had the night before. She still couldn't believe that this was all happening, that John, her friend, her boss, the man she'd slowly but surely devoted her heart to over the last few months, was a traitor.

His face, when she'd told him she would give him until today to sort out his affairs, haunted her. His gaze had not held hers for long; they had been drawn like a magnet back towards the hotel. Towards *her*. His deepest fears were not for himself. No. His expressive bright green eyes had given it away. His fears were for *her*. Scarlet Drew. Even then, as he faced the prospect of losing everything, it was her he thought of. And that struck like a hot knife through her heart.

Why had he done it? Why had he thrown his lot in with that cold, lawless murdering bitch? She couldn't wrap her head around it. The woman was stunning, that much she couldn't ignore, much as she'd like to. But looks weren't everything in this life. What happened to loyalty? What happened to upholding the law? What could he possibly have seen in her that he couldn't have found elsewhere? That he couldn't have found in her?

She closed her eyes and let the last tear fall. The last, she decided, for today. At least until she was back here later and alone with her thoughts once more.

Standing up, she walked away from the window and slipped her feet into the shiny black boots by the door. Moving to the mirror, she pinched her cheeks and blinked the last of the dampness out of her eyes. She cast her gaze over her uniform, checking all was in order.

In just over half an hour, she would be walking into the office she'd shared with John every day for the last few months. The office she'd entered each day with a smile and a hopeful heart. But her heart wasn't hopeful today. It was cold and hard and ready for vengeance. Today, when she walked into the office, she would go to a different floor. She would find Jennings and tell him everything. Then together they would find John, find the evidence he stole and she would pay back that murdering siren in full.

She stepped out into the corridor and marched forward with purpose. Scarlet Drew would pay for what she'd taken from her. And she would pay for what she'd taken from John. Ascough still didn't know how she had made such a strong man turn his back on all that was good in his life, and maybe she never would. But she would not rest until she had won. She would not rest until Scarlet Drew was behind bars and she could throw away the key.

EPILOGUE

Cillian pulled up a long dirt track and past a large barn where they held a lot of their stolen goods, and continued up to a grassy area just before a line of trees. It was a pretty area, quiet and out of the way. The best place they could find to do this, under the circumstances. Several other cars were already parked up, and a group of people stood waiting.

Lily, Scarlet, Isla and Jimmy stood together on one side of the small mound of freshly dug earth, with Ray and two of his men a few feet away. Connor and Billie stood together, a few feet apart from the rest of them.

Pulling to a stop, Cillian got out of the car and walked slowly round to the passenger side to open the door.

It had been a week since he'd broken out of hospital, and while he was still a bit sore, he had been able to get back to normal, day-to-day things such as driving and walking around. The nightmares still woke him every few hours in the night, and he was still coming to terms with what had happened to him. But Billie was by his side, full-time now that she had moved in with him, and with her and Connor's support, he was getting there mentally too.

To his surprise, no one had yet been dragged in for questioning about John and Scarlet's relationship. The police had raided John's flat and set up surveillance outside Cath and Scarlet's house, but as yet they were keeping their cards close to their chest. Cillian imagined they were trying to track John down first in the hope they could get him to crack, before going full force on the Drews. They were, after all, already facing harassment complaints. But it would only be a matter of time before they came and then all hell would be let loose.

One of the first things he'd done upon leaving hospital was call in on Ray. Not to talk about the family bombshell Lily had dropped – and he'd made that perfectly clear – but to ask him for one last favour. Ray had secured the old farmhouse that hid the entrance to the bunker, after everything had happened, knowing that they would need to make sure it still appeared occupied if they were going to avoid people nosing about and potentially finding the horrors that lay beneath. The last thing Cillian wanted to do was go down to the place that haunted his dreams, but there was something down there he still needed.

Ray had gone down with a team of men to retrieve Barnes's body a couple of days later. Cillian would never be able to get over the devastation that his friend had died such a painful and terrible death. But the one small thing he was grateful for was that Joe hadn't yet got round to disposing of his body, the way he had Gary's. At least now they were able to bury him and say goodbye with love and in peace, somewhere the sun would shine down on his grave. At least this way, his mother could say goodbye properly. Being as close as he had been to being Joe's next victim, Cillian couldn't help but hope that if he had been, someone would have done this for him.

While he'd been down there, Ray had also collected Joe's body, getting rid of it quietly and efficiently. Cillian didn't know where he was buried, and he didn't particularly want to know either. The main thing was he'd been put somewhere that no one would ever find him. And should someone one day come across the bunker for any reason, there would be nothing left there but perhaps an old bloodstain.

Cillian held his hand out to Barnes's mother now, and she took it, pulling herself out of the car with a strength and dignity he admired. He walked her over to where they'd laid Barnes, wrapped in a white sheet so she'd never see the state of his body, and he picked up a handful of dirt, offering it to her to throw in first. He stepped back next to Connor and Billie, and as Jimmy began reciting a prayer, the simple, peaceful burial began.

Cillian looked around at the broken groups around the grave, and their troubles lay heavy on his shoulders. This family, once so strong as one whole entity, was now fractured. Where once there had been trust, there were secrets and suspicion. Where there had been unity, there was now war. By his mother's side was a girl that none of them even really knew, instead of her sons, the way they always had been in the past.

Scarlet met his gaze, and the coldness and determination he saw there scared him. He knew that she was looking for Ruby, and if she found her, she would mete out her revenge. In turn, Scarlet knew that *he* was looking for Ruby too, and if he found her, he would protect her at all costs. He didn't want to have to choose – he loved them both. But Ruby was his sister, the closer blood relative of the two. He often found himself praying that she would just stay lost, so that this never had to come to a head. But he knew her too well to believe that would happen.

Lily looked up at him, and Cillian cast his gaze aside, the familiar pain and anger rising up inside. He wanted to forgive her. He missed her and loved her. But he just couldn't move on. She had betrayed them both, him and Connor. And up until that moment, Lily had always been the one person they thought held no secrets, that they thought they could trust more than anyone else on the planet. But it had been a lie. How could they ever trust her again? How could they ever look her in the eye with respect again?

He'd have no choice but to face her for work, especially now they'd bought the boxing club. Lily had laid out her plans to spruce it up and start turning a profit, and there was a lot of work ahead of them. A lot of work where they were all involved and working in close quarters. It was going to be tough. There were dark days ahead, storms and sieges between warring factions of their firm. Of their family. And only time would tell how that would go.

He watched Ray's hard, brooding expression as they lowered Barnes into the grave. He and his men had helped dig it earlier that day, but none of them had talked beyond what was absolutely necessary. He was here out of duty, because Barnes had been one of his men. He was not here for Lily. If anything, her presence seemed to be making him angry. And for once, Cillian could understand his feelings towards her.

As the short ceremony ended and Connor led Barnes's mother away, Cillian watched as all the broken pieces of their circle left in different directions. Glances were thrown, tensions held, and the feeling that a storm was coming settled in like a dark, sinister fog within his soul. A fractured firm was vulnerable. A firm where no one trusted each other was dangerous. Had friends really turned into enemies? Had family really turned into strangers?

Taking a deep breath, Cillian tried to brace himself for what was to come. Because although he wasn't yet sure what that would be, he knew, without doubt, that it was going to either make or break the Drews for good.

———

As the procession of cars filed out from the almost-concealed dirt track and back onto the country road, two pairs of eyes watched from the car hidden behind the trees in a small copse across the way. The family looked uneasy with each other, they noted, though as yet they didn't know why. They didn't know whose funeral this was either, or how it had come about. But that didn't matter. What they *did* know, at this point in time, was that one of their own had managed to nestle herself right in the heart of the Drew family firm.

As she came into view, the man in the driver's seat smiled, his dark brown eyes crinkling at the sides, full of mischief, and his gold front tooth glinted in what little sun still reached them.

'Our little Isla,' he said, giving a deep throaty laugh.

'In the flesh,' hissed his companion.

'She's got their trust already,' he mused.

'She always was good at that though. The quiet ones always are.'

As the last of the cars disappeared down the road, he started up their own engine and pulled out, turning away. They'd seen enough for today.

'I think this is gonna be a good little earner, this one,' he said, his anticipation rising.

'It is indeed,' his companion agreed.

'And the best part is,' he said with a dark smile, 'they'll never see it coming.'

A LETTER FROM EMMA

Dear readers,

Thank you so much for reading *Her Payback* and I hope you liked it. If this is the first of my books you've picked up, then welcome to the world of the Drews! And if you've been on this journey with me from previous books, welcome back, friends. If you would like to hear more about the series, sign up here. Your email address won't be shared and you can unsubscribe at any time.

www.bookouture.com/emma-tallon

Some books are a joy to write and some books, for reasons that still escape me, fight me all the way. This book was a prize-winning fighter! But it's come together in the end.

On a character level, we've really seen two very different sides to a few of the Drew family members. And it's funny, because although I write these books and I plan them out to a degree, it's like the characters often take on a life of their own under my fingertips. I don't always know what they're going to do until they do them, which is exciting – and at times shocking.

With all that's gone on, I'm really looking forward to hearing what your thoughts are on everything. Even my own opinions are a little torn on things that have gone on in this book.

I think the next book is going to be particularly explosive

and I, as much as anyone, look forward to seeing what happens between all these strong characters. I hope you'll journey with me through that book too, and in the meantime, stay safe, stay well and stay happy.

All my love,

Emma Xx

http://emmatallon.com

 facebook.com/emmatallonofficial

 twitter.com/EmmaEsj

 instagram.com/my.author.life

ACKNOWLEDGEMENTS

First of all, a huge, heartfelt thank you to all my readers. Thank you for every copy you buy, every post you share, every review or recommendation you make. I appreciate it more than I can express.

I want to acknowledge a couple of people behind the scenes here: my in-laws, Pauline and Chris. It's not easy writing, editing and releasing two books a year with two small children, but no matter what's going on, however much my husband and I have to juggle, they're always there lending support and helping with the kids so we can do everything we need to. I appreciate that support immensely. Thank you so much, both of you.

I'd also like to send a big thank you to an old colleague, Phil Walker, who was kind enough to share some of his very valuable knowledge about how a piece of land in London may be valued. Whilst I have still used some creative licence around a certain deal in this book, that has helped immensely in keeping me decently close to the mark.

And lastly, there are so many supportive author friends I have to thank, but in particular, Casey Kelleher and Victoria Jenkins. These two have supported my writing journey on a whole other level. They have motivated me, celebrated with me, talked me off the ledge of despair, made me laugh, made me cry (in good ways) and have shown me the deepest levels of friendship at every turn. You girls are my tribe and I couldn't imagine life without you.

Printed in Great Britain
by Amazon

84721093R00192